Sweet SPOT

REBECCA JENSHAK

Copyright © 2020 by Rebecca Jenshak
All rights reserved. Except as permitted under the U.S. Copyright Act of 1976, no part of this book may be reproduced, distributed, transmitted in any form or by any means, or stored in a database or retrieval system, without written permission from the author.

www.rebeccajenshak.com

Cover Design by Lori Jackson Designs
Cover Photo by Wander Aguiar
Editing by Edits in Blue
Proofreading by My Brother's Editor
Formatting by Mesquite Business Services
Paperback Formatting by Jersey Girl Design

The characters and events in this book are fictitious. Names, characters, places, and plots are a product of the author's imagination. Any similarity to real persons, living or dead, is coincidental and not intended by the author.

Books by Rebecca Jenshak

Smart Jocks Series
The Assist
The Fadeaway
The Tip-Off
The Fake

Standalones
Sweat
If Not For Love
Electric Blue Love

For Craig

"*Hitting a driver is easy,
it's the size of a tennis racket.*"

– Craig M.

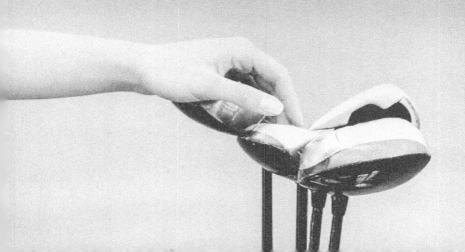

CHAPTER ONE

Keira

I'm not good at very many things.

I never learned to play a musical instrument. I can't draw. I'm messy, unorganized, and hot-headed. Pop-Tarts are a staple in my diet so, obviously, maintaining a balanced diet isn't a talent of mine either. I don't understand classic literature, and I'm hopeless at video games. None of it ever mattered to me. Nothing but golf.

Wedge in hand, I bounce the ball off the clubface as if it's a paddle. Each time, the ball lands squarely in the center—right on the sweet spot—with a light tap.

Tap. Tap. Tap.

The noise soothes and excites me. Body poised, right forearm extended slightly in front of me, the tip of my tongue between my teeth. That last part isn't strictly necessary, but it's a habit any time I'm concentrating this hard.

My teammates stand to the side, watching my every move.

I've done this trick a hundred times, but I know better than to look anywhere except at the ball. Even the trickle of sweat at the nape of my neck and the stray hair that's fallen in my face won't distract me.

Tap. Tap. Tap.

I move the club behind my back.

Tap. Between my legs. *Tap.* Club forward. *Tap. Tap. Tap.* Right foot hop and kick, letting the ball bounce off the sole of my shoe before catching it. *Tap. Tap. Tap.* Deep breath as I track the ball, move into my final position, and swing.

A shot of pride zips through me as the ball sails through the air, a white dot in the bright blue sky. My teammates cheer, finally breaking their silence.

"That's incredible," Abby says, offering me a high-five. "And on the first try. Is this how you spent all of winter break?"

I shrug. "It didn't take that long to perfect it."

Erica stares at her phone, thumbs moving rapidly over the screen. "I'm posting it. Your trick shots get more likes and comments than anything else I post." She looks up at me. "You're more popular than I am on my own account. That's screwed up." She snickers and goes back to her phone.

The other girls are giving me the appropriate props when Coach's voice bellows from the clubhouse. "Ladies, hit the bunkers."

I swear he glares right at me as if I'm the only one standing here. I glare back, refusing to cower. He looks away first, and I call that a victory until he adds, "You too, Keira. Your fancy trick shots won't help you in a tournament."

I open my mouth to argue that we were on a water break, so it wasn't as if I had been wasting practice time, but Abby steps in front of me, blocking him from view. "Come on."

I grab my bag, and we head for the sand traps with the rest of the team.

"You have to stop letting him rile you. It throws you off all practice."

"He hates me."

"He hates everyone." Abby and I walk a few paces behind our teammates. She finger combs her silky, black hair into a ponytail and adjusts her visor. "He just picks on you the most because he knows he can get a rise out of you. Stop giving him what he wants."

I mumble my acknowledgment. It isn't that I'm argumentative by default, but Coach Potter pushes all my buttons. If the man were a Pop-Tart, he'd be the unfrosted kind—a total disgrace to the Pop-Tart brand.

"How was break?" she asks as we reach the group and set our bags on the ground.

"It was fine. Yours?"

"Good. What'd your dad get you this year?"

My dad's Christmas gifts are . . . entertaining. I raise my arm to show off the bright neon-pink unicorn scrunchie, which is one of twelve of varying colors he gave me this year. Last year, I got a pair of cat ear headphones. I'm convinced he thinks I will forever be thirteen years old.

Abby laughs. "Why doesn't he just get you a gift card or golf stuff?"

"Oh no, he never goes the gift-card route. And I have so much golf stuff that I'm sure he would have no idea what to buy."

"Let me guess, you told him you loved it?"

"He's always so proud of what he picks, how could I not? Besides, I could be into unicorns."

She snorts. "It's actually pretty cute. Maybe I need to get on the Christmas list next year."

We spend the next half hour hitting shots from the bunker and then Coach lays the pin down behind the hole and instructs us to keep going until we've each hit it three times in a row.

It takes a few minutes to stop overthinking it, but soon, I have two consecutive hits and am lining up for my third.

"Open the clubface a little more. Address it off the toe. You're looking rusty. Come on ladies, focus," he barks loud enough that I know it's advice meant for the entire team, but Coach's presence directly behind me makes me grip the club tighter. The man sets my every nerve on edge. His personality is completely abrasive, making me firmly believe either he hates coaching, golf, or maybe both. He certainly doesn't like me.

I'd rather swing the wedge at his head, but I breathe and refocus. Unfortunately, as soon as I make contact with the ball, I know it's going right. Coach walks off without a word.

I'm the last to finish and head back up to the putting green. The boys' team has already arrived. They practice right after us, but a quick glance at my phone tells me we still have more than thirty minutes left. They're never this early.

Abby's holding her putter, leaned over as if she's eyeing the line, but the only thing she's eyeing is her boyfriend Smith. He's on the driving range, staring right back at her.

"You two are ridiculous, sneaking glances at one another like you're in middle school," I say, dropping a few balls onto the green and joining her.

My friend blushes. "What? He's cute. Let me stare without your judgment."

I shake my head. "What are they doing here so early, anyway?"

"They have a clinic today with some big shot swing coach."

"Figures. Why do they always have people coming in to offer extra coaching? We've had a better record for the past two years, but do fancy swing coaches come to see us?" I don't wait for her answer. "No, they do not."

She shrugs, not the least bit bothered by it, and honestly, I don't know if I'd be upset if it weren't for the fact our coach barely speaks to me, let alone coaches me.

We've never seen eye to eye, but when I was holding my own in tournaments, he didn't seem to loathe me quite so much.

While we finish putting, Coach strolls over to review this week's schedule. We have a tournament upstate this weekend but only five will travel and play.

I keep my eyes glued to the ground as he says the first four names. Our top three rarely changes. Erica, Kim, and Cassidy are our most senior members and have earned their spots by consistently placing well in tournaments. Then there's Abby. She's streaky, but as of our last tournament in December, that streak is holding. That leaves only one spot. My spot. Or it was. One bad tournament last October and Coach was all too eager to replace me. I've been trying to claw my way back to his good graces ever since. Unsuccessfully, I might add.

"And finally, Brittany will join us."

I glance up in time to see his cold, gray eyes sweep over the team and lock on to me, waiting for a reaction. It's as if the man gets off on my anger. I plaster on a congratulatory smile and clap for my teammates. I will not let him see how much it hurts.

He places both hands on his hips. "Weak practice today, girls. Get your heads right and show up tomorrow ready to work harder."

After everyone separates, I approach him. "Coach, can I talk to you for a minute?" My big, fake smile is starting to make my cheeks hurt.

"What is it, Keira? I'm not going to change my mind on the girls going to the tournament."

Oh my God, why is he such a dick?

"I understand. I was just going to ask what I might do to improve so I can have my spot back? Or, at least, a chance to earn it back. Before break, I was consistently scoring with the top three in practice."

"I can't give you the answers. You have to prove it out there." He points toward the course. If it's some sort of voodoo mind trick, I'm clueless. He's the coach, the sole decider of who plays. Of course, he has the answer. And I *am* proving it out there.

"Right."

"Put the work in and give your best every time. And your attitude needs a serious adjustment." His brows raise, and his eyes widen as he waits for me to respond. He's expecting me to argue, I'm sure.

"Yes, Sir."

I'm screwed. I'm already the hardest worker on the team, and he knows it. Golf is my passion. I love it. I want to be the best, not just on our team but in the world. I don't think that's out of reach for me. I'm good—really good—but I can't prove that if I'm not playing.

Abby waits for me by our bags. "What did he say?"

"Nothing useful. Go ahead. I'm gonna stay and hit a bucket of balls."

"Seriously?"

"I have to get my spot back. I'll sleep here if I have to."

She chuckles. "Just don't sleep with him."

"Ewww." Bile coats my throat at the idea of seeing that vile man naked. He's young-ish, late thirties, and reasonably attractive, but his personality kills any and all sexual vibes.

I'm still swallowing my disgust when Abby elbows me. "Look, that must be the swing coach. *Damn.*"

Slowly, I scan until I locate him. He isn't hard to find. Tall, dark hair, bronzed skin set off by dress pants and a crisp white polo that he fills out nicely. His body language, even from this far, gives off an air of confidence.

He smiles at something the boys' coach, Coach James says, and it's hard to look away. So hard it's annoying. I'm totally annoyed by his good looks because *of course* he's good-looking. Probably a real jerk, too.

Okay, I might just be projecting my hatred for Coach Potter on all mankind, but I also really despise how the boys' team always seems to get the outside attention and help.

Abby pulls her hair from the ponytail. "We should go introduce ourselves."

"Why?"

"Because I want to see that man up close. Don't you?"

I laugh. "What about Smith?"

"See him; not jump him. Come on, it can't hurt to make nice."

"No thanks." I pick up my bag and shoulder it. "See you back at the dorm later."

"Don't forget that we're going out tonight with Erica and Cass."

"Oh, I haven't forgotten. The promise of alcohol is the only thing that got me through that practice."

"All right, well, I'm headed back to shower and get ready. Don't stay too long."

"Just long enough to work out my frustration."

"Please, it'll be dark by then." She smiles smugly and walks off toward the parking lot.

I head to the clubhouse, splash some water on my face in the bathroom and try to wash away my irritation from practice. I grab a bucket of balls and walk over to an open mat on the driving range. The boys team huddles off to the side, Coach James and hottie swing coach the center of their focus.

I don't need them, and I don't need Potter. I'm going to prove I deserve that spot all on my own. I bounce the ball on the clubface a few times, the concentration it requires and the familiar movements calming me instantly.

I can do this.

CHAPTER TWO

Lincoln

Starting a new business is hard. Exhausting. No, exhausting doesn't even cover the half of it. Travelling the world, a different city every week, early mornings, late nights, sporting event after sporting event. It's basically everything I ever dreamed of.

Except for the crappy jobs that need to get done but can't be pawned off on anyone else, which is my current state at the Valley University golf course. Ah, the joys of being the boss. I'm trying hard not to think about the box seats I had to turn down for today's Cardinals playoff game. A cold beer and a million-dollar view would be pretty great about now.

I find Coach James on the driving range, instructing his team to warm up and give each of their clubs a few swings. A few of the guys notice me, but I hang back until Mark lifts a hand.

"Hey, Mark. Long time. Good to see ya." I nod to toward the guys and smile.

"You too, Linc." We shake hands, and then he motions for me to follow him. "Let's chat before I introduce you to the team."

He leads me into the clubhouse and to a small office. "Thanks for coming."

"Thank you for inviting me," I say as we take our seats. "This should be fun."

He grunts a laugh as if he doesn't believe my optimism. Yeah, I don't either. The Cardinals haven't made it this far in the season in years, and instead of watching the game, I'm going to spend my Sunday afternoon giving pointers to a bunch of college kids who expect me to sweep in and make big changes to their game in two hours of work. Not even I'm that good.

I lean back and rest my interlocking fingers at my waist as I study my old friend. It's been almost twelve years since I've seen him, but he's the same arrogant kid I knew in high school—minus a little hair and plus a little weight around his midsection.

"It's fine. Happy to do it. You've been a big supporter of the new coaching site and I appreciate it."

"But?"

"How do you know there's a but?"

He arches a brow pointedly.

"But any one of my guys could have done it. Why am I here?"

"Because you're the best."

Well, I can't argue there.

"Look," I reason with him, "I'm glad to help how I can, but this isn't really what I do. Analyzing and fixing an entire team of kids' mistakes in a single afternoon . . . I'm not a miracle worker. Usually, I work with individuals over weeks, sometimes months or years. And the group clinics I offer cover a single aspect of the game like downswing sequencing or setup. A few hours giving pointers to ten kids isn't going to make the same kind of difference that I see with my personal clients. I want to make sure you understand that."

"Well, you're welcome to stay for as long as you need to get these boys on track. They're excited about meeting you. They're a young group, making all sorts of rookie mistakes, but I think they have potential. Smith Jacobson has a good, clean swing I think you'll appreciate."

"You can't afford for me to stay that long." I smirk. "Let's just focus on what you think would be the best use of their time for today."

Leaning forward in his chair, Mark grins back at me. "Fair enough."

After chatting about what he views as the biggest weaknesses of the team collectively, we decide the best use of everyone's time is for me to do a few quick drills on adding length and accuracy to their drives. Then I'll spend time with each kid before giving them targeted feedback.

We don't talk individual players because I don't want to walk out there with any preconceived notions about them. If I'm looking for a specific fault right off the bat, I might miss something else.

"All set?" Mark stands. "The guys are probably getting anxious to meet you. A few of them were here an hour before practice already stretching and warming up."

"Let's do it."

The bright blue Arizona sky is flawless, not a damn cloud as far as the eye can see. That, and the nonexistent breeze make it spectacular golfing weather for January.

A man approaches as we step onto the grass and Mark slows.

"Lincoln, this is Wyatt Potter. He's the coach of the girls' team."

"Pleasure to meet you. I hear your record is pretty good this year."

"Top two consecutively since I took over three years ago."

"Impressive. I'm happy to include them in the clinic today or—" Before I can offer my services another day, he holds up a hand, which annoys the fuck out of me.

"No offense, but no one coaches my girls but me. Too many outside influences confuses them and makes it hard to keep them motivated."

I quirk a brow. Is this guy for real?

Mark jumps in, "Lincoln's a hell of a coach. He played professionally and—"

I clap a hand on Mark's shoulder to stop him from saying more. It's obvious this guy has no interest in my qualifications or background, no need to waste my time.

"Even still," Coach Potter says, voice and face full of condescension.

What a prick. I dig deep for some professionalism and manners, despite his lack thereof. "Well, the offer is always good if you need anything. Good luck on the season."

I step away, and luckily, Mark follows. When the boys spot us, they stop warming up and move in our direction, clearly ready to get started. There's so much excitement on their faces that I can't help but feel a little more energized myself.

Mark and I stand in the center as they form a half circle around us.

"Everyone, I'd like to introduce you to Lincoln Reeves. It's a real honor to have him here today. He knows more about golf than all of us combined, so if he tells you something, take it as gospel."

I bite back a laugh, knowing it probably cost Mark a little pride to give me that much credit. It isn't as if he doesn't mean it; I'm here because he wanted the best. But the relationship Mark and I had as kids included a lot more ribbing and jokes at one another's expense than flowery compliments. Blame it on growing up together, competing against one another, and knowing all each other's embarrassing childhood shit. Regardless, I appreciate him having my back with that asshole coach of the girls' team and with his guys.

After thanking Mark and saying hello to the boys, I lead the group to one end of the driving range and go over some tips on technique specific to the driver, demonstrating as I talk. It isn't overly complicated to understand, but putting it into practice is much more difficult.

When I'm done, I send them off to work on it, giving them about five minutes before I grab my camera and tripod. Going down the line, I film each of their swings from behind and the side, offer a few quick tips or corrections, and then move on. I don't have time to completely analyze each swing, but I can pinpoint fundamental issues on the fly, so I do my best to give each of them helpful, individualized feedback.

I keep it lighthearted and fun, knowing they'll perform better if they're relaxed instead of worried about being perfect. Clinics are supposed to be inspiring, otherwise, what's the point? I even find myself smiling and enjoying myself as I stand back and watch each kid take a couple of swings.

There's always this moment as a coach or a lover of any sport where you're holding your breath, hoping to be awed. I'd be lying if I said any of them succeed.

Smith Jacobson, Mark's star athlete, has a decent swing, but it lacks power, and he's missing confidence and tenacity. Every time he hits a bad shot, he takes five minutes setting up for the next, overthinking it and second-guessing himself. But, all in all, they're a good group of kids, and with some work and experience, they'll be all right.

"You're good with them." Mark nods toward his players. "If the site flops, I could use another good coach here." He elbows me so I know he's joking. "Love to have you back any time."

We're standing back twenty feet or so from the range. Time is up, but all the guys are still working, so I linger. I bet they've each hit close to two hundred balls. They have to be exhausted, but they're pushing through on fumes and dreams.

"I'll try to get the videos uploaded and sent to you tomorrow."

"No rush. I appreciate it," he says earnestly. "In a year or two, you're going to have so much business you aren't going to be able to keep up. Your grandfather would be proud."

I soften at the mention of Pop. "Thanks, Mark. That's a problem I'm looking forward to solving."

Mark extends his hand, and we shake. "It was good to see you, Lincoln. Don't be a stranger."

By the time I pack up, Mark and his team have moved down the first hole. The late afternoon sun has started to descend, casting the sky in pink and orange. I stop and take it in, trying to remember the last time I hit a few balls for fun.

Another year, maybe two, and then I will be able to find a better balance. I've already found more success than I ever could have imagined when I'd had a moment of drunken brilliance to take the business my grandfather started forty years ago and expand it.

It's taken longer, been harder, and required more sacrifice than expected, but it's also brought a sense of pride and accomplishment that is beyond anything golf alone has ever given me.

I step back, scanning the horizon and soaking up this feeling so I can pocket it for a reminder the next time I'm going on two hours of sleep and want to give up.

A pure, hard *thwack* snaps me from my daydream. I find and follow the ball as it sails beautifully high and straight down the line.

"Damn," I mutter and start toward whoever hit it. I need to shake this kid's hand and, more importantly, see if he can do it twice. Anyone can get lucky and hit a shot like that once, but great golf comes from consistency.

My pace slows as I get closer. Confusion sets in, not because I was wrong and a chick hit it but because this girl in particular looks nothing like I would have expected. For one, she's small.

The average woman on the LPGA is only five foot four, but I don't think this girl is even that tall. And she's thin. Toned, but not overly muscular like I'd expect someone driving the ball that far. Otherwise, she looks the part in a black golf skirt and matching long-sleeved shirt.

I don't know where she gets her power, but I'm intrigued. She's setting up another ball, so I hang back and watch. Crossing my arms over my chest, I wait to see what she can do.

She lets out a long breath as if she's trying to calm herself. Dark hair, which has a reddish tint under the remaining sunlight, hangs over her shoulders and falls in her eyes. She jabs at it twice with one hand, only to have it fall right back in her face.

Resting the grip of the club against her stomach to free her hands, she pulls the long mane back into a ponytail and secures it with a bright-pink scrunchie from her wrist. Her frustration is evident, but I don't think her hair is the problem.

Finally, she's ready, and I find myself holding my breath as she swings. She's more powerful than most the guys I helped today, swinging in a way that makes me wonder who the hell she's picturing as the ball.

I watch as she hits three more awe-worthy shots before I approach her. "Nice swing."

"Thanks," she says without looking back at me. She switches from a driver to a seven iron. This time, she doesn't hit the ball square on, and it hooks to the left. Her jaw tenses, and instead of taking her time and a minute to compose herself, she goes right for the next ball with a similar result. It takes five shitty shots before she growls her frustration. "Damn it."

"Can I offer you some advice?"

Her dark eyes lock on to me, and her brows rise as if I've totally offended her, but she doesn't speak.

Trying to diffuse the situation, I step closer and offer my hand. She stares at it but makes no move to take it, so I shove both hands into my pockets. "I'm Lincoln Reeves. I just finished a clinic for the boys' team. I'm a golf instructor and owner of an instructional sports website. You have power. Those shots you hit with your driver were really nice. Best I've seen all day."

Her demeanor softens only slightly. "Thank you."

"If you let me record a couple of swings, I think I can show you where it's breaking down and help you hit it more consistently." My body buzzes in anticipation. I really want to see what this girl is capable of. God, I love this job.

"No thanks. I got it." She brushes me off with a flick of her ponytail and tees up another ball.

Well, that's never happened before. Golfers tend to be open to feedback or will, at least, humor tips from pros at the driving range. It's such a complicated and yet simple thing, hitting a golf ball.

"Are you sure? It's no problem." I can't get a read on this girl. She's out here putting in the work, so I know she's determined, and her body language makes it clear she knows a good swing from a bad.

"On camera, it's easier to see the nuances. You're spinning your hips. Your timing is good, so it isn't affecting every shot, but when it does, you're hooking it."

She stands tall, which isn't really that tall, but my spidey sense tingles, alerting me to danger. I've pissed this girl off, though I don't know why.

"Figures you're helpful now."

"Excuse me?" I smile, which is absolutely the wrong thing to do because she glowers back.

"Guys like you show up and offer all your wisdom to the boys' team like just because they have penises, they deserve all the advantages. Did it ever occur to you to offer a clinic for the girls' team?"

"I—"

"No, of course not. It doesn't matter that we have a better record, year after year, or that I can out drive most of them." She scoffs, tees up another ball, and gets into position. "So, no thanks. I don't need another man who thinks he's God's gift to golf to offer advice that he probably picked up from the Golf Channel."

Before I can speak, she draws back and smokes it. Chills run up my fingertips all the way to the back of my neck. "Holy shit," I whisper.

A pleased smile tips up her lips.

"You're right. Doesn't look like you need me at all."

She stalks off, that smug expression painted firmly in place. I watch her until she disappears from sight, the smile on my face so big and awestruck I think it might have been worth trading those Cardinal tickets for.

AFTER LEAVING THE GOLF COURSE, I MEET UP WITH ONE OF THE GUYS who works for me, Heath, for a quick dinner before I head out of town.

"Can I get you guys anything else?" our waitress at The Hideout asks, her eyes not leaving Heath.

Amused, I rest an arm on the back of the empty chair next to me and wonder when she's going to realize she hasn't put down the beer she's holding on her tray. *My* beer.

"Just that Bud Light you got there," Heath says with a wink.

"Oh, right, of course." Flustered, she sets the pint in front of Heath, gives him one last awkward smile, and then scurries off.

Heath wraps his hand around the glass and lifts it.

"Give me that." I reach out and take it from him before he gets a drink. After a long pull of the cold beer, I ask, "You wanna get us both in trouble?"

"Relax, it's just a beer. Besides, I look twenty-one."

"Oh, well then, I guess it's perfectly fine since you *look* old enough."

"I've drank here lots of times. It's no big deal."

I'm about to lecture him, or at least tell him not to tell me shit like that so I don't have it on my conscience, as a couple of guys walk by the table and then backtrack when they notice Heath. He stands and the guys chat for a few minutes before he motions toward me and tells them he'll meet up with them later.

I officially feel like an old man. He's making plans to go out after dinner and the only thing I have scheduled is a night alone, probably working.

"Looks like things are going well for you. Try not to get yourself into trouble. You get caught drinking underage and—"

Heath groans. "Save it. Between you and my brother, I've had this same conversation nearly every day since I got here five months ago. *Five months.*" He holds up a hand and wiggles his fingers for emphasis. "I made it through one semester, didn't I?"

His sullen expression makes him look like the teenager he is, and I hold back a laugh.

"Noted. Tell me about the team."

Heath gives me the rundown on school and the Valley U hockey team while we eat. He's a good kid. Typical freshman looking to jump off the deep end and enjoy everything college has to offer.

I feel a sense of responsibility for him, almost like a kid brother. I met his real brother Nathan last year through a mutual friend.

He worked for me through his senior year of college, coaching aspiring basketball players. Their home situation wasn't the best at the time and they both needed some extra cash, so I hired Heath to field the hockey questions that come in from other athletes trying to get an edge.

Though my background is golf, my coaching website spans multiple sports and is growing faster than I can keep up with. Heath is just one of the many experts and stars in their field mentoring the next generation of great athletes.

Heath's a talented kid who won't need my help for long if he keeps himself out of trouble.

The waitress drops the bill on the table and slides it in front of me as she gives me a timid smile. It's the first time she's given me much notice. Her eyes flash to Heath and he gives her a wink as she hurries away.

"Thanks for dinner," Heath says. "You wanna meet some of the guys?"

Do I? A glance around the busy bar. Since we sat down, the college hangout has gone from a handful of empty tables to standing room only. Classes start back tomorrow, and everyone is ready to see their friends and party, totally undeterred by the chaos. I'm sure I was the same way, but that feels like a million years ago.

I suppress a groan. No, I definitely don't want to mingle in this crowd. Thirty isn't exactly old, but the years that separate me from these kids are dog years. However, if I'm looking out for him like a big brother would that probably includes hiking up my old man balls and tucking them into my waistband so I can meet the people he's spending time with.

CHAPTER THREE

Keira

Abby and I meet some of the team at our favorite local restaurant and bar. It's crowded, which isn't all that surprising. A new semester starts tomorrow and the best thing about going on break is coming back and catching up with friends.

And this is the perfect place to do that while also bumping into lots of other people. Frat guys, sorority girls, jocks, nerds . . . The Hideout is beloved by just about everyone. Greasy food and cheap drinks, you really can't go wrong.

We give up on finding a table, grab drinks from the bar, and then make our way over to Erica and Cassidy. The four of us stand in a tiny circle, basically shoulder to shoulder.

"It's so packed," Erica says as someone bumps into her from behind and sends her stumbling forward, her vodka and cranberry spilling over the side of the glass.

Abby grabs her elbow and steadies her. "You okay?"

She nods but still shoots a dirty look to the guy behind her.

"Be right back," Cassidy says. "I'm gonna do a lap and see if I know anyone sitting at a table. Maybe we can squeeze in."

After she disappears, Abby looks to Erica. "How was break?"

"It was good. I went to North Carolina with Cassidy. You guys should see her dad. Holy silver fox. I mean, I'd seen him a few times before at tournaments, but when he's at home in old concert T-shirts and sweatpants..." She tilts her chin toward the ceiling and sighs.

"You're ridiculous," Abby says. "And if Cass hears you, she's never going to invite you back home with her."

Erica just shrugs. "What about you guys?" She looks between Abby and me.

"Smith and I split the time between our families. He came to Texas for Christmas, and I went to Alabama for New Year's Eve."

Both girls glance to me expectantly.

"It was nice."

Erica snorts. "That's code for boring as hell because you spent the entire time playing golf instead of enjoying break."

She isn't wrong, but golf is what keeps me sane. Well, golf and nights out with my girls. But in their absence, I might have spent more time than usual with a club in my hand.

Before I can defend myself, Cassidy returns with four shots, and is grinning as she holds them out to us. "I didn't find a table, but if you can't beat 'em, join 'em."

Erica grabs one excitedly and Abby laughs as she takes one, eyes the lime wedge, and then sniffs the alcohol. "Tequila? This early?"

"I told the bartender to surprise me."

Cassidy dangles the last shot glass in front of my face. "Ready to get drunk enough we can't feel how much our feet hurt from standing in these heels?"

"Some of us were sensible enough not to wear five-inch heels to the bar." I lift a foot, showing off my chunky heel boots.

"Cute," she says, eyeing them with appreciation before holding up her shot glass. The rest of us join in, raising our glasses to the center and clinking them together before throwing back the strong liquor.

We all grimace, and Erica gags a little as she sucks on the lime.

"No more shots," Abby says, and we all agree.

Ah, the best laid plans.

One hour and two shots later, my face is flushed pink and I can't stop smiling. I'm holding on to Cassidy as we make our way back from the restroom. The place has only gotten busier, but the alcohol is doing its magic, and I'm less annoyed when people bump us from both sides like we're inside a human pinball machine.

Cass leads the way, a step ahead of me, her blonde hair swaying side to side with each short, bouncy step she takes. Every two seconds, she stops to say hello to someone. She's definitely the most social and outgoing of my teammates.

As the top-rated girl on our team, it should be easy for me to think of her as competition, but she's just too dang nice to dislike.

Tonight is exactly what I needed. A carefree evening with my girls. I've no sooner thought about how much fun I'm having when I spot Abby with Smith at the bar. I stop, and Cass looks back as our hands start to separate. She follows my line of vision.

"Awww, they're so cute." When I don't comment, she adds, "You don't think so?"

"No, they're perfect together. I was just having a good time spending the night with just us girls. Since they started dating, I barely see her outside of practice."

She gives me a reassuring smile. "Come on. Let's find Erica."

When we eventually find the missing member of our party, she's sitting at the end of a table with three of the golf guys.

"Hey," Erica says, "look who I found."

"What's up, Keira? Hey, Cass." Keith stands and offers me his seat. He smacks Griff on the shoulder as he's mid drink. "Get up, man."

Cassidy and I take their seats across from Erica and Chapman.

The guys somehow manage to find two free chairs and drag them up to the ends. Keith gets another pitcher of beer and more shots magically appear.

I can't have another drink. I'm already riding the line between puking in a public restroom toilet and passing out peacefully as soon as my head hits the pillow. The latter is my preference, obviously. But I know myself and one more shot and I'll think I'm invincible to the effects of alcohol.

"No," I say when all eyes fall to me and the last shot glass on the table. "I can't."

"Come on, one more shot and then we'll go dance," Cass pleads.

"Dance?" I ask and look around. "Where?"

"Anywhere and everywhere," she singsongs with a laugh.

I glance to Erica for backup, but she looks just as excited as Cassidy. I have no idea where these two are storing their liquor, but they don't seem nearly as drunk as I am. They're only slightly taller than me, and we have similar builds. I could toss either one of them over my shoulder like a rag doll.

Okay, actually that's a lie, I'm too scrawny to toss anyone like that except maybe an actual rag doll, but I'm definitely stronger than them so why am I the only one feeling it so hard right now?

Someone slides the shot glass from the center of the table to just in front of me. I open my mouth to protest again, but Cassidy looks at me with those big, brown eyes. The girl is some sort of sweet ninja with her ability to make me want to do things.

I don't usually care about going along with people just because I can stand on my own—maybe too much sometimes. But if Cassidy were holding a torch gun in one hand and a bottle of moonshine in the other, I'd probably want to tag right along to see what she was going to get into.

She's the scary type of friend who makes everything seem like a fun time until you're sitting in the back of a police car or holding your head over the toilet while you sit on the dirty floor of a frat house bathroom. That first thing hasn't happened yet, but the second has on more than one occasion.

I knew she had this effect on me within two hours of meeting her freshman year, so I shouldn't be surprised that right now as she tries to push a shot glass in my hand, my fingers curl around it and effectively sign me up for wherever the night might lead.

Cassidy squeals with victory as I raise the shot. "Cheers!" she exclaims merrily, making sure to clink glasses with everyone.

I give a little mini salute with mine and then bring it to my lips. I tip the shot glass back ever so slightly so just a taste falls into my mouth, and my stomach clenches in warning. Nope, not happening. Absolutely not.

As discretely as I can, I move the glass to the left and quickly toss the remaining liquid over my shoulder. I glance around to see if anyone noticed, but everyone is busy squeezing their eyes closed and grimacing. Freaking tequila.

I giggle at the ridiculousness and set my empty glass on the table at the same time Cassidy does.

"That wasn't so bad, right?" she asks.

"No, it really wasn't," I say with sarcasm that goes totally missed.

Success. I'll just tag along tossing my good intentions and my drinks over my shoulder with no one being the wiser.

CHAPTER FOUR

Lincoln

I hate to admit it, but I'm not having an awful time. I feel a little old as these kids talk about lounging around their parents' houses all break and how bummed they are to start waking up for eight a.m. classes again, but I can't remember the last time I had a night out that was this carefree.

Sure, I go to games and get to booze and schmooze, but I'm there to make connections, not to get shitfaced. As such, there's always a certain level of professionalism I have to maintain so when business talk slips in, which it always does, I'm ready to make my pitch.

I stand from the table of hockey players, which is more difficult than it should be thanks to the crowd. I sidestep at the same time as something wet hits my neck and trickles down the back of my shirt.

What the hell?

My hand instinctively wipes away the liquid, and I turn my head to survey the spot on my white shirt. The smell of tequila hits me, and a cold shiver runs down my spine. Tequila and I are not friends. That bitch screwed me over years ago, and I still haven't forgiven her.

I look up to find wide, brown eyes staring at me, horrified. I glance between the soaked fabric and the empty shot glass in her hand.

"You," I say at the same time she blurts out, "Oh my God, I'm so sorry."

The girl from the golf course yells at someone to hand her napkins, but no one at the table is paying attention, so she finally leans over to the holder, grabs a handful, and turns to shove them toward me. Seeing her flustered after she was all confidence and sass earlier is comical.

"If you were aiming for your mouth, I'd say you missed."

"My aim was dead on, but I wasn't expecting someone to walk into it."

Ah, there it is. I lied. Her sass is far more amusing than her fluster.

"You were trying to toss tequila on strangers?"

"Not on strangers, just anywhere but my mouth."

I chuckle at her response. I feel that.

"I can't take another shot," she adds with a wobble of her head.

I look to the group she's with. They still haven't noticed she's gone, and by the number of empty shot glasses on the table, I can assume they are all drunk.

I can't tell if she's in the same boat, but since she's chucking shots over her shoulder, I'd say it's likely she's either drunk or out of her mind. Someone bumps her from the side, and I reach out to catch her, cupping her small shoulders. Her long, reddish-brown hair falls forward, teasing my fingers.

There's no way for me not to check her out this close up. Tight jeans wrap around her legs and come up high on her waist, meeting a white sweater that seems twice as short as a normal shirt should be.

My lips twitch at the same hot pink scrunchie from earlier circling her wrist. And are those unicorns on it?

People have been bumping into me all night, but this is the first time I haven't minded the contact. I inhale, catching a whiff of raspberries and tequila.

Heath appears beside me, and her gaze momentarily flits to him before resting back on me. She steps back and tries again to hand me the napkins, but I shake my head. "I'll live."

Heath snickers. "Don't mind him. He could use a shot or two." Then he turns to me. "Linc, I'll be right back."

"Keira!" A girl in a tiny black dress appears at her side and hugs her arm. "I thought you ditched us and went home."

I test her name out, saying it in my head as I look her over. *Keira*. It fits.

"No, sorry, I just ran into . . ." She stops as if she's trying to remember my name. *Ouch*.

"Lincoln," I say, saving her.

"Hey, I'm Cassidy." She pulls her arm free from Keira's and smiles—one of those big, Julia-Roberts grins with so much teeth it's a little scary. "Come, both of you should sit before someone else tries to squeeze in."

Cassidy and Keira slide in, and I step up to the table.

"Holy shit. Lincoln Reeves." One of the guys at the table stands, runs a hand through his hair, and then thrusts his hand out, takes it back, and then smiles sheepishly. "Hello, sir, or Lincoln. Mr. Reeves? I mean, hey, man."

I'm having trouble remembering where I met the kid before until Smith Jacobson steps beside him and places a hand on his shoulder. "Hey, Lincoln. We weren't expecting to see you here."

Ah shit. Figures Keira would be sitting with a bunch of guys from the golf team.

I rub the back of my neck. "Hey, guys. Good to see you. I was just about to head out."

"No, no way," Smith says. "Stay and have a drink with us."

I don't see much of a polite way out, so I nod. "All right, one beer."

Smith grabs me a chair, which I pull up next to Keira, and a glass is filled and pushed into my hand. Then it's twenty minutes of constant questions before the guys take a break long enough for me to take a drink and glance at Keira.

She fidgets with the pink scrunchie on her wrist, tugging and twisting it. I keep staring and finally she looks up as if she can feel the weight of my gaze on her. Her lips curve up, not exactly in a smile, but she no longer looks like she's plotting my death.

Someone orders a round of shots, and I take the opportunity to slide my chair closer until my arm brushes the soft fabric of her sweater. "Let me know which way you're tossing so I can stay dry."

I raise a shot glass and a brow, daring her to do the same. Keira brings it to her lips first as if she's considering drinking it just to spite me, which wasn't my goal at all. If she says she's too drunk to have another, I believe it.

While she sits frozen, summoning the courage or whatever, I keep my eyes locked with hers and chuck the contents over my shoulder. Her pink lips tilt up into a relieved smile and then she does the same.

She holds my gaze as we both set our empty glasses on the table.

"Let's go to The White House!" someone exclaims, breaking the moment. "I heard they're having people over for after hours!"

Keira looks away first, and I shake my head, trying to make sense of the weird turn this night's taken.

There's some back and forth over it, but the general consensus is they're all ready to take the party elsewhere. Keira stands to let her friend out, and I unfold myself from my chair to make room.

She fiddles with that hot pink scrunchie on her right arm and peers up at me through dark lashes. "I'm sorry," she says when everyone else has gone to the bar to close out.

"What's that?" I ask, leaning down and holding back a smile. I'm totally messing with her, and she knows it.

She lets out a long breath. "I said I'm sorry. I was pissed at my coach, and I took it out on you."

"And the tequila?"

"*That* was an accident."

"Maybe we should start over." I grin and offer her my hand. "I'm Lincoln. Swing coach, business owner, non-creeper."

She stares at my hand for a beat before placing her palm in mine. A shot of pleasure races up my arm.

"Keira. Golfer, college student, skeptic."

A deep chuckle escapes from my chest. "Nice to meet you, Keira."

We stand smiling at one another, taking the other in, until someone bumps into her again. I motion for her to have a seat so we're out of the way and then take the chair next to her.

"I think you made a few lifelong fans," she says, and I follow her slight nod to where Keith and Chapman stand talking.

Chapman lifts his beer in a salute, and I wave before responding to Keira. "Believe it or not, most people were excited to see me today."

"I thought we were starting over."

"Fair enough. I won't mention it again, but just so you know, I did offer my services to your coach."

Her eyes widen in surprise. "Really?"

"He said no, obviously. My guess is that I'm not the first person he's said no to, if that helps your hatred toward all mankind any."

Her jaw clenches and her features go from gorgeous to glower, which also happens to be gorgeous—so long as she isn't glowering at me. "Why would he do that?"

"Some coaches like things a certain way and think bringing another person in messes with their system." Do I think it's bullshit? Yes. But I'm not about to admit that.

"I'm never going to get my spot back." She meets my gaze. "I was travelling with the team until last fall."

"What happened?"

"I had a bad tournament, lost my head." She shrugs. "Coach replaced me, and I'm pretty sure he's going to punish me indefinitely for it." Her dark lashes flutter closed as her voice softens. "I miss it. The early morning smell on the course just before the first group tees off and the buzz of energy as the last pair walks onto the green on the final hole." When she opens her eyes, her face flushes adorably.

I clear my throat and take a sip of my beer. "I'm sorry. That's tough."

"Are you speaking from experience or just being nice?"

"I got looked over plenty of times," I assure her.

"What did you do?"

"Worked harder, proved I belonged out there."

She rolls her eyes. "I could win the freaking US Open, and it wouldn't make a difference to Coach Potter. He hates me."

"So, do it. You don't need him to go the professional route."

She scoffs, but I'm not wrong. Playing college golf isn't the only way to go pro—or even the best way.

"No, but I do need coaching and experience, neither of which I'm getting. And now I know he isn't letting anyone else come in and help me either. What a prick."

"He really that bad?"

"He's a dictator, ruling with fear instead of respect. He makes the game less fun for everyone." She sits up a little taller and lets out a deep breath. "Anyway, not your problem."

"Still, he's managed to have some impressive seasons."

"That's because the team is crazy talented. Coach Hanson, the coach before Potter took over, was amazing. Everyone loved him. He's the reason the team is stacked. He recruited hard, and everyone wanted to play for him. He left to coach at a smaller school closer to family, and Coach Potter took over right before my freshmen year. Really regretting not going to Duke about now," she mumbles the last part.

Smith and his girlfriend appear at the table, interrupting what I'm sure was likely to be a much longer tirade.

"Hey, Lincoln," Smith says, near empty beer in hand. "I just wanted to say thanks for all your tips today. I worked on them all evening. My release is already looking better. I took video, just like you said. And I signed up for an account on your site."

"Good, I'm really glad it was helpful."

"Keira, are you ready?" Abby asks. "We're heading out."

She stands. "Yeah, can you guys drop me off on the way? I'm ready to crash."

Smith nods, finishes his beer, and places the empty glass on the table.

"Well, it was interesting," Keira says, hanging back as her friends start to leave.

"It was really good to meet you."

"Same." And with that, she moves to follow her friends out of the bar.

I call out before she gets lost in the crowd. "Keira."

"Yeah?" She angles herself between tables and groups of people on each side. Those brown eyes soften, and warmth spreads through my chest. I think about asking her to stay. I want to keep listening as she talks about golf with a passion that vibrates off every word. I understand it and respect the hell out of it.

Instead, I go with something much more appropriate. "Work hard, keep your head down, you'll be okay."

She seems to let my advice sink in for a moment before she gives a slight head bob and then ducks into the crowd.

CHAPTER FIVE

Lincoln

I sit up with a groan and look around the small, drab hotel room. I slept like shit. By the time I found Heath and got out of the bar, it was almost midnight.

I'd planned on going back yesterday afternoon as soon as the clinic was over, but Nathan found out I was at Valley and wanted me to check on Heath and then, well, the night slipped away.

I only had two beers but driving the nearly three hours home that late with any amount of alcohol in my system seemed like a bad idea. Then, I couldn't fall asleep because I was too busy thinking about Keira and her fiery hatred of her coach.

I don't pretend to know if she's a good golfer just from watching her swing, but I know she has the potential to be, and that's even more exciting as a coach. So, why isn't Potter playing her?

I looked through everything I could find on the guy. He jumped around a few junior colleges before landing at Valley, decent records at all of them. Really, nothing out of the ordinary.

I followed that with looking up Keira.

Keira Brooks. Twenty-one, junior. Played on her local Valley high school team with all-state honors her junior and senior years. Since coming to Valley, she's placed in a handful of tournaments, missed the cut at the championship last spring, and had her first individual win a few months ago.

After that, I could only find one more tournament she played where she led until the last day and then bombed with three bogeys in a row and tossed a driver into a water hazard. I laughed at that because I could totally picture it. And then saw it for myself when I found a clip on YouTube. Guess that was what she meant by losing her head.

By the time I drag myself through getting ready for the day and get in my vehicle to head back to Scottsdale, I'm behind schedule. But I can probably take care of most of the things I missed last night and this morning with a few phone calls during the drive. When I get home, I can get to my client emails, and shit, I need to check in with all my direct reports too.

There's really no escape. Anything I put off one day just gets piled onto the next. Still, I think last night might have been worth it; although, I need some caffeine.

At the end of the parking lot, I hesitate to turn right toward the freeway. I rub at the back of my neck and let out a sigh.

It's none of my business. I have better things to do. I shouldn't get involved. I have my own shit to handle. I absolutely shouldn't be angling for ways I can see Keira again. Not only would that be a bad business decision, but also a terrible personal decision.

Fuck.

I turn left.

At the Valley U golf course, I head through the clubhouse and out to the driving range, where I find Mark hitting a few balls. He leans on his driver and waits until I reach him before he says, "Hey, Linc. What are you doing back?"

Shifting awkwardly, I wonder if I made a mistake coming here without calling first...or just coming at all. I'm winging it, and I hate winging shit.

"I took a look at the videos from yesterday and thought it might be useful if I could sit with the boys and talk them through what I see."

"Yeah, of course." He gives me a weird look. "I don't have the budget to pay for another day."

I hold up a hand. "No, of course not, and in fact, I'm crediting you back for yesterday. We're friends—or, at least, we used to be. I just want to help. They seem like good kids, and like I said yesterday, I really appreciate that you've been such a big supporter of my business. I should have offered long before you reached out."

"All right, don't get too soft on me or I'll think too hard about why you're being so accommodating. The truth is that I don't care why. I need all the help I can get. Practice isn't for a few hours still though."

I nod. "I figured. Uh, one other thing. Do you think it would be okay if I offered my services to anyone that comes by today?"

His brows furrow. "You mean like a public clinic?"

"Sure. To anyone. Not all my clients are competitive athletes, you know?"

"Yeah, I don't see a problem with that. Just tell me what you need."

Mark and I drag a table and three chairs outside and he erects a sunshade over me while I setup my laptop.

I'm actually a little disappointed I didn't think to do this yesterday. Yeah, it takes more time, but it'll be easier to provide specific and hopefully helpful feedback when I can show them exactly what I mean on the video.

It's slow for the first hour. A handful of people come by the course, but only one is interested in help.

Lou is a retired Valley professor who, according to him, is trying to figure out what to do with his days now that he's no longer teaching. He's a nice guy, and I enjoy chatting with him, but I cringe as I watch his swing back on the screen. There are so many problems that all I can do is help with his setup and grip. Feels like a shallow victory when he masters that and heads off to the driving range.

Mark let his team know I was here again today, so they drop in early, which is nice since I'm twiddling my thumbs and triple guessing being here.

As I suspected, showing them slow-motion clips of their swings gives them a better understanding of what they are doing wrong and where they can improve. The real challenge comes from their ability to change habits that have been ingrained with thousands of golf balls. But it's a start.

I'm finishing the last review when she arrives with a few other girls she was with last night. Her eyes narrow in confusion and she slows her pace. The girl to her left, Erica, I think, says something that Keira waves off.

I meet her halfway.

A small smile tugs at the corners of her mouth. "You're back."

"So are you."

She tilts her head toward the girls she walked away from. "We have practice in fifteen minutes. What are *you* doing here?" She looks past me to my tent setup and smirks. "Another clinic with the boys' team?"

"No. Well, yes, but not them exclusively. It's a free clinic and it's completely open to the public."

"The public?" Her voice lifts an octave while she puts it together. A slow smile spreads across her face.

"Maybe you could let the *public* know? What time is practice over?"

"Five." She's still looking at me as if she maybe doesn't believe I'm for real. "You'll still be here?"

"I'll still be here."

The hopeful and pleased look she gives me makes my day seem not quite so wasted.

As the girls' team heads off to practice, the driving range gets crowded with locals. I'm too busy to watch the time pass, but two hours later, the Valley U women's golf team starts to fill my line. Though Keira is nowhere in sight.

I'm helping the first one of his players, when Coach Potter storms over. "What's going on here? I thought I said I didn't want you offering your services to my girls?"

The young girl in front of me, a freshman named Clarice, wilts in his presence.

"It's a free swing review. What could it hurt?"

"Clarice, go on now," Potter instructs. "Practice is over for the day."

I step to him, giving Clarice and the rest of the girls my back, and lower my voice. "I get that you want to be the end all be all to these girls, but you might consider that I have something to offer them, as do a lot of other people."

He scoffs, shoots me a glare, and then sends one over my shoulder to the girls as well. What a prick.

"My way. My rules," he grits out and pushes past me, telling his girls to go home and rest up.

One by one, they shuffle away, looking defeated. Once again, I look around for Keira, finally finding her on the driving range. Her gaze follows Coach and her teammates, eyes blazing with hatred I'm finding it hard to blame her for.

She walks toward us with purpose, ponytail swinging side to side with every determined step. She stops and briefly chats with one of the girls, jaw tightens, and then she marches toward me.

Her teammates watch her with something like admiration, and when she reaches the tent, she hesitates for only a second before walking in and taking a seat.

"Are you sure about this?" I ask quietly.

She meets my gaze and then lets it slide to the left so she's glaring at her coach. "Definitely."

I try to forget about everything else around us and focus only on Keira, which isn't really that difficult. Any hope I had that my fascination could be easily expelled by setting things right is shattered when I see her in action again. Everything about the way she moves with a golf club excites me.

It takes maybe two minutes to record her swing from every angle and upload it to my laptop so I can show her. In that time, her coach has disappeared, and her teammates have gathered back around.

I play her video as she sits in the chair on the other side of the table.

"You have a good swing...really good, actually. Nice and smooth. A few tweaks, and you'll be hitting greens all day long."

Her lips curve up as she laces her fingers together in her lap.

I freeze the video and then turn the screen so I can show her. "Right here, see how you're extending early? You're shifting your swing plane. I've seen much worse cases, but I think it's where your inconsistency comes from. It also looks as if you're holding back a little in a few of these."

"I've had issues in the past with opening my hips too quickly. Coach Potter doesn't want me swinging as hard as I can because I'm not consistent enough to control it."

I grind my teeth a little and bite my tongue. "Yeah, it's all related. But you have power, and you should use it. Let me show you something."

Standing, I come around the table and walk her through a drill I use on clients with the same issue. She watches, brown eyes following my every move with interest.

"You wanna try it?" I ask when I'm done.

Silently, she stands and gets into position with her club.

"Do a few without the club first to get a feel for it. Bring it back to the basics. Changing motor functions requires breaking it down to the simplest movements."

She tosses her club to the ground, and I step in front of her and get in position. Sometimes people are self-conscious, so doing the training with them helps remove barriers.

We move together, her mirroring me. I'm so close I can smell the fruity scent of her hair and a hint of sunscreen with each gust of wind.

"Nice, there you go. Can you feel the urge to push off that right leg?"

"Yeah, I really can." She does it again, mouth set in a determined line and the tip of her tongue between her teeth.

"Do that about a thousand times and then add in your arms." I extend my hands out in front of me and do the same motion. "And then you can add the club back to your swing."

She nods again, but this time, it's with a lot more enthusiasm. "Thank you."

"I didn't say anything any guy with a Golf Channel subscription couldn't have." I wink and grab a business card off the table. "I'd love to hear how it works for you or if you have any questions. You really do have a beautiful swing. Best I've seen in a long time. If I had a swing like that, they'd be fitting me for a green jacket."

The tips of her fingers brush mine as she reaches for my card. Neither of us makes a move to break the contact right away, and her pale skin dots with pink on her neck and cheeks. "Thanks, Lincoln."

She pulls away, tucking the card into her pocket and grabbing her club. As she walks backward out of the tent, I find myself holding her gaze. I can't seem to look away. With the flip of her ponytail, she's gone and the next girl steps through.

CHAPTER SIX

Keira

By the time I shower and scarf down a Pop-Tart, I have to sprint across campus to make it to my evening physical chemistry lab. I slip into my chair with only seconds to spare.

Professor Teague lifts a brow and glances at the clock. The head of the department is a huge stickler for attendance and being on time.

I catch my breath and hurriedly drink my Red Bull while he goes over the syllabus and then gives a brief lecture for today's lab. He removes his glasses and holds them in front of him as he says, "You may get started."

I swivel in my chair to face Keith. He's a chemistry major like I am, and we've been partners for nearly every lab since freshmen year. He's big on following the rules and does so to the point of basically brown nosing. Our friendship causes him great anxiety, I'm sure.

"Are you trying to get on his bad side on the first day?" he asks as he shakes his head. "You know he'll dock us points if you're late."

"Relax, I made it."

"I'm gonna get an ulcer if you cut it that close every week."

"Practice ran late."

"Oh, I heard," he says as he sets up.

I skim over the instructions and the questions we'll need to answer as we go along. "You heard what?"

"That you caused a scene after practice," Keith says, tosses me a disapproving smirk, and then tries to read the handout upside down. "Tell me, do you try to make waves everywhere you go, or is it just a special gift?"

I know he's mostly teasing, but I still bristle. "Coach Potter is a jerk. There is no reason we shouldn't get the same extra resources you guys do. How'd you hear about it already anyway?"

"Everyone was talking about it at the house before I left."

Keith lives in an off-campus house with Smith and Chapman. I'm pretty sure I have Abby to thank for Keith knowing, not that it wouldn't have gotten out anyway. But, screw it, I stand by my actions. I learned a lot from Lincoln, so it was well worth whatever punishment Coach plans on doling out.

"Look, I don't blame you. Lincoln Reeves is the best there is. I don't know if I'd have gone against my coach's wishes and made a scene like you did, but I get it."

"Your coach would never do that to you."

He shrugs and we start on the lab, easily falling into sync. We've worked together enough that we don't waste time deciding who does what, we both jump in and do what's necessary.

"What do you mean, he's the best there is?" I ask a few minutes later.

He looks up, the protective goggles on his face making it hard to tell he's raising his brows in question.

"Lincoln Reeves," I explain. "You said he was the best there is."

"Oh, right." He scribbles something on our paper before continuing, "You don't know who he is?"

"Just that he's a swing coach. Abby said he was a big deal." I lift one shoulder and let it fall. "He seems to know his stuff."

"Lincoln Reeves is going to be a legend. Reeves Sports, his online coaching website, is still new, but it's already one of the best out there. It has every sport you can imagine. Baseball, football, lacrosse, rugby, pickle ball, curling. And the athletes he has coaching?" Keith raises his goggles so they rest on the top of his wavy, brown hair. His blue eyes widen with excitement, and there's a faint outline from the goggles making him look funny. "He has pro-level coaches answering questions, providing tutorials, and creating training plans. When you sign up, you're getting the best of the best as your personal coach. If I had the funds, I'd totally sign up."

"Is it expensive?"

"Nah, but it's still out of my price range."

"Pretty cool," I say, but the excitement that hums through my veins makes me want to open my laptop right here and check it out. And maybe check out Lincoln some more while I'm at it.

He's...well, hot, of course, but there's something about his rare smile that makes my stomach flip. Mostly, those smiles seem to come at my expense, but I still can't help but admire them.

"Yeah, it really is."

"So, why would he come to Valley?" I ask, stopping any pretense that I'm working, and take a seat. "No offense, but you guys aren't exactly attracting media attention."

"He and Coach James played together in high school."

It's weird to picture Lincoln and Coach James as being in the same age bracket. Coach James is a younger coach. It's his fifth year at Valley and second as head coach. Still, that has to make Lincoln, what? Thirty? The way he holds himself and the experience that oozes off him make him seem like he could be that old. But last night at the bar, he seemed like one of us—a hot grad student maybe.

"Did he play college?"

"They both did; although, not together. Coach James went to ASU. Lincoln went to Texas for a couple of years before he went pro."

"He's a pro? How come I've never heard of him?"

"He didn't tour for long. He struggled the first year, missed a lot of cuts, and almost lost his eligibility. Then, as soon as he started placing and gaining momentum, he had some back issues that took him out for a year. They were speculating that when he returned, he'd be the next big thing, but when he resurfaced, it was as a swing coach for one of his friends on the tour. He worked with several pros before starting his company."

"Really? He coaches the pros?"

"Yeah, well, he did. I heard him say he only personally coaches a handful of clients now so he can focus on the business."

I nod, lost in my thoughts. Keith pulls his goggles back down over his eyes, and we get back to work.

After lab, Keith walks me back to the dorm on the way to his car.

"Thanks," I say as we approach the front of Freddy. "See you in class tomorrow."

"No problem, and, uh, maybe be on time. Need me to text you?"

I roll my eyes. "I got it."

Inside my room, I toss my bag on the bed, lie down beside it, and stare up at the ceiling, exhausted. My reprieve only lasts a few seconds before I sit up and grab my laptop and the card Lincoln gave me earlier.

Lincoln Reeves, Owner Reeves Sports. It lists the website URL, his email address, and phone number.

I place it on the bed next to my laptop and type in the web address. My pulse quickens as the logo appears in the left-hand corner. There's a video on the main page, Lincoln's build and those full lips of his are frozen on the screen.

Smiling, I click play and listen intently as he gives a thirty-second pitch for the site. His tone is serious, no smiles or enthusiasm—all business.

From there, I navigate to the golf portion of the site and watch another video, then two more. He holds a seven iron casually in his left hand, standing on a driving range, swinging the club lightly as he talks to the camera. He goes through a proper setup and then a few drills. It's an introduction video, beginner stuff, but his command speaks to the breadth of knowledge I now know he has.

He isn't saying anything I don't know, but it's the way he moves, and the memory of how being coached by him felt. Even now, my face warms like it had as his confidence and guidance wrapped around me earlier, making me feel as if I could do it—I could be exactly who I want to be. Nothing else mattered, only golf. I wish I could bottle that feeling.

There are a lot of videos. Some are by different coaches, and others feature current pros—men and women. I must view twenty videos, each one from start to finish, afraid I might miss the smallest piece of advice.

I click through every single one with Lincoln. He really is the best. His explanations are clear and concise, and he's able to break it down in a way that makes sense.

I press play on another. In this one, he's teaching the stinger. After a few minutes of explanation, he sets up to demo it. His swing is a beautiful, effortless thing. The ball rushes down the fairway, low and straight, before it bounces onto the green and rolls smoothly toward the pin and in.

His smile turns boyish with surprise at the hole in one he just caught on video. He treks down the green with the camera at nearly a run. When he pulls the ball from the hole, he holds it up and smiles with pride and excitement. Pressing pause, I smile back.

I open my email, type in his address, and then pause, going back and forth over how to address him. Lincoln? Mr. Reeves? Eventually, I decide to leave off all formalities.

Thanks for today. I've never seen Coach Potter so mad.

Keira

P.S. Sorry again for insinuating that you might be a creeper...and for throwing tequila on you.

After I press send, I get ready for bed and watch a few videos on my phone.

There's a nine-year-old kid in Florida who has his own golf channel where he does trick shots. It's one of my favorites, and I watch his newest video as my eyes get heavy.

He's blindfolded and stands in front of five golf balls teed up about a foot apart. He goes down the line, hitting each one dead on.

It's impressive, and his young face beams as he removes his mask.

His love and joy for the sport leaves an uncomfortable ache in my chest. Coach Potter makes it easy to forget how much I love golf, but today was a good day, and I want to savor it before he ruins it tomorrow.

I LOADED MY SCHEDULE TO TAKE MOST OF MY CLASSES ON TUESDAYS and Thursdays so that I can get in more practice time on my light days and so I can check in on Dad and take him to doctor appointments, as needed.

I'm eating a bowl of noodles for lunch when I finally check my email and see that Lincoln responded. I open it with a giddy smile.

> **You're welcome. I hope you aren't in more trouble with your coach. Working on the drills?**
>
> **Lincoln**

Still chewing, I type out a quick response.

> **Headed to the course early to practice. I'll find out what sort of punishment Coach has in store for me in a couple of hours. Whatever it is, it will be worth it. Are you still in town, maybe going around door to door to see if there's anyone else you can help?**
>
> **Keira**

"DAD," I CALL OUT AS I COME THROUGH THE FRONT DOOR LATER THAT evening.

The television is on, but he isn't in his favorite recliner. I stop at the dining room table and strip off my jacket and place it on the back of a chair.

The floor creaks, and his cane knocks on the hardwood before he shuffles into view.

"Hey, kiddo. Wasn't expecting you."

He hobbles the rest of the way to drop a kiss on my forehead, pausing before his lips press to my skin. "You smell like golf."

I snort. "Like golf?"

"Yeah. Fresh-cut grass and sweat with a dab of Hawaiian Tropic." He drops the kiss, and I smile into his quick embrace. "How was practice?"

"Shot seventy-two." I smile for the first time in a long time when thinking about practice. Even Coach ignoring me all afternoon can't take away my excitement. "Best score on the team today."

He takes a seat in his chair and mutes the basketball game. "Proud of you."

"I thought I'd make dinner for us."

"Already ate," he says, not quite meeting my gaze.

"You didn't?" I ask and move toward the pantry. When I see the empty frozen meal box in the trash, I groan. "Dad, no one should eat those. Ever. Ever, ever."

"The Suns are playing. I didn't want to bother with cooking. Besides, they really aren't that bad. Tell me about golf. When's your next tournament?"

He's deflecting, but golf is always a good way to distract me. I tell him about the upcoming tournament. "I'm not going. Coach still hasn't moved me back to top five."

"You'll get there."

I shrug, not wanting to think too hard on what it'll take to get Coach to see that I deserve another chance. I change the conversation to school and fill him in on my class schedule this semester. He pretends to be interested while I take out ingredients for his favorite casserole.

My schedule, outside of golf is pretty short and uninteresting, and within a few minutes, we fall silent. With the exception of the occasional outburst at the television, neither of us speaks again until I cover the top of the dish in tin foil and set it in the fridge.

"Put it in the oven at three hundred fifty degrees for about thirty minutes. I'll be by later this week to take you to your doctor appointment."

He makes a dismissive grunt of acknowledgment. He hates feeling like he can't do stuff for himself, but since his accident, he needs me more than he's willing to admit.

A fall from a roof left him with a broken leg and a knee that needed extensive surgery to repair. It left me with a grumpy parent who is arguably the worst patient in all of history.

I tried to move back in with him at the end of last semester, but he wouldn't have it. He even went as far as to block my entry into the house when I'd arrived with an overnight bag.

I drop a kiss to his cheek. "Bye, Daddy. Stay away from the frozen dinners."

"You stay away from the junk food," he fires back.

I'd say it's unlikely either of us is going to heed the other's advice.

CHAPTER SEVEN

Lincoln

Gram hands me a New Balance shoebox. "Here are all his old client records, like you asked for."

I lift the top and laugh even as I cringe. "This is how he organized them?"

Index cards that don't appear to be in any kind of order take up most of the box. Underneath those are a yo-yo, a half-empty pack of Big Red gum, and a notebook my grandfather carried to jot things down during client sessions.

I shuffle through the cards, admiring his familiar handwriting. Some include addresses or phone numbers, but most don't. I take one out and read it aloud, "Mary Lou always wears purple."

I raise my eyes in question, and my grandmother smiles. "I remember Mary Lou. She was a snowbird and came down every year January through April from Wisconsin, I think. She passed a few years ago."

"Wears purple?"

She nods. "Always. Without fail."

I don't bother throwing out her card. My guess is they're all about as helpful.

My grandfather was a great teacher. People came from all over Arizona for lessons with him, sometimes farther. He was patient, encouraging, and smart, so freaking smart. And I'm not just biased because I looked up to him my entire life. He taught me the game, so I can attest to how much his teachings have stayed with me over the years. Everything I know about golf leads back to him in some way.

He wasn't as good of a businessman, it seems. Guess he didn't need to be. He was satisfied with the life he and my grandmother built here. If he were still alive, he'd probably balk at how much I've expanded the idea behind his small business. Reeves Sports is a tribute to the man I loved and a motivation to push harder, find success for myself, and ultimately, solidify my grandfather's legacy.

"These ought to be good for a laugh, if nothing else," I say and drop the box onto the dining room table. It's formally set with placemats, napkins, and dishes. And just like always, there is a bouquet of fresh flowers in the center. My gaze drops to the third setting. "Are we expecting someone else?"

Gram smiles. "I invited Patty's granddaughter, Autumn. You remember Autumn, right? She graduated and moved home."

I sigh. "Yeah, Gram, I remember her." I also remember that she dated my brother Kenton for two years. I use the word *dated* loosely, but either way—that's a hard limit for me. "I'm not interested in dating right now."

"Oh, you don't mean that. You're just scared after the way your marriage went up in flames."

I chuckle against my better judgment. Leave it to Grams not to pull any punches. "It isn't just that. I'm busy. The travel and long hours..."

"The right girl will make all of those excuses seem silly. You'll see."

No matter how many "right girls" Gram sends my way, I'll never be the *right* guy to be what they need. But I don't have the energy or headspace to try to convince my stubborn grandmother of that, so I accept defeat. "What can I do to help?"

"She'll be here in ten minutes, so go freshen up and let me worry about everything else." She cups my cheek lovingly and then darts off to the kitchen with more energy than I'd expect from someone her age. Energy that has been dead set on getting me a new wife since the day I signed the divorce papers a year ago.

Right on time, the doorbell rings. Gram shoos me to the door, and I drag it open with a forced smile.

"Hey, Lincoln." Autumn holds a bouquet of flowers in one hand and steps inside slowly.

"It's good to see you," I tell her and offer an awkward one-arm hug.

"You too." She looks around as if she's expecting someone else. "When your grandma invited me over to have dinner with her grandson, I assumed she meant Kenton."

Ah, well this makes more sense. No wonder she agreed to a setup. "Sorry about that."

She smiles, and it eases some of the tension for the night ahead. Gram appears, and Autumn steps forward. "Hi, Milly. These are for you."

"Oh, how lovely."

"I remember how you always had fresh flowers out. I used to love that."

Grandma's eyes sparkle, and her gaze slides over to me. "Isn't that nice, Lincoln?"

Good lord, I'm sure she's already imagining the flowers at my and Autumn's wedding. Pump the brakes, Gram.

"It sure is." I reach for the flowers. "Let me take care of those."

"Nonsense, you don't know what you're doing. You kids grab a drink. Dinner will be ready in fifteen minutes."

We do as Gram instructed and head out on the patio. Maybe the fresh air will help me feel less like I might suffocate at any moment.

Autumn is exactly like I remember her. Tall and thin with long blonde hair. Back when we were kids she was all tomboy, but if her dress and high heels are any indication, I'd say she's given up playing in the dirt and chasing lizards.

Our grandparents have lived next to one another for as long as I can remember, so we've bumped into one another a lot over the years. She and Kenton spent lots of weekends exploring the neighborhood while I tagged along with Pop when he went to work. He'd take me to the range, get me a bucket of balls to hit, and when those were gone, I'd sit on the ground and watch as he worked with clients. If it rained or when he travelled, I'd be forced to stay behind and hang out with my little brother and the girl next door.

"Relax, Lincoln, it's just dinner," she says after we're seated. "You look like you're ready to take off in a dead run down the ninth hole." She inclines her head toward the golf course behind Gram's house.

"Just dinner?" I laugh quietly. "You don't remember my grandma as well as you think you do."

She rolls her eyes and settles back into her chair, obviously more comfortable than I am. "What have you been up to? It's been years. I was sorry to hear about you and Lacey. I always liked her, she was really nice."

"Still is." I take a long, *long* drink and then fill her in on the major milestones of my life, which takes an embarrassingly short amount of time. "What about you?"

"I went to school upstate. Graduated last May, spent some time travelling Europe, and now I've accepted a position teaching middle school. It's a long-term sub gig for now, but hopefully it'll lead to a full-time job next year."

"A teacher?" I ask in surprise. Then she shoots me a glare that I bet makes her pre-pubescent students wet themselves and wipes the look off my face.

As she's telling me all the reasons she chose teaching as a career path, my phone rings with a call from my IT guy. Gram walks out to let us know it's time to eat and eyes the phone in my hand with a disapproving scowl.

"It's work. I'll be right there."

"Work can wait."

"Five minutes."

"Two," she states firmly. "Come on, Autumn. I want to hear about your plans now that you're back."

"Yes, ma'am," Autumn says, and they disappear into the house.

I place the phone to my ear. "Hey, Will. What's up?"

"Hey, boss man. Site crashed."

"How long?"

"Just happened. Looks like it was an operating system update. I'll have it back shortly, just wanted to give you a heads-up."

"Okay. Send me more information when you have it. Anything

else?" I ask, mostly to delay going inside. Will is one of those guys who needs minimal supervision, which I appreciate more than he knows. I barely have time to manage myself.

"All good. We're probably gonna need to add another server sometime in the next six months to handle the traffic, but we're okay for now." I can hear his fingers flying over the keyboard. "And we're back. A few emails came in at the same time, I'll put them in a zip file and re-send."

"Thanks."

"No problem. Later, boss man."

The call ends, and instead of hustling into the house like I should, I pull up my email. I really need to set up a filter to weed out the hundreds of spam messages I get every day. One from Keira Brooks catches my eye, and a smile spreads across my face as I open it. We've sent a few back and forth over the last couple of days as she's checked out the site and worked on the drills.

Saw your video with the hole in one. Impressive.

Keira

There's a video attached. Under any other circumstance, I might wait or have a second of hesitation about opening an unsolicited video from a girl I barely know, but since I'm avoiding dinner with my brother's ex, I click play.

The camera faces a blank, white wall. Keira comes into view, long hair pulled back into a ponytail. She glances back at the camera and smirks before holding up a red cup in her hand and then setting it on the floor.

She backs up about five feet, grabs a wedge and a ball, and stands sideways to the camera so I can see her profile. She takes a deep breath and then tosses the ball with her left hand and catches it with the club in her right.

She bounces the ball off the clubface in a steady rhythm. After a few bounces, she moves the club behind her and between her legs, keeping that rhythm and holding command over the ball.

Then she goes into trickier moves, catching it on the top of her shoe between bounces, kicking it with the sole of the other shoe behind her. It's really something to watch. I've seen plenty of trick shots, but she has a graceful, fluid control that most don't possess.

For the finale, she bounces the ball a touch harder, moves the club behind her back, taps the ball, and somehow hits it into the cup.

My eyes widen in disbelief. I watch it twice. If she somehow spliced the video, I sure as hell can't tell.

I send her a quick email in response.

How many tries did that take?

Lincoln

I'm smiling at my phone, watching the video a third time when another email from her comes in.

One.

Okay fine, three.

Keira

I kick my feet up and lean back, sending another reply.

Nice. How's the swing coming?

Lincoln

As if she's waiting for my email, the same way I'm waiting for hers, the reply is quick.

Just got back to my dorm. I'm going to work on the drills after I study.

Keira

The reminder that she is in college is a swift kick to the old man balls. She has a life outside of golf that I can't relate to anymore. I sit forward in my seat and send one last email.

Sign up for a free account on the site, there are a ton of videos that you'll have access to, and you can get one free swing review each month from someone on my team.

Even though I told myself the email was my final reply, I still wait for hers. It comes just as quickly as the others.

Your team, huh?

Keira

"Lincoln."

"Hmm." I raise my head slowly from my phone and find Gram scowling at me.

"I said your name three times before you answered. Put that phone away and come eat. Whatever it is, it can wait."

I place my phone in my pocket. "Sorry, Gram."

Dinner passes relatively quickly, and it isn't even that awkward because it's clear neither Autumn nor I are interested in the other. After thanking Gram, I walk Autumn out to her car.

"How is Kenton? Do you talk to him much?"

Hands in my pockets, I follow her slow pace. "He's good. Still in

L.A. playing soccer."

"He always said he was getting out of Arizona. I guess I should have believed him." She looks a little sad, and I don't know what to say. Kenton is . . . Kenton. Carefree and fun, incredibly hard working and successful but somehow still manages not to take himself too seriously. "Tell him I said hello."

I nod and open her car door. "It was good to see you. Congrats on graduating and good luck teaching."

"Thanks, Lincoln." She slips into the car and grabs a pen and scrap piece of paper from the console. She scribbles on it and then hands it to me. "Call me if you want to get together again."

A flicker of attraction in her eyes that wasn't present until just now surprises me and has me standing mute as she closes the door and starts the car. Well, that was unexpected.

When I get home, I grab a beer from the fridge and head into my office. I drop Pop's shoebox of contacts on my desk and open my laptop.

I check email first, curious as hell to reread the conversation with Keira, then shoot her a quick response.

Did you sign up?

Lincoln

I switch over to the site and log in so I can check my messages and swing submissions for the day. The notification for Keira's reply pops up in the bottom of the screen, and I click on it.

Yes. I submitted a video and someone named Simon is reviewing it.

Keira

I search through Simon's inbox, something I alone have the site privileges to do. When new members sign up, their inquiries are routed to one of three of my golf coaches. Simon has the least experience, but he's sharp.

I can see he's watched the video but hasn't responded yet. That isn't altogether surprising since it only came in an hour ago. We promise a response in twenty-four hours, so I expect he'll get back to her tomorrow.

I watch her swing, noting that she's worked on her weight shift. It isn't quite there, but the initial turn is better. My fingers itch to do her review myself, but there just aren't enough hours in the day. I really shouldn't be holding on to the few clients I have now, but coaching helps me remember why I'm doing this in the first place.

My phone rings, and I go to silence it but pause at the name on the screen. *Lacey.* It keeps ringing while I decide whether or not to answer. It isn't like her to call or text unless it's absolutely necessary. We aren't on bad terms exactly; we just have nothing to say to one another.

"Hello?" I try to keep my tone totally neutral as I answer. Maybe it's a butt dial.

"Hey, Lincoln. It's Lacey," she says, voice tight.

I find it humorous she thinks I've deleted her contact. Even if I had, hers is one of only a few numbers I could recite by heart.

"Hey. Uh, everything okay?" I wince and try another approach. "How are you?"

She laughs, breaking some of the tension. "I'm fine. Sorry to call, but I wanted to remind you that we have to get everything out of the storage unit. We pre-paid through April, after that there are additional fees."

"Right. The storage unit." I think back, trying to remember what's in it. It felt like my whole life at the time, yet I've managed just fine without any of it.

"I'm going tomorrow if you want to meet me there. There are a few boxes we should probably go through together anyway."

"Tomorrow's no good for me." I rub at the back of my neck. "But feel free to go through them and take whatever you want. You know better than I do what's what anyway."

She's quiet, and I check the phone to make sure we didn't get disconnected.

"Lace?"

"I spent our entire relationship taking care of things when you were gone or too busy or maybe just didn't want to be bothered, so don't take it the wrong way when I say that it isn't my job anymore to go through your shit."

That wasn't exactly what I meant, but years of guilt gnaw at me and keep me from lashing back. She isn't completely wrong, a lot of things did fall on her, and I guess I got used to depending on her. It's easy to slip back into those same roles, even now. "I can't tomorrow. Is there another day? Next week I'm travelling, but maybe the week after?"

She sighs, and it's a long, exasperated sound. "Yeah, sure. Give me a call when you're ready."

She disconnects first, leaving me with dead air and a thousand regrets. I drop my phone to the desk and stare at my computer screen.

The end of Keira's video is paused so that she's frozen in position. I hit play one more time, letting her swing bring a little bit of joy to this shitty night, and then force myself to get to work.

CHAPTER EIGHT

Keira

Wednesday's practice is nearly identical to Tuesday's. We break into groups to play eighteen holes and then spend some time with Coach working on individual drills. Well, except for me and a few freshmen he doesn't get to before time is up. I'm positive that isn't a coincidence that he somehow didn't get to me two practices in a row.

After everyone else leaves, I stay at the driving range, working on my swing until it's too dark to see the ball. I'm trying to incorporate the things Lincoln said, but I can't feel if I'm getting it right, and it's beyond frustrating.

I head back to the dorm, checking my text messages as I walk the stairs to the second floor. Abby is at Smith's apartment, per the usual. Since she started dating him last semester, she rarely sleeps here.

I shower and pick through clothes on Abby's bed. I've taken to using it as a storage area for my clean-ish clothes—the ones I've only worn once but am too lazy to hang back up in the closet. Erica and Cassidy texted that they were having people over, and since I'd rather go out than sit here alone, I get ready and call an Uber.

With eleven minutes to kill until my driver picks me up, I open my email. Simon from Reeves Sports has completed my swing review, and the write up has way more details than I expected. He's even attached a slow-motion video of my swing like the one Lincoln had done, and talks through what he sees. I'd been expecting something much more generic. This is really cool.

I grab my seven iron from my bag and hold it as I listen, pulling back and trying to get the feel of my weight shift like Lincoln had said that first time. Honestly, what Simon says is much the same, so either it's standard advice they give everyone or Lincoln was right. I don't know why that continues to surprise me. Everything about him radiates a confidence that can't be fake.

The thing is that, pro or not, it doesn't automatically mean he's qualified to give others advice. The best mentor I ever had was my high school coach, whose only qualification was that he loved golf. He worked hard and genuinely wanted his players to succeed. That, in turn, made us work hard.

The Uber driver calls to say he's pulling up outside of Freddy, and I grab my purse and hustle downstairs. When we're on our way, I send Lincoln an email.

> **Simon was more helpful than I expected. The site is really cool. I like the video feedback.**
>
> **Keira**

His response comes as the driver stops in front of Erica and

Cass's place. I thank him and walk to the front door slowly, reading.

I just saw his feedback. It's pretty spot on with what I thought after watching it.

I can hear people inside the house, but I pause at the front door and email him back.

You watched it?

Keira

An unexpected thrill shoots through me at the thought of him taking the time to follow up on me. I wait out front for a minute, and when I don't get a new response, I head inside.

A lot of the guys and girls from the golf teams are here hanging out in the living room watching television and drinking. Erica and Cassidy are sitting at a table in their small dining area with Chapman, Keith, and a sophomore named Han.

"You made it," Cassidy squeals and hugs me.

"I did." I squeeze her back and smile at the rest of the group. "I'm surprised you two are drinking the night before a tournament."

"Tomorrow is just a practice round, plus we can sleep on the ride," Erica says. "Help yourself, we restocked the booze."

I'm pouring vodka and Red Bull into a cup when Brittany comes up to me in the kitchen. "Hey, Keira."

"Hey, Britt." I offer her the vodka. "Drink?"

"No, I'm not drinking tonight."

I nod in understanding. Of course, she isn't. She knows as well as I do what it's like to be left behind while the team travels. I wouldn't be drinking either.

"I'm sorry about taking your spot. I know how hard you've

worked and—"

"Don't be sorry. You've worked hard too. Coach made his decision, and as much as I disagree with it, it's good for you. Take advantage of it. I know I would be."

She nods, and I step away before the conversation tanks my mood. "Good luck this weekend, Britt."

After a couple of drinks, we clear the table and set up for beer pong. Erica and me against Chapman and Han. Cassidy and Keith stand off to the side watching us. Cass has switched to water, and Keith holds a Natty Light in each hand.

Erica and I get smoked three games in a row. My bloated stomach can't take another loss, but I've managed to distract myself from thinking about the tournament this weekend. Well, sort of.

"We're getting thrashed. Do you have a couple of wedges around we could use so we have a chance in hell of winning the next one?"

Erica's eyes narrow and then widen with understanding. "Definitely."

She returns with a golf ball and two wedges.

"All right boys, ready to switch things up?" I go first, tossing the ball and catching it with the club. I bounce it a couple of times before hitting it into the air, flipping the club around, and tapping it toward the cups. The ball hits the rim and bounces away, nearly tipping over two cups in the process. Guess there's a reason we use ping-pong balls.

Han shakes his head but gives it a try. After each of us has taken a turn, we've managed to spill half the beer, but no one has made a shot.

"How about you use empty cups, and then the loser has to chug?" Cass suggests.

"Good idea," Erica says. We wipe down the table and re-start. Slowly, we garner a crowd, and they're watching me closely as I bounce the ball off the clubface. This time, when I send it sailing toward the cup, it goes in. I drop the wedge to the floor and throw my hands over my head in victory as Chapman and Han chug their beers.

"Oh, man. I'm glad you made that because I need to pass out." Erica holds a hand over her mouth as she yawns.

"What happened to sleeping in the van tomorrow?"

"Sorry."

"Han and I are going over to The White House if you want to come," Chapman says at the same time I look around to see everyone has left or is preparing to leave. My teammates are headed off to sleep so they can play well this weekend and that makes me want to keep right on drinking, so I don't have to think about how I won't be there.

"I'm in."

Chapman, Han, and I walk the block to The White House, an off-campus house where some of the basketball guys live. Parties at The White House are always big and crazy fun. They had a foam party in their backyard once. It was insane. I've never seen anything like it.

Loud music greets us inside and there are people everywhere. We head out to the back patio. Chapman grabs us beers, and we mill around.

I spot the guy who was with Lincoln the night I tossed tequila on him at the same time he does me. I leave Chapman and Han and walk toward him. He stares at me for a second as if he's trying to place me, and then one side of his mouth pulls up into a grin. "Tequila girl."

"Not tonight," I say as I lift the cup of beer I'm holding. "You play basketball?"

He scoffs. "Nah, I'm on the hockey team. Heath," he introduces himself. "I don't think I caught your name."

"Keira." I glance around hopefully. "Is Lincoln with you?"

"No way. Linc be caught at a college party?" He laughs. "He went back to Scottsdale, I think. He travels so much it's kind of hard to keep track of him."

I nod like I know. "How do you know him? Is he a friend of yours or..." I'm trying to piece together how a college hockey player knows a pro golfer.

"Sort of." He bobs his head from side to side. "Friend, boss, pain in the ass. He's tight with my brother, so he's like a second big brother in some ways."

"Did you say boss?"

"Yeah, you know his site? Reeves Sports? I work on the hockey portion of the website and do the occasional in-person job. Last summer, he got me a gig coaching at a kids hockey camp."

"Wow. That's awesome. I've only checked out the golf stuff so far, but it seems pretty impressive."

"You play golf?"

"Yeah."

"Well, Lincoln is the guy to know then. He's the very best and a really decent guy on top of it. You know, when he isn't acting like an overprotective ass."

"Do you provide reviews like he does—perfect hockey puck shooting form or something?"

He barks a laugh. "Not a big hockey fan, huh?"

"I grew up in the desert."

"There's hockey here."

I raise a brow.

"All right, I get your point. And no, my job is to answer questions that come in. Like, which shot is the hardest for a goalie to stop or how does someone increase the speed on their slap shot?"

"That's pretty cool."

Heath nods and flashes a cocky grin that reaches his dark blue eyes. "Just until I make it pro."

He says it so matter-of-fact that I believe him. If he's half as good as he is cocky, I have no doubt.

Someone yells across the party, and Heath's head lifts. He nods to whoever was calling his name and then his eyes flit back to meet mine. "I gotta go. Nice seeing you."

"You too."

I find an empty chair in the corner of the crowded living room and pull out my phone.

I entered Lincoln's number from his business card into my phone. I'm not even sure why, I never intended to use it, but my finger hovers over his name in my contact list. I bite my lip, close my eyes, squeal quietly, and tap.

He answers on the third ring. "This is Lincoln."

A small giggle escapes my mouth at his tone, which is totally serious and not fazed in the least about the time. Makes me wonder if he's used to getting calls at one in the morning.

"Hello?" he asks, voice bordering on annoyed.

"Ah, much better. Do you really answer the phone at one in the morning without so much as a hello first?"

There's a beat before his deep baritone slides over the line. "Anyone who calls this late is delivering bad news. Might as well get right to the point."

"I guess that's true."

"What bad news are you delivering, Keira?"

Maybe it's the alcohol or maybe it's because it's late at night and I likely woke him, but my name on his lips sounds like straight sex and my body warms. "It's good news actually."

"Yeah?"

"Yep. I've decided that I want you to take over for Simon and be my swing coach. I signed up for the daily review plan." Saying the words aloud makes me realize just how much I want it. I want to remember how it felt when he was standing near me, scrutinizing, and coaching me like he believed in me more than anyone else ever has.

"I saw."

"You did?" I ask, pleased that he's keeping tabs on me.

"It's my job." He's silent for a moment before asking, "Did Simon do something wrong? We have other coaches if you don't think he's a good fit."

"No, he's been fine. But you're the best. Everyone says so. I want the best."

He chuckles softly. "I'm not taking new clients. I'm having a hard enough time keeping up with the three I do have."

"And I'm not taking no for an answer."

There's commotion in the entryway, and I look up to see some guy wearing a bear helmet riding a scooter. People are laughing and cheering, a few start chanting his name. "Datson, Datson, Datson."

"Where are you?" Lincoln asks.

"At a party. By the way, I ran into your friend Heath."

"Heath is there?" He grumbles something and then adds, "I hope he isn't drinking. Was he drinking? Never mind, don't tell me."

"You're changing the subject."

He sighs. "I'm sorry. I can't. It wouldn't be fair to you or my other clients. I don't have time right now. I will get Roy to take over for Simon. He's the most senior of the staff, and he's just as good as I am."

"I highly doubt that." I was so sure I could convince him that the rejection stings.

"How's practice going? Did everything smooth over with your coach?"

"He added an extra thirty minutes of conditioning to our weekend workout, and he's basically ignoring me, but it's fine. Totally worth it."

"Keep your head up. You'll be okay."

"Yeah, all right." The alcohol and the late hour crash into me. "It's late. I should go."

"Be careful and don't call any other boys this late. It screams booty call."

I roll my eyes. "I assure you that if I call anyone else, it *will* be a booty call."

Another deep chuckle tickles my ear. "'Night, Keira."

CHAPTER NINE

Keira

I wake with a groan and find Abby standing at the side of my bed. "Wake up, sleeping beauty."

I groan louder.

"Your phone has been going off nonstop." She tosses it on top of the comforter. "You missed your eight o'clock. If you get up now, you can still make your next one. I'd suggest a shower first, though, you smell awful."

I hurl my pillow at her, but it misses by several feet.

Laughing, she hands me my water bottle from my desk. "Do you still have the black Adidas jacket I loaned you before break? I want to take it with me."

"On the bed," I croak out, ignoring the pang of disappointment that I'm not going.

My voice is scratchy, throat dry, and head pounding. I close my eyes and feel around for my phone. Wrapping my fingers around it,

I turn onto my side and slowly open my lids again.

Curse vodka. Or maybe it was the beer. Maybe it was the mixing. Maybe it was the sheer volume. After Lincoln's rejection, I softened the blow with a game of flip cup, and then I think there were a few games of quarters. Groan.

I have a dozen texts from people I ran into last night, ranging from concern to laughing emojis at how drunk I was and calling me a lightweight. There are two from Keith—one asking where I am and the next assuring me that he'll take notes and we can meet up at lunch so he can fill me in.

The newest message, though, makes my already rolling stomach lurch.

> Lincoln: I've sent over a training plan. We may need to tweak it based on your practices, so I'd like you to detail everything you do in practices for the next week. This morning get the run in and do the weight training. After your practice, we'll adjust the swing drills as needed.

The time stamp is from ten minutes ago. I read it several times before I notice the messages above his from me, sent early this morning. I scroll up, heat making my face burn. There are three of them just after four a.m.

> Me: What do I have to do to convince you?

> Me: I'll work harder than any of your clients. You say, "Jump," I'll ask, "How high?" Or in this case, you say, "Swing," and I'll ask, "How many times?"

> Me: Please? This is important to me. It's all I've ever wanted.

Oh God. I throw an arm over my face to shield me from the blast of embarrassment. My head is pounding, and I squeeze my eyes shut.

"You okay?"

I moan in response, but then his text sinks into my foggy brain. "He said yes." I sit up fast, too fast, and gag.

Abby sits on her bed folding the pile of clothes, mostly mine. "Who said yes?"

I check my email but don't see the training plan that Lincoln mentioned. My laptop is on my desk, so I swing my legs off the side of the bed and stumble the few steps to get it and bring it back to bed with me. Abby grabs her mug off the Keurig and joins me.

"You're acting weirder than normal. What's going on?" She crosses her legs and takes a sip of the coffee.

"Ugh. The smell of that coffee is making me want to gag."

"Don't blame the coffee. You're the one who lost three straight games of beer pong. For someone who deals in small balls, you have shit aim throwing them."

"I don't see it."

"I'm pretty sure I got some video of it if you want to see just how bad you were."

"Not that. Lincoln said he sent a training plan, but I can't find it."

"Lincoln? Lincoln Reeves, the swing coach? The one you threw tequila on?"

"Will no one let me live that down?"

"Why is he emailing you?"

I keep my eyes firmly on the screen as I admit the embarrassing truth. "I drunk dialed him last night. And then drunk texted him."

"Keira!" She laughs. "What did you say?"

"I asked him—no, I begged him to coach me."

Her eyes widen. "And he said yes?"

I log into the Reeves Sports website and see I have a message waiting from Lincoln. His profile picture makes me laugh—a stoic expression, ball cap on, blue polo shirt. He's still gorgeous but far too serious. "Ah, I found it!"

Abby stands. "I gotta get to the van, and you need to get to class." She picks up her phone. "Keith is texting me now. Will you put that poor boy out of his misery and tell him you're up and on your way?" She grabs her bag and heads to the door.

I tear my eyes away from the screen. "I will. Good luck this weekend. I put something in the side pocket of your bag."

She reaches in and pulls out the blue unicorn scrunchie.

"Go be a badass unicorn scrunchie-wearing superstar."

Her smile is sad. "It matches yours."

I lift my arm. I still haven't taken off the pink one. Maybe my dad knows me better than I think.

"Thank you." She slips it on her wrist and lingers in the doorway. "Part of me wishes we could trade places. I don't really feel like going, if I'm honest."

"You're just dreading the drive." Abby hates car rides. She doesn't even like going across town to run errands with me.

"You're probably right. Okay." She lets out a long breath. "I'll call you later and let you know how it goes tonight."

"Bye."

When she's gone, I read over the training plan with a huge grin on my face. It's detailed and a little intense. A two-mile run? And there are at least twenty different flexibility exercises in addition to weightlifting.

It all seems like overkill. We do conditioning and weights as part of our normal training, but it's nowhere near this much. Regardless, I'm excited to try some of it.

It'll have to wait though. I have to get moving if I'm going to get a shower and manage to stomach some food before my nine o'clock class.

I slide into a seat next to Keith just as class begins. My stomach cramps from the Pop-Tart I ate, and I'm sweating out alcohol from the half jog that was necessary so that I wasn't late.

Keith shakes his head disapprovingly, and I stick my tongue out at him. Then I regret it because it makes me gag.

Fifty minutes has never felt so long. When class finally ends what feels like a decade later, I have to go straight to my next class and sit through another lecture. I'm dragging when Keith and I make it to University Hall for lunch.

"Do you want anything? I'm gonna grab a sandwich?"

"No, definitely not. My stomach is still really angry." I look around at the food options and then end up changing my mind. "Well, maybe some chips."

He nods, and I place my head on the table until he returns. I do my best to pay attention as Keith catches me up on what I missed in organic chem.

"I'm going to email you my notes too since I know your brain is still foggy."

"You're a prince."

"I have to rush off to get my workout in before our next class. Don't skip measurements class. Professor Anolf docks a grade for too many absences."

"I won't," I assure him. "I have to take my dad to the doctor, but I should be done in plenty of time."

"Today?"

I nod. "It was their only available appointment all week."

When Keith leaves, I read through his notes and the accompanying chapters from the textbook. Since it's still the first week, one missed class won't kill me, but I can't afford to fall behind. The season is just about to pick up and study time will be hard to find.

An alarm on my phone goes off with a one-minute warning, and I silence it and continue to hold the phone until it rings.

"Hey, Mom," I answer.

"Hi, honey. How are you?" Her warm, upbeat voice makes me smile.

"I'm good. Between classes."

"Does this time still work for you this semester?" she asks.

"Yeah, it's fine."

"Good. I look forward to our calls every week."

"Me too."

I try not to think too hard about the fact I've been relegated to a time slot much like dropping off dry cleaning or grocery shopping.

I was sixteen when she and my dad divorced, and she moved back to Maryland where she grew up. Last summer she got remarried. My new stepdad (super weird to think of him as that), Bart, is a doctor at the same hospital where she works, and he seems nice. I've only met him a few times. Mom's happy, though, which is all that really matters.

"How's school? Busy schedule this semester?"

I give her a quick summary of my classes and then tell her about golf. I play down my disappointment in not being with Abby and the others at the tournament this weekend and give her my standard cheerful line, "I'll just keep putting in the work until I get my spot back."

"You will. I know you will," she says.

"How's everything else? Any boyfriends I should know about? Or girlfriends," she adds quickly.

I snort. "No, Mom. No boyfriends or girlfriends."

"Well, you'll find someone."

"I'm not worried."

"When I was your age, I was already married. Not that I'm rushing you."

I snort again and stop myself from pointing out the obvious—that it ended in divorce, but her thoughts must drift there anyway. "How's your dad?"

"Stubborn." I check the time. "Speaking of, I need to run so I can take him to the doctor."

"All right, honey. Call me if you need anything."

"I will." I pause before saying goodbye. "I miss you."

"You too, baby."

Dad's waiting on the curb when I pull up outside his house.

"You're late." Sweat beads on his forehead.

"I'm right on time. Your clocks are fast. I keep telling you that."

"If you aren't five minutes early, you're late."

"I don't think that counts for doctor's offices since they're going to make us wait at least fifteen minutes."

I get him in the passenger seat and drive over to the hospital.

"Wait here, and I'll grab a wheelchair to take you in."

"I don't need a wheelchair." He opens his door and swings his good leg out.

I hurry to help and bite down on my molars. Five very long and very exhausting minutes later, the sliding doors open and the air conditioning blasts my sweaty body. "We made it," I say breathlessly.

My dad's leaning on me, and my shoulder aches from the

pressure, but he seems completely oblivious to my exertion. Damn, stubborn man.

"Mr. Brooks." One of the nurses rolls a wheelchair in front of us, shoots me a sympathetic smile, and then bats her eyelashes at my dad. He grins at her and lowers himself into the chair without complaint, and I try not to roll my eyes as I go to the reception and sign him in.

When I take a seat beside him in the waiting room, he finally looks more at ease. Depending on me and not being able to get around like he used to is harder for him than it is for me, and I feel guilty for all the frustration I felt. "I'm sorry I was late."

His mouth twists into a half smile that says bullshit. "You're a good kid. I know you have better things to do than cart your old man around. Hopefully this is the last appointment you need to drive me to."

"Optimism... I dig it." I raise my fist for him to bump, but he just stares at me confused.

He grabs my hand and squeezes tenderly. "Love ya, sweet pea."

SINCE COACH POTTER IS WITH THE TEAM TRAVELLING TO THE tournament, it's a pleasant afternoon at the golf course. We divide into two groups and play eighteen holes and then work on some individual drills.

When I get back to my room, I face-plant onto my bed. I still have study group tonight before I can nap. Or maybe I'll just go to bed really early. Reluctantly, I sit up and open my laptop and send Lincoln a message through the website that details today's practice and the schedule through Sunday.

I've just started in on the swing drills he gave me when a message pops up.

Lincoln: How was the morning conditioning session?

Me: I didn't get to it. Just starting in on the swing drills now.

I take a step back from the laptop to start again just as a call request from him pops up on the screen.

Tentatively, I press accept. "Uh, hello?"

"What do you mean, you didn't get to it?" His voice is agitated and clipped. The screen is black, and I'm tempted to turn on the video so I can scowl at him.

"I didn't have time today."

"There's always time."

"I had classes all day, plus I had to go to the doctor, and I still have study group tonight, but I'm getting in what I can now."

A notification on the screen indicates he wants to turn on video for the call—guess he had the same idea—to turn on video to scowl at me. I tuck my hair behind my ears and do a quick scan around the room. There isn't much I can do about the mess, so I ignore it and press accept.

When his face appears, I forget to breathe for a second. His hair looks like he's been pulling at it, and he's frowning in a decidedly hot way—who knew that was possible? "Are you okay?"

"Yes?" I answer, a bit confused until I realize what I said. "I'm fine. I had to take my dad to the doctor. He can't drive."

His shoulders relax, but the frown stays firmly in place. "You have to make time for the training. You can't skip it because you stayed out too late and felt like shit this morning."

"That hardly seems fair since I didn't know about the training plan until after I made the decision to drink my troubles away." I smile at his ridiculousness, but he doesn't return it.

"No excuses. If you want this as much as you claim, then you'll make time. The next time you decide to skip the plan I line out for you, we're done."

I open my mouth to apologize or yell back, I haven't chosen which, when he asks, "How much time before your class?"

"An hour."

"All right, let's get to work then."

CHAPTER TEN

Keira

It's still dark outside when my alarm goes off. I don't bother changing clothes since I passed out in yesterday's workout leggings and tank. The last two days have been a blur. After Lincoln scolded me like a child on Thursday night, I was at the field house until midnight getting in the training he outlined.

I thought he'd be pleased, but yesterday, he was in the same pissy mood. And maybe it's delusional to think my getting up early on a Saturday morning to hit the gym will please him, but a girl can hope.

It isn't that I want to please *him* exactly, it's that I want him to know that I'm willing to do what it takes to be the best and he didn't make the wrong choice in taking me on as a client. I saw that look on his face at the clinic when he helped me with my swing. He believed in me. I want that look back.

I jog over to the field house with my eyes half open, hoping that by the time I get there my body will be warmed up and I'll be more awake. The weight room is basically empty. A few people are running on treadmills, but I have the free weights to myself.

I text Abby good luck on her second day of the tournament and then put my headphones on, trying to deceive my body into thinking I'm excited to be here by playing fun, peppy songs.

Today is upper body with a heavy focus on back, and apparently my *everything* is weak because every time I choose a weight to start, I have to go down by fifteen pounds and try again.

I note everything in the online workout journal Lincoln set up for me. Number of reps, amount of rest between sets, weight, and I add in my own notes of displeasure for certain exercises just for fun. Next to burpees, I let him know that it's a dumb exercise with a dumber name. It's too early to be clever.

I'm working my ass off for him, but I want to make sure he knows I think he's ridiculous and overbearing.

While I'm between exercises, I pull up the swing review he completed for me last night. His deep, clipped voice takes my breath away as he commentates through the video. It's gritty and raw, absolutely no frills. He goes right into it without so much as a hello.

He pauses at certain spots to highlight things I'm doing wrong and offer advice on how to correct it. Three minutes and twenty-five seconds of painfully honest feedback with absolutely no attempt to try to sugarcoat my weaknesses. It's a little hard to take, but I hang on his every word anyway.

The video ends as abruptly as it started, and I hit replay. Each time I watch it, which is basically every time I rest, I'm filled with the same overwhelming desire to do more, try harder, dig deeper.

As I'm finishing, Abby texts back to thank me and tell me she had a good warm-up and she's about to tee off. She also assures me that Coach is still a dick—as if there were any doubt. Sometimes, it's good to know I'm not the only one who feels that way though. Apparently, he spent most of day one with Cassidy and ignored the rest of the team.

I head to the outdoor track for a mile run. Today is supposed to be light conditioning, and I guess it is since I'm running one mile instead of two like yesterday, but it sure doesn't feel easy.

Two hours, a shower, and a quick nap later, I head to the driving range, only to have it start to rain. Big, cold drops soak my clothes and hair. I shoot a glare at the dark clouds that are ruining my training session.

Seriously? It couldn't have rained while I was running earlier?

I try to keep going even as my teeth chatter, but I can't video my swing in this condition, so I head to my dad's.

"Hey, sweet pea. You look like you ran over. Coming down pretty good out there." He glances out the window from the recliner.

"I got caught in it at the driving range." I take off my shoes and then go to my old bedroom to swap out my shirt for a dry one.

Back in the living room, I take a seat on the couch and wrap the throw blanket hanging over the arm snug around me. "Did you eat lunch?"

He nods to the counter. "Yeah, I ordered pizza a couple hours ago."

"Any left?" I stand and walk toward the kitchen.

"*Mm-hmm.* A slice or two."

It's cold, but I devour a slice of sausage pizza while I open the fridge and rummage around until I find a Diet Mountain Dew. I hide them in the vegetable drawer and behind condiments he rarely uses.

"Dad, do you still have my old golf mat and net?"

"They are in the garage, I think."

I take my soda with me and sigh as I see the disorganization of the garage. It's clear where I got my messy tendencies.

I manage to find them, and I'm standing on a ladder, hanging the net from the hooks in the ceiling, when Lincoln calls. I hesitate to accept the video call and seriously think about sending him to voice mail, but somewhere deep down (like really deep down), somewhere that can forget what a sadist ass he is and how sore I am, I know I need him.

"Hello?" I answer, putting it on speaker and setting the phone on the top of the ladder so I can continue to hang the net.

"Keira?"

I move my head in front of the phone so he can see me. "I'm here. One second."

"What in the world are you doing? And why do you look like a wet rat?"

I ignore the last comment because I totally do, and he looks perfect as usual. "I'm trying to hang my old golf net in my dad's garage. It's raining out."

"It is?" It sounds like he moves around before he speaks again. "Huh. It's raining here too."

"Where are you?" I ask, glancing at the screen and staring past him at the background. Blank, white walls that tell me absolutely nothing.

"At home. Let's see this net."

I get the last loop over the hook and step down the ladder. I switch the camera so it's front facing and show him the setup.

"How old is that mat?"

"I don't know. Maybe five years. I got it and the net for my sixteenth birthday."

"Well, you won't need either today."

"What do you mean? The training plan says two hundred reps."

"That's why I'm calling. Scratch that. I want you to go back to practicing without a club. And double the reps. That turn and weight shift need to be perfect. Your power is your best asset, but in order to swing as hard as you can, everything else has to be dialed in."

"But—" I start to object and think better of it. "All right, whatever you say."

For the next hour, I continue to bite my tongue and follow his instructions. Lincoln insists I need to slow down and rebuild my swing—something few people would dare try to do in the middle of a season.

But it's listen to Lincoln or keep hoping Coach Potter suddenly notices how much I deserve to be out there. And the latter seems as likely as Lincoln telling me to take tomorrow off and enjoy a nice bubble bath.

"Pause at the top of the turn and concentrate on using your legs—your arms are just levers."

It takes a few minutes of him nit picking every single part of my body.

"Your knees are bent too much."

"No, now not enough bend."

"You're tilting too much."

"Your pushing with your right."

"Your shoulders are too stiff."

But I listen, and soon, his commentary falls silent and I settle into a rhythm, focusing on the feeling of my body and trying to commit it to memory.

"I think I have it," I tell him once the correct way starts to feel natural. I stop and face the camera, waiting for the next step or maybe a compliment.

"Keep going. I'll let you know when to stop." He steps out of view, and I stick my tongue out at him.

The door from the house into the garage opens, and my dad smiles as he sees me standing on my golf mat.

"I'm gonna heat up a frozen dinner. Are you staying to eat, sweet pea?"

Oh God. I don't dare look at my phone to see if Lincoln is watching. "Oh, uh. I'll make dinner for us. Don't eat that garbage. Just give me a bit to finish up first."

He waves me off. "I'll cook two Hungry Man dinners so I can prove that they aren't garbage. Frozen packages of delight, those things are." He shakes a finger at me as he goes back in and then lets the door fall closed.

I glance at the phone and find Lincoln almost smirking.

"Don't say a word," I warn him.

"Wouldn't dream of it, *sweet pea.*" He smiles, and I consider picking up a club and throwing it at his head, but don't want to destroy my phone. "Go, have a delicious dinner with your father and then get another three-hundred reps in. Message me later and let me know how it goes."

"Three hundred?" My eyes widen and my brows rise, but Lincoln's face remains completely serious.

"Take advantage of the setup at your dads while you're there. It's better than your space in the dorm. We really need to figure out how to make it where you can hit balls there when the time comes."

"Yeah, my neighbors would love that," I mutter quietly, but the man misses nothing.

"Enjoy your Hungry Man." He full-on smiles, and it looks good on him. I forget how annoying he is when he smiles like that.

"What are you having for dinner? Do you cook? Pizza delivery? Or are you more of a takeout kind of guy?"

"Actually, I'm having dinner with someone." He lifts his arm and checks the time on his expensive-looking watch. "I should get going. Have a nice night, Keira."

Irrational jealousy heats my face. He's going on a date and I'm having a microwavable dinner with my dad. Figures.

Focusing all my frustration, I set the camera up to record and do all three hundred reps. And then fifty more.

CHAPTER ELEVEN

Lincoln

I walk through Gram's door a half hour early. It's a first, and I catch her checking the time on the microwave before she speaks. "Lincoln, what are you doing here so early?"

"Can't a man show up early to help his grandmother with dinner?"

"He *could*, but I can't remember the last time he did."

"Well, I'm here now." I put the wine on the counter and push up my sleeves. "What can I do?"

She laughs. "Pour me a glass and grab the rose plates from the top shelf in the china cabinet."

I grab two wine goblets, fill them, and take a drink of mine before her request sinks in. "The rose plates? We only use those on special occasions."

They were a wedding gift from her mother, and I can count the number of times she's used them on one hand. Most notably her and

Pop's fiftieth wedding anniversary and five Christmases ago when we first found out he had cancer.

"I made a vow this year that I would use the things that bring me joy more often. I'm not going to be around forever, you know?"

"Really, Gram? Playing the death card?" I cross my arms over my chest and wait for the real reason we're busting out her precious china.

"Also, I invited my friend Margie and her granddaughter over for dinner."

I groan.

She rolls her eyes, the second woman to do that to me today. "You act as if having dinner with a pretty young woman is the worst way you could spend a Saturday night."

She turns her back to me, stirring something on the stove, and I move to the china cabinet and pull down the rose plates.

"I'm in no position to date right now."

"You keep saying that, and I keep ignoring it."

I chuckle, well aware she's ignoring me. I can't figure out how to make her understand that I don't have anything to offer at the moment.

"Listen, honey, I know Lacey made you feel like it was all your fault that things didn't work out, but that's rubbish. She was just as much at fault."

"Eh..."

"She was. Marriage is hard work, but dating doesn't have to be. Have dinner with Sweetie and just try to enjoy yourself, that's all I'm asking."

"*Sweetie?* Her name is Sweetie?"

There's a knock at the door and Gram scans the place quickly.

"Everyone's early tonight. Get the door, will you?" She turns back to the stove, and I shake my head.

"This is the last time," I tell her quietly over my shoulder. "No more setups. I mean it. I'll stop coming over."

She hums a response that I'm pretty sure is her total disregard for such a threat. And she's probably right. I'll keep coming back, hoping one of these times the girl at the door will make me believe Gram's optimistic outlook.

Sweetie turns out to be the perfect name for the woman sitting across from me. She's blonde with blue eyes and a soft, syrupy-sweet voice. Everything about her says feminine, right down to the light pink dress she's wearing and the pearls around her neck.

It's impossible to dislike her or not enjoy myself, but there's absolutely zero chance she and I would work out. I'm a grumpy asshole, and this woman looks as if she'd burst into tears if I so much as looked at her the wrong way.

If I do ever start dating again, it'll be with someone who can take my shit and call me on it. Like Keira does. Or did. Since we started working together, she's less vocal. The girl was holding back so many words today I thought she was gonna bite her tongue off.

My phone vibrates in my pocket, but I know Gram will be pissed if I take a call at the table. A few minutes later, though, Sweetie's phone rings.

"Oh, good gracious. I am so sorry. I forgot to turn this thing off," she says as she rummages through her purse and pulls out her phone. She bites her lip as she looks at the screen and then gives Gram and Marge big, puppy dog eyes. "I'm so sorry. I have to take this." Then she looks at me. "I'll be right back."

I wait until she disappears into the living room before I look at my phone.

Keira: 350 reps done. You're a sadist asshole. I can't feel my arms.

And another that came in a few minutes later.

Keira: I don't see anything on tomorrow's plan. Same as today?

I love that, even when she's calling me an asshole for putting her through the wringer, she's asking for more. And I don't have to ask if the extra fifty reps she did was a silent fuck you—I know it was.

"Lincoln," Gram admonishes.

I glance up from my phone as I tap out a text to Keira. Gram's expression changes from annoyed to something I can't place, curious maybe.

"Sorry, Gram." I fire off the message and pocket my phone.

After Marge and Sweetie leave, I help Gram clean up.

"Dinner was fantastic. As usual."

She smiles and hands me another plate to dry.

"And I saw Marge eyeing these dishes with envy."

She laughs softly, but the quiet surrounds us again. There is a look of melancholy on her face that makes me wonder, but not ask, if she's thinking of Pop.

After the dishes are done, Gram flips off the kitchen light and walks me to the front door.

"Same time next week?"

"*Mm-hmm.* And maybe bring whoever you were texting earlier. It'll save me a phone call or two to find your next date."

I try to picture Keira at dinner with Gram but shut down that train of thought fast. Do I think it would have been more fun, if not hazardous to my being, than sitting across from Sweetie all night?

Yes. Is it highly inappropriate that I think that? Also yes.

"That was a client, Gram. I told you I'm not dating right now. Well, unless you count the blind dates you keep setting me up on, then I guess technically I am dating, but it's very solidly against my wishes."

She doesn't bother apologizing. I'm sure tonight's missed love connection has just made her that much more determined. "A female client?"

I hesitate to answer a second too long, and Gram smiles all too knowingly. I think back to texting Keira, but I don't see how anything I did or said could have made Gram think it was a woman. Maybe I'm not as good as I thought at hiding how much I'm enjoying working with Keira.

"Yeah, so? I have lots of female clients." Keira is my only *personal* female client, but the website has many, so Gram doesn't know any better.

"I saw that look in your eyes. You were smiling, for heaven's sake."

"I smile." Though as I say it, I realize I'm frowning.

Gram laughs and touches my cheek with her palm. "I love you. Don't work too hard. Have fun. Enjoy this time in your life. It goes fast."

I'm still thinking about Gram's words when I get home. I grab a beer, turn on ESPN, and open my laptop. Gram doesn't understand this is fun. I love my job. The pride and satisfaction I feel when a client succeeds is better than any high.

And, yeah, I miss having a woman to come home to sometimes, but any time that longing gets too heavy, I think about the look of disappointment Lacey wore like the latest fashion for the last year of our marriage.

Yeah, no thanks. I'd rather be single for the rest of my life than go through that again. Perpetually disappointing the person you care about the most chips away at you. Touching people's lives by making them better at something they love, inspiring them to be the best they can, isn't a bad way to spend my days.

It's late Saturday night, so I don't call or text Keira about tomorrow's training plan. I send instructions via the site, which will notify her by email.

I press send and reach for my beer, but as I'm setting it down, she messages me on the site's chat feature.

> **Keira:** Are you feeling okay? Have you been body snatched? Did someone hack your account?

I chuckle as I respond.

> **Me:** Sunday's are a recovery day. Stretch out, get a few turns in, and spend the rest of the day preparing for the week.

> **Me:** And eat something besides a Hungry Man frozen dinner.

> **Keira:** No worries on that. If I never eat another, it'll be too soon. How was your date?

It takes me a second to realize she misinterpreted my words earlier today when I told her I had dinner plans. I know I didn't say date, but seeing as how it ended up sort of being a date, I don't bother correcting her.

> **Me:** It was fine.

> **Keira:** Fine? *snort* Wow, lucky lady.

> **Me:** If you go out tonight, take it easy on the alcohol and make sure you still

get enough sleep. Don't derail all your progress.

Keira: Wow, you're a real conversation buzz kill. Do you ever stop thinking about training?

Me: It's my job to think about it. Every decision, no matter how minor you may think it is, plays a part in your success or failure.

Shit, I do sound like a buzz kill. It's true, though.

Keira: I have no plans to go out tonight, and I'm already lying in bed. Happy?

Well, no. Now I'm picturing her lying in bed. So, I'm not happy at all.

My thoughts run away from me for long enough that I picture her bare legs and that gorgeous sun-kissed hair splayed out begging for me to run my fingers through it. Perving on a client—super douche move.

Me: Good. Enjoy your day off.

I log out of the chat before she can respond and spend the next two hours working on her training plan for next week and trying hard not to be the creeper she accused me of being the first time we met.

CHAPTER TWELVE

Lincoln

Over the next week, I push her harder than I have pushed any other athlete I've ever coached. Ever. I need to know she's serious. That she'll work as hard as I will.

Adding another client might seem like a small thing, but I spend a minimum of fourteen hours a week on a client. That's an average client. I'm spending double that with Keira because of how much I believe in her. And if I'm spreading myself this thin and putting my *hope* in her, then I have to know that we're in this together.

On Tuesday night, I fly out to L.A. to see my brother and interview a woman to manage my tennis coaches. Kenton plays soccer for the L.A. Stars. Despite—or maybe because of—our family history with golf, he was never interested in it.

He's waiting at the bar near my gate. Turned in his seat so he can watch the passengers walking by, his hat is pulled low so he's hard to recognize. Not that it fools me; I'd recognize his tall, lanky ass anywhere. The slight tilt of his shoulders and the way he sits on the stool with one foot resting on the top rung and the other on the floor is all so familiar.

He stands as I weave through people to get to him.

"Linc." He embraces me and gives me a couple of good slaps before stepping back. "Been too long, brother."

Smiling, I nod and look him over. He's taller than I am by an inch, but his build is smaller—leaner from all the conditioning he does. I'm damn proud of him even if it means the time between seeing him seems to get longer each visit.

"You look good. Nice game last night."

We each take a seat, and he slides a beer toward me. "Thanks. You catch it or watch the highlights?"

I take a sip before I reply, "Come on, you really think I'd miss my little bro in action?"

He raises a brow.

"Fine, I caught the last twenty minutes or so."

"Did you see that header in the last minute?"

"I did." I hit the bill of his cap. "Should have picked a sport where you don't have to use your head so barbarically. Or at least one with a helmet."

He just grins.

We chat mostly about the team and what he's been up to in L.A. as we grab dinner and drink more beer. Then I fill him in on Gram and her latest setup attempts.

We're both dog tired so we make it an early night and head back to his house.

I chuckle as he leads me into his new place. It's the first time I've seen it since he moved in six months ago and it's as extravagant as I expected. "This place is ridiculous, Kent."

"I know, right? Check out the view."

I follow him through the entryway and into the living area with floor-to-ceiling windows that showcase the lights of the city at night.

I drop my bag to the floor and fall into the chair where I can appreciate the skyscape.

"I'm gonna shower. I got you all set up in the spare room." He motions with his head to the right and walks off toward the left. "Glad to have you here, bro."

I lean back in the chair and blow out a breath. Looking around the place, I smile. It's over the top sleek and modern, but in a way that is totally fitting for my baby brother. I'm proud as hell that he's been so successful.

My small apartment back in Scottsdale is a dump by comparison. I rented it after my divorce, not particularly caring about where I lived as long as it met two conditions: it was not with my ex and it was on a golf course.

With my business, I can live anywhere or everywhere. I travel a lot, but Scottsdale is home, and the weather is great year-round for golf.

Tired as fuck, I pull out my laptop and check email. I'm cc'ed on more than fifty emails, but there are only a few that require me to respond. I tackle those and then log into the website to check in with my clients.

Simon and Roy handle the majority of our golf clients, and I have a couple of team members who answer questions and do an occasional review if needed. It's a big market and we're growing faster than any other department.

Initially, I kept a few clients simply because we didn't have enough people to support the demand, but now, I keep a hand in it to remind me what fuels my desire and love for the company.

I have an up-and-coming pro golfer who'll be a household name soon, a twelve-year-old kid whose parents' ambitions are set on him being the next Tiger Woods, and a retiree who just wants to be able to show up his buddies on their weekly golf outings. And now, Keira.

I check in with my other clients first, leaving Keira for last. She sent her swing video, a detailed write-up of what they did in practice today, and notes on the morning training session I gave her.

I read over it, watch the video a handful of times. I'm watching her swing one last time in slow motion when Kenton appears. Hair wet, basketball shorts and a faded Nike T-shirt, he looks a lot more like my little brother like this.

"I thought I heard you still out here." He grabs two beers from the fridge, takes a seat on the couch across from me, and offers me one.

"Thanks," I say absently, staring at the screen.

"How are things going with Reeves Sports?" He crosses one leg over a knee and holds the neck of a Bud Light with his fingers.

"You should know." Kenton is a silent partner, so he's copied on all the executive reports, which he clearly doesn't read.

"You don't really want me sitting in on those long conference calls, do you?"

I huff a laugh, and he shakes his head.

"I didn't think so." He sits forward and cranes his neck to look at the screen. "Got any fun clients I can see?"

Turning the screen, I press play, and we watch Keira's swing. She took the footage at the driving range, so the scenery of Arizona and the sun setting over the mountains is the backdrop.

Even after seeing it so many times, I get a little rush and goose bumps dot my arms.

I glance over at Kenton. He doesn't look all that impressed, but I'm not surprised. It isn't Keira's ability alone that excites me; it's her potential. I wouldn't expect most people to see it. In fact, my career is as successful as it is because most don't.

"Not bad. Pro or amateur league?"

"Neither."

His gaze meets mine, and he lifts a brow in question.

"I did that clinic at Valley University for Mark James. He's the coach there now. Anyway, I met Keira there." I motion to the screen. "She's on the girls' team."

I press play again. "She's a little unfocused and impulsive, but she has a lot of promise."

"She's hot." Kenton continues to stare at the screen as he quickly drains the rest of his beer and places the empty on the coffee table.

I turn my laptop so he's no longer able to see her. "Anyway, I should get back to it."

"I can see it's a real hardship." He snorts. "Enjoy the view. I have to get to bed. I have an early workout in the morning. Lunch tomorrow?"

"Yeah, sounds good."

When he's gone, I play her video again feeling more protective than is rational. Keira's young and beautiful, any dude with a pulse could attest to that, but Kenton voicing something I can't bothers me more than I'd like to admit. I can't exactly be jealous of every guy that looks at her and sees the obvious, though that feels exactly like what just happened.

I carry my stuff into the spare room, change into fresh T-shirt and sweatpants, and grab another beer before I call her. Pacing the room, I stare out into the L.A. night while I wait for her to answer.

"Hello?" Her voice is groggy like I woke her up.

I check the time. "Sorry if I woke you. I assumed you'd still be up."

"It's fine. I must have fallen asleep reading my chemistry notes."

I snort. "Can't blame you there. We can talk tomorrow."

"It's okay. I'm awake now."

I should insist she go back to sleep, but our training has become something I look forward to every night. "All right. Grab your seven iron. I want to talk you through what I'm seeing."

"Hold on."

The website allows for video chat, though I've never used it with clients before her. Typically, the feedback I send is in email format. If I need to get more detailed, I record a video of my screen as I watch their swing in slow motion and talk through any issues I see.

We've used all those features, too, but with Keira, the live sessions together have proven to be invaluable.

"All right, I'm set."

I hang up the phone and start the video call on the website. She answers almost immediately, and her face appears. With no greeting, she steps away, checking back once to make sure she's in full view of the camera.

Her dark hair is pulled back in a messy ponytail and falls over one bare shoulder. She's wearing some sort of tank top with straps so small I can barely see the pink material against her skin. The tiny shorts she's wearing aren't any better.

I'm frustrated by my inability to ignore how gorgeous she is. Fucking Kenton. It isn't really his fault, he didn't tell me anything new, but now it's fresh on my mind.

"Lincoln?"

"Yeah, sorry." I slide my gaze away from her legs and hope she didn't catch me gawking like a perv. "Let me see what you worked on today."

She's set up in her dorm room, standing in the space between two beds. She has just enough space to swing. It isn't really ideal, but I can't very well ask her to head to the gym at this hour. Though, the thought did occur to me.

"So, what do you think?" she asks after she's done three swings.

"It's hard to tell. Your swing changes with a ball in front of you. Right now, it looks good, though. I can tell you've been working the drills. How's the weight training?"

She groans. "Awful. My legs are so sore I could barely walk up the stairs today. And who knew going *down* stairs would be worse?"

My eyes sweep over her legs again and up. "You're going to need to be stronger. It'll help with consistency, and it'll also allow you to trust yourself more when it comes to those big, key moments where you have to let go and just believe you've worked hard enough to pull off whatever the gods of golf throw at you."

"The golf gods." She smiles, tosses the ball in the air with her club, and begins to bounce it. She does it often between drills as we're chatting. The move seems to calm her. She barely looks at it, feeling the ball with the clubface and trusting the movement. It's sexy as hell.

"How'd you learn to do that?"

She stops as if she just realized what she was doing, and the ball drops to the floor. "Saw Tiger do it when I was a kid, and I practiced. A lot."

"Tiger, huh? He was your favorite?"

"Of the men." She abandons the club and sits on the bed, bringing the laptop closer to her face. She has a hint of sun on her cheeks, but the rest of her skin is smooth and flawless.

Keira on a bed, in a bed, or near a bed are all combinations that stir things I haven't felt in a long time.

"Who's your favorite?"

I consider just going with a canned answer. I looked up to Tiger a lot, but it was never him I was trying to emulate. "My grandfather."

"Did he play professionally?"

I shake my head. "No, but he played in college and taught me everything I know about the game. Coached a lot of other people too. He was a golf pro in Scottsdale."

"Is he willing to come out of retirement to take on a new client? I bet he would be nicer. Old people love me. I'm spunky." She yawns.

A chuckle escapes. "Sorry, you're stuck with me. He passed two years ago."

"Oh, I'm sorry." Her mouth falls into a frown, and her eyes lift from mine. "Where are you? Is that a different room in your place?"

I look behind me to the picture hanging on the wall over the bed. It's a black-and-white nude of Kenton's naked back and the top of his ass, holding a soccer ball at his hip. It's an artistic shot and probably (hopefully) not meant to be sexy, but it's still my damn brother's ass above the bed I'm supposed to sleep in.

I turn back to face her. "I'm in Los Angeles staying with my brother for a couple of days. He plays soccer for the Stars, and apparently, he likes to welcome his guests with uncomfortable artwork."

"Any other siblings?"

"No. You?"

"No, I'm an only child." She yawns again, and I check the time.

"You should get some sleep. Your body needs recovery time. Drink lots of water too."

She rolls her eyes, but her voice is soft. "Yes, Coach."

"'Night, Keira."

CHAPTER THIRTEEN

Keira

"You came!" Erica jumps up from her spot next to Chapman on the couch and rushes to hug me.

I laugh and try to speak, but she has a vise grip around my neck and shakes us from side to side. When she releases me, she links our hands and jumps with excitement. "You have been hiding away for weeks."

Cassidy joins us in the entryway and hands me a drink before nodding her agreement. "Seriously. The only time I see you anymore is at practice."

"I can't drink this," I say after smelling the contents of the cup.

"Just one!" Erica says. She and Cassidy share matching pouty expressions.

"Nice try. I'm not drinking tonight." I hand the cup back to Cassidy.

"Well, fine, as long as you'll still dance with me. The White House is having a party, and I need to dance it out." Cass closes her eyes and sways her hips from side to side.

"Dance what out?"

"She's waiting for Peter to call her," Erica supplies.

I glance between them for the story. "Peter?"

"Peter Kurtis, he's a hockey player Cass is crushing on ha-ard," Erica sing-songs the last word.

"I am not," she says but then smiles. "He asked for my number a week ago but hasn't called or texted."

Erica nudges me. "I have a class with Peter's roommate, Tiny, and he said they're going to The White House tonight."

"Will you come and be my dance partner?" Cass begs.

"Of course, I will." I fight a yawn. "Do you have any Red Bull?"

AT THE WHITE HOUSE, CASSIDY PULLS ME OUTSIDE TO WHERE A DJ IS setup and a few people are dancing on one side of the yard. Erica is sitting near the pool with Chapman.

The beat of the music relaxes my aching muscles and the caffeine temporarily makes me forget how tired I am. The last couple of weeks have been exhausting in the best way. Classes, practice, and hours of training with Lincoln.

Cass leans forward, her blonde hair falling around her face and shielding her from everyone but me. "He's here."

Casually, I glance around. "Where?"

"He just walked out onto the patio with another guy. White hat, gray sweater."

I find him easily enough. He's scanning the crowd in the way people do when they first get to a party to see who else is there. He finds Cass and turns to his buddy to say something. And as luck would have it, I know that buddy.

"Come on, I know his friend." I drag Cass with me.

Her hand grips mine hard, and I laugh a little at how nervous she seems. She's gorgeous, sweet, and super talented. I can't imagine any guy not being into her.

Heath notices me as I approach, and his mouth draws into a wide smile.

"Hey, Keira." He takes a sip from the beer.

"Hey, yourself." I yank Cass closer to me. "Heath, this is my friend Cassidy."

"Hi." She gives a small wave and steals a glance at Peter. "Hey, Peter."

"You two know each other?" I play dumb.

"Yeah, of course. Hey, Cassidy." I swear this big, hunky hockey player is blushing. "Can I get you a drink?"

She stares at him, frozen and mute until I elbow her, then she sputters out, "Yeah. Great."

Heath and I watch them disappear into the house.

"She likes him." I shrug.

"Yeah, him too. He's been talking about her all week, trying to figure out when to call her and what to say. I've never seen someone obsess so much over calling a girl." He looks at my empty hands and then asks, "You need a drink?"

"Nah, I'm not drinking tonight."

He raises a brow in question.

"I have to get up early tomorrow to work out."

"Me too." He looks around the party. "I'd wager half the people here have practice or workouts in the morning."

Cassidy and Peter rejoin us at the same time Erica and Chapman do. Once everyone is introduced, Erica tries to hand me another drink.

"No thanks," I say. "Still not drinking."

"Boooo." She gives me a thumbs-down and then holds her hand out. "Give me your phone."

"Why?"

"I'm going to call mister hottie swing coach and tell him that you need a night of drunken fun."

I keep a strong grip on my phone because there is no chance I'm letting her call Lincoln.

"You're still working with Linc?" Heath smiles.

"Yeah, he's helping me with my swing."

"That's cool." He takes out his phone as he continues to talk. "Do you like working with him? He isn't too tough? I met this kid he worked with last year, he said Lincoln had him running a mile every day and weight training three to four times a week, getting something like a thousand swings in. All that on top of his regular team practices."

Heath's eyes are wide with disbelief. "All that for golf? I mean, no offense, I know you gotta be in shape, but that seems like a lot of work just to walk along the golf course and hit the ball. Is that what he has you doing?"

I grind my teeth as I answer. "Yeah, something like that."

"Here, smile." He holds his phone out in front of us and takes a picture before I can do anything but stare dumbly ahead. He chuckles as he taps on his phone and then pockets it.

"What was that?"

"I was texting Lincoln."

"You told him I was here?" I look around like he can somehow see me from Scottsdale… or wherever he is today. I can't keep track of him and believe you me, I've tried.

"Well, no. I just told him I bumped into you at a party and that he should go easier on you."

"Great." I wince as my phone vibrates in my front pocket. One guess who that is.

I pull it free and show the screen to Heath. "You did this!"

He plucks it out of my hand and answers. "What's up, old man?"

I shoot a death glare at him, but he just gives me a wide, cheeky grin in return.

"Yeah, she's right here." He winks at me. "Nah, of course, I'm not drinking." He takes a big swallow of his beer. "All right. Sounds good. Talk to you tomorrow." He shoves the phone at me. "He wants to talk to you."

Yeah, no kidding. I knew I should have stayed in. Three weeks of nonstop training. I've pushed my body harder than I thought possible. I've made more progress than I have in two years with Coach Potter too.

Working with Lincoln is amazing. I don't want to screw it up, I just need a night out with my friends to unwind. Another tournament is coming up this weekend and Coach announced the starters today. I didn't make the top five, again, and it stung.

I'm trying not to think about it, but it's hard not to. And it isn't as if I'm planning to slack off on my training tomorrow. I already have three alarms set so I'll be sure to wake up with plenty of time to get in the run and weights before my first class. I might be tired, but I'll push through.

I plan to tell Lincoln all of this as I take the phone with a shaky hand and put it to my ear. "Hi."

"Are you all right?" he asks, the harshness I expected in his tone absent and instead he sounds genuinely concerned for my wellbeing.

I give Heath one last glare for good measure and walk away from the group to find a quieter place to talk. "Yeah, I'm fine. I just needed to get out of the dorm for a bit. I'm heading home soon."

"I saw the roster for the tournament this weekend. I'm sorry."

I sink into one of the patio chairs, embarrassed that he knows and that I hadn't been the one to tell him.

"Am I . . ." I start, and my voice breaks. I feel like I'm hanging on by a thread. "Am I ever going to be ready?"

"You've made huge strides already. We just keep working at it."

I nod.

"Keira?" His deep voice somehow sounds tender as he says my name.

"Yeah, I'm here. I heard you."

I lean my head back and stare into the night sky. The helplessness and defeat that I've been fighting all day finally hits me. I may never get my chance. I'm not even sure I deserve it anymore. Maybe Coach Potter is right.

"You have more raw talent than any person I've ever coached. Ever. I can't predict the future. I don't know if I can make your dreams come true, but I promise that I will do everything I can to make sure you get your shot. You may hate me for how hard I push you, but it's because I want to know we've done everything we can. We're a team. If you fail, I fail."

A lump the size of a golf ball lodges in my throat. I don't have to ask if he means it, I heard the sincerity of his tone and Lincoln has never, not once, tried to pad my ego. It's one of the many reasons I like working with him. But he fails if I fail? That seems like a lot of pressure for him to put on himself and on me.

Suddenly, my grumblings about his methods and how tired I am feel bratty. Although . . .

"I heard a rumor tonight that your usual training only includes a *one*-mile run and *three* days of weights per week."

He curses quietly away from the phone. "Heath has a big mouth."

I don't argue that.

"None of my clients ever have the same regimen. It isn't some generic thing I pass from player to player. You get what I think you need."

"And I need to do twice as much as the others?" I can't hide the note of hurt in my voice. Am I really that awful?

"The better the player, the harder they need to work."

I scoff. Really, that's the best he's got?

"I'll never ask you to do anything that isn't necessary to get you where you want to be. You're capable of so much more than you think. Get out of your own way. Can you do that? Can you just trust that I only want what's best for you?"

I'm nodding again like he can see me. "Yes, I trust you. Tell me what to do."

He lets out a sigh of relief. "Tonight, have fun with your friends. We'll get back to it tomorrow."

The next day at practice we split up into groups to play nine holes. I'm grouped with Abby and Brittany.

"You're quiet today. Everything okay?" Abby whispers as we stand back and wait for Brittany to tee off on the third hole.

"Yeah, I'm all right." I meet her gaze and find her staring back unbelieving. We may not spend as much time together as we once did, but she still knows me better than anyone. "I'm disappointed about the tournament and starting to wonder if I'll ever get back to the top five."

"You will."

"I don't know." Brittany swings, and the ball sails high and drifts slightly from left to right, leaving her in good position on the green. "She's good."

"So are you."

We make our way down the par five. Abby is lining up a five-footer while Brittany and I wait. She rests the club against her leg and grabs her right wrist with her left hand and winces. "Shit."

"Are you all right?"

"My wrist is achy today. I think I'm gonna walk back and see if I can ice it."

"Do you want us to come with you?" I offer.

"No, I'm sure it's fine. Can't be too careful this close to a tournament."

"Right." I try to smile reassuringly, but the reminder that she's playing and I'm not hurts, and I'm not good at faking anything It's one of the many things Coach Potter dislikes about me.

Golf is a country club sport where players are supposed to school their features and always appear completely dignified. But I've always felt too strongly about the sport to pretend to be unfazed by how I'm playing. If I'm happy with a shot, I'm going to show it. And if I'm so mad I want to throw a club...well, I throw a club.

"What's up with Brittany?" Abby asks as we head to the next hole without her. A par three with a wicked sand trap on the right side.

"Wrist is bothering her. She decided to call it so she's ready this weekend." I really try to keep my voice from sounding bitter, but I fail. Bad at faking *everything*.

Abby and I play better when it's just the two of us. We're comfortable, we joke, and we egg each other on. We still play hard, our competitive spirits making everything a game, but it's way more fun. I miss her, spending time just the two of us. Don't get me wrong, I'm happy for her and Smith, but selfishly I want more moments like this.

We're laughing, and I'm lighter than I've been in weeks when we finish the ninth hole and walk back to the clubhouse.

A group of our teammates are standing outside the door, and when they spot us, they go quiet.

Erica smiles at me as we approach. "Looks like you're up."

Abby and I share a confused look.

"Brittany has tendinitis in her wrist. She's out, which means . . ."

My heart races. "I'm in."

CHAPTER FOURTEEN

Keira

"When do you leave?" His brows draw together in hard concentration, and his face shows none of the excitement I expected after telling him the good news.

"Thursday afternoon. The practice round is Friday and the tournament takes place Saturday and Sunday."

He stands and brings me with him to another room via the laptop in his hand. He sets me down and sits in a big office chair. There's a picture behind him—the first evidence of personalization I've seen in his house.

I stare at it, trying to make out more of the photograph while he does whatever it is he's doing and not paying attention to me. It's a picture of two people standing on a golf course. One is definitely Lincoln. There's no mistaking that dark hair and build. The man next to him looks like he could be his father or grandfather. I'm guessing the latter since he told me that's who taught him to play.

"I can move some things around, but I wouldn't be able to get to Valley until late Wednesday night." He frowns. "I'd really like to see you before the tournament. I suppose video will have to do. Can you clear Wednesday night to get a long session in?"

"Sure. I'm free after class on Wednesday. I'm done around ten."

He nods his approval but still looks disappointed and not directly at me.

"I could come to you."

His focus finally snaps to me. "To Scottsdale?"

"That's where you live, right?" I shrug. "If it's easier, then sure."

He considers it for a few quiet seconds, but slowly, I see the agreement in the relaxing of his shoulders. "I'll send you the address. I have another client at three, but if you can get here early then we can get time in before and after."

A whole day of golf and Lincoln? "I'll be there," I say too eagerly.

I SPENT THE MORNING IN THE HOT SEAT WHILE HE WATCHED MY SWING and offered critiques. It felt good, as if we were finally making real progress.

While I sit in the golf cart and eat a sandwich from the country club restaurant, Lincoln chats with Tommy, a local high school kid. He's different with Tommy than he is with me. More hands-on, nicer even.

Lincoln is hard to get to know. He's all business all the time. We've only had a few small moments where we've shared that personal connection, but I want more of it. And I want more of this shiny, fun Lincoln in front of me. I mean, the guy just laughed. Full-on, head back, laughed.

He left his phone in the cart with me. Light music he turned on earlier still plays and I'm starting to get an idea of his taste in music—mostly rock, like dudes with big hair screaming about drugs and rock and roll. It makes me giggle.

I'm enjoying being in his world and learning these small things about him. When he finally walks over to me, his demeanor changes with each step as if he's retreating back into himself and only allowing me to see the serious and professional side of him.

"I'm just gonna grab some water, and then I'll be ready."

"There's no rush if you want to get lunch." He made sure I ate but I haven't seen him eat anything all day.

"I'll grab something later."

He returns from the clubhouse with two waters and gets into the driver's seat of the golf cart. When we pull up to the tee box at the first hole, there's a hint of a smile on his face. "Let's see what you got."

"I get to play?" I'm giddy as I step out and grab my driver before he can change his mind.

This course, what I can see of it anyway, is breathtaking. Nicer than any other I've played.

Lincoln gets out of the cart but stays off to the side as I set up. For some reason, this is more nerve-wracking than having him pick apart my swing all day, every day. All our work will be graded here on the course.

"Just relax. It's going to take time to translate everything from practice to playing. There are more distractions and your old tendencies are still going to show up. Relax, focus on only one swing at a time."

I close my eyes and take a deep breath. When I open them, he's standing closer. His masculine scent and the smell of grass wrap around me, adding another distraction I should ignore.

"Let me see you at the top of the backswing."

Once in position, he walks a circle around me. "Good. Now pull with your lead leg. Focus here." He places a hand on my left thigh. "Here," he says again. "Got it?"

I'm holding my breath, the skin-to-skin contact doing funny things to me while he seems totally unaware and completely focused on golf. He removes his hand and stands tall. I realize I still haven't answered when he steps into my line of vision.

"I got it."

"All right." He steps back. "Show me what you got."

By the third hole, I finally relax, and by the sixth, I'm smiling at how much more consistent my drives are. I still have work to do, but I'm playing the best round of golf in my life.

We catch up to a couple of guys just ready to tee off at the seventh.

"Lincoln?" An old man in the standard-issued country-club getup of polo with khakis walks toward us. "I thought that was you." He flashes a smile under his Sam Elliott style mustache.

"Hey, Bob. Nice to see you."

"Are you playing today? Hank and I could use a little friendly competition."

"Nah, just working with a client. Bob, Hank, this is Keira."

"Pleasure to meet you, young lady." Bob's brown eyes twinkle as he smiles at me. Based on first impressions, he's impossible not to like.

"You too."

Hank shakes Lincoln's hand and then nods to me. "You two go

ahead and play through. If I get back to the clubhouse before five, I'll have to go to dinner with my wife and her *sister*. That woman sends back everything. The water is too warm. The burger is too rare. The vegetables are touching the rice." He rolls his eyes and puts the cigar in his left hand to his mouth.

I look to Lincoln for my cue on whether I should go ahead. He smiles, a crooked grin that makes my stomach flutter. "Go ahead, Keira."

As I'm grabbing my driver, I overhear Bob ask Lincoln, "How come you aren't playing today?"

"It's been a while. Maybe he can't hack it anymore, Bob," Hank says on an exhale of smoke.

I fight to keep my lips pressed together and laughter inside.

Lincoln shakes his head. "Today is just about Keira. She has a tournament coming up this weekend."

"Sounds likes she could use some competition then." Hank nods toward where I walk to the front tees.

Lincoln smiles but doesn't move. His clubs are in the back of the cart, so I know he doesn't have that as an excuse not to take the guys up on their offer. "I'm just here for some last-minute instruction."

"I think I'd feel better *supported* if a pro came up here and showed me how it was done."

Bob and Hank whistle and chuckle.

"I like her," Hank says.

I stare at Lincoln with a smug, challenging set to my jaw, but I don't really expect him to grab a club from his bag. He carries it under his arm and walks toward me as he puts on his glove.

The tiny victory I feel at goading him into showing me his swing disappears when he leans over to place a tee on the ground and then again to place a ball on top. It's hard not to check out his ass. Some women love football pants, some love baseball pants, but a man in dress pants swinging a golf club—that's my weakness.

With his eye on the fairway, he swings the club lightly just in front of him. "See that tree on the left side just before the sand trap?"

"Yeah."

"Closest ball wins."

"Wins what?"

A cocky smirk twists his lips. "When I win, we're going to finish nine and then head back to the driving range so you can do two-hundred more solid swings."

"What about if I win?"

"If you win, then you're done for the day. You can drive back to Valley in time to hang out with your friends or whatever it is you do when you aren't practicing."

As if there's time for anything else. Also, I don't want to go back. I want to stay here and play until it's too dark to see the ball.

And I want him to keep smiling at me like he is right now.

"All right. You're on, but if I win, you have to buy me dinner first."

A rough huff of a laugh rolls out of him. "I have dinner plans."

"Not if I win you don't."

"Ladies first." He raises both brows in a friendly challenge.

I step back. "Oh no, age before beauty."

Hank and Bob stand off to the side. It sounds like they're placing bets, but I focus only on the man next to me as he steps up to the ball.

His chest rises and falls with a long breath. He shifts his weight around until he's comfortable, and then he stills. I hold my breath as he pulls back and hits the prettiest shot I've ever seen in person.

My mouth is wide open when the ball drops near the tree and he turns to face me.

"That was...beautiful." I'm too impressed to be embarrassed by the awe in my voice.

He seems a little taken aback by my compliment, and there's an awkward beat of silence as he grabs his tee and pockets it. "You're up."

More so than any time he's watched me, I feel his gaze like a weighted blanket—though, not at all as comforting as people claim. I do my best to ignore everything but the club in my hands and the tree I'm aiming for, take a deep breath, and swing.

For the first time, I feel it. That elusive sensation that only comes from hitting the ball pure and exactly where I intended.

"Wooooweee," one of the guys—Hank, I think—calls as my ball sails through the air.

Chills run up my right arm, and Lincoln steps up beside me, driver held loosely in his right hand. "Nice shot." He rests the clubface on the top of his shoe. "It's gonna be close."

"She won. Pay up," Hank says to Bob as the two head for their cart.

"You can't see that far." Hank rolls his eyes and hops in next to Bob.

Lincoln and I exchange an amused smile and follow them. Even as the balls come into view, it's impossible to tell whose is closer.

I'm about to ask how we're going to determine the winner when Bob grabs a laser rangefinder from his bag.

"That thing won't work, it's too close. I'm going to walk it out," Hank starts counting his steps from Lincoln's ball to the tree while Bob continues pressing buttons on his rangefinder.

"That was the best drive I've seen from you yet," Lincoln says as we stand back and await the results.

"Thanks. Yours was really good too. I saw it on some videos, but they didn't do it justice. You have a great swing."

"I'm rusty," he says with a small chuckle. "I don't get a chance to play much anymore."

"Five steps on Lincoln's," Hank calls and moves to do the same for mine.

"I can't imagine not playing." I breathe in the smell and lift my head to the sky enjoying the way the late sun beats down on my face.

He's quiet, and when I look over, he's staring at me with a strange expression. Sometime this afternoon he's developed a five o'clock shadow that I find myself wanting to reach out and touch, see if it feels and sounds the way I imagine as I lightly run my nails along his jaw.

"She won! Four and a half steps!" Hank exclaims, breaking the moment. He walks over to me with extra pep in his step and hugs me and bounces us around, shaking laughter out of me. Lincoln watches, looking happy and young, and I think I fall a little in love with him.

"Where are we going? I'm starving." I sit in the passenger seat of Lincoln's SUV. It's nice; sparkling leather without a trace of dust, floors and compartments clean and tidy. He has one of those center console organizers where everything is put in its perfect place. It's so very Lincoln.

We left my car at the country club and I'm collecting my winnings before I head back to Valley.

He turns into a subdivision where the lawns are green, and the houses get bigger with each one we pass. "Wherever you want, but I need to make a stop first."

He slows in front of a beautiful tan-colored home with a large rose bush out front. It isn't the type of place I expected him to live. "Is this your house?"

"No." He laughs and pulls up behind a silver Mercedes. He puts it in park and sits back in the seat, making no move to turn it off. "Shit."

"What?"

"Gram did it again."

Knowing this is his grandmother's house makes more sense. "Did what again?"

He rakes a hand through his hair and squeezes his eyes shut. Seeing Lincoln irritated at something that isn't me is new and much better for appreciating how hot he looks when he's grumpy.

"Is that her?" I point to the woman coming out the front of the house. She's wearing a floral apron and looks an awful lot like Betty White with a head of big, white hair and bright pink lips.

Lincoln shuts the engine off and opens his door. "I'll be right back."

He embraces the woman, and they exchange words I can't hear. She looks past him to me, and a big smile lifts her lips up even higher and then falls. She focuses back on Lincoln and there's more back and forth.

Obviously, they're talking about me, and even though he told me he would be right back, it's completely rude of me to just sit here and not even say hello. Also, I kind of want to meet her.

I step out and walk a few steps toward them before either of them notices. Lincoln is telling her he'll call later when his grandma stops paying attention to him and looks to me.

"Hello." Her smile puts me at ease, and I close the remaining distance.

"Hi. I'm Keira."

CHAPTER FIFTEEN

Lincoln

"It's lovely to meet you, dear. I'm Milly, Lincoln's grandmother."

"I was just telling Gram that we had dinner plans and can't stay." I place a hand at Keira's back and then remove it, flex it and try to rid the burning sensation working up my arm. I'm about to crawl out of my skin with all the ways this is fucked up.

I brought a client to my grandmother's house, which is unprofessional enough without all the ways my body is reacting to said client—none of which are the least bit professional. And now she's a door away from seeing the blind date Gram has waiting for me. I should have known. The woman never gives up.

Gram seems to really like Keira, or maybe she just likes that I willingly brought a woman over. Gram was never supposed to know. I was just gonna slip inside, tell her something came up with a client, and then Keira and I'd be on our way. I should have called.

"We have dinner together every week. He's a good boy."

"That's sweet." Keira smirks at me, obviously loving every second of my discomfort.

Ha! If Keira knew the thoughts going through my head, she wouldn't be calling me sweet. I scan the length of her. Her little golf skirts are going to be the death of me.

Gram nods. "I made tamales tonight. It's Lincoln's favorite, and I've invited my friend Jenny and her granddaughter."

"That sounds delicious," Keira says and presses a hand against her stomach, the movement lifting her shirt to show off the smooth skin just below her belly button. "I'm starving."

I can see the wheels turning under Gram's big hair.

"We can't. Keira has to get back to Valley." And away from me before I screw up and touch her again.

Keira shrugs. "It's okay. It's been a while since I've had a real home-cooked meal."

"Well, let's get you inside. The more the merrier. There are chips and guacamole you can snack on while I finish dinner." Gram herds Keira inside, and I shove my hands into my pockets so I don't rip the hair out of my scalp. Or touch her.

Keira turns her head as they enter the front door and smiles at me, sweet and playful. Gram continues inside, but Keira waits for me to come unglued from my spot.

"Come on." She rolls her eyes, steps to me, and takes my hand, pulling me along.

Her small fingers wrap around mine and squeeze before she leaves me in the entryway and heads toward Gram in the kitchen. She washes her hands and then snags a handful of chips.

I move to the dining room to say hello to Jenny, who's one of Gram's friends I actually remember; though, I've never met her granddaughter Whitney. I apologize to them both, fumbling over what exactly I'm apologizing for since I had no clue, but I did just bring another chick to a blind date, so saying something seems like the right thing to do.

"I'm sorry about this. Gram must have mixed up the dates." She definitely didn't mix up the dates, and anyone who knows her, knows she's still whip-smart. "Keira is a client, and she has an important tournament coming up this weekend."

"Your grandmother said you're a golf coach. Is that right?" Whitney asks.

I give her and Jenny a brief overview of the company. As I talk, my gaze randomly falls to Keira. She hasn't left Gram's side in the kitchen, and more surprising is that Gram hasn't shooed her out. That might be because she wants to keep Keira and Whitney apart, so her matchmaking wasn't in vain, but they're both smiling an awful lot.

I do my best to entertain Jenny and Whitney while only allowing myself small glances at Keira. Making conversation has always come easy to me. I'm not as charismatic as Kenton, but I like people and I'm generally good at making them feel at ease and welcome. It's part of the reason I travel so much. I'm more persuasive in person.

It's nice out, so Gram and Keira set the table on the back patio, and we all sit to eat.

"Anyone want more wine?" Gram asks, bringing bottles of red and white to the table.

I prefer beer, but since I know there isn't any in the fridge, I take the red and refill Jenny and Whitney's glasses before giving myself a small pour. I'd like to guzzle the entire bottle to make this less awkward, but since I'm driving Keira, I won't.

"Would you like some wine, dear?" Gram asks Keira, she's the only one without a wine glass in front of her. "There are more glasses inside. Lincoln, why don't you grab her a glass."

Keira holds up a hand. "Oh, no thanks. I have to drive back to Valley tonight." She takes a bite of her tamale and groans. "This is so good."

Gram smiles while I watch on amused. Keira has totally bewitched her. If Pop were here, he'd be smitten too...just as soon as he saw her hit a golf ball, anyway.

"Lincoln was saying you have a big tournament this weekend." Whitney passes a platter to me but speaks to Keira.

Keira glances at me while nodding. "Yeah, that's right." She squirms in her seat, pushes some food around her plate, and takes a drink of water, clearly uncomfortable with being in the spotlight. Put a golf club in her hand and she'd be giving them a show, but without one, she's less sure of herself.

"Keira plays at Valley University. She had back-to-back top ten placings at the Pac-12 Championships and NCAA Regionals, was named Player of the Month in September, made first team all-Pac-12, almost advanced to semifinals of the NCAA Championship, too." I finish and take a sip of wine. It's still silent when I place it back on the table.

Gram's smile couldn't get any bigger, and Keira looks dumbstruck, as if she didn't expect me to know her stats. Did the girl really think I took her on just because she begged and pleaded?

"Wow." Whitney is the first to speak. She looks between Keira and me a couple of times. "That's really impressive."

"It sure is," Gram says, eyes not leaving my face. I shake my head because I know exactly what she's thinking. Just because I know the girl's history, it doesn't mean I'm interested in dating her.

And even if I were, it's simply not possible. Putting aside the fact I'm her coach, I care too much about seeing Keira succeed to screw it up by getting in her way.

CHAPTER SIXTEEN

Keira

Lincoln went to walk Whitney and her grandmother to their car, but I stay on the patio with Milly, enjoying the light breeze and the last heat of the sun.

"Your house is beautiful. I can't imagine waking up to this every day." Lincoln's grandmother's house has a beautiful view of the golf course.

"George, my husband, had coffee out here every morning, and a lot of evenings too. I don't sit out here nearly as much now that he's gone, but it always makes me think of him."

"Lincoln talks about him a lot—or, as much as he talks about anyone."

"He started following George around as soon as he was able to walk and never stopped."

I pull my legs under me as I try to picture a young Lincoln.

"My parents moved out here from Maryland when I was little.

My grandparents were always far away so I never really had that type of relationship with them. I think it's nice that he did. And nice that you two are still so close."

"That must have been hard."

I shrug. "They've passed now, but they would send cards, and we talked on the phone occasionally. I never felt like I missed out. Well, not too much. Seeing you and Lincoln together makes me think it would have been nice to have lived closer."

"I'm sure Lincoln would love to have me across the country right about now. He's one blind date away from never speaking to me again."

I giggle, which is something I'm finding I do a lot around Milly. "Why do you do it if you know he hates it?"

She sighs. "Because I'm afraid that, if I don't push him, he'll spend so much time fixing people's golf swings that he'll forget to fix his own issues and live his life. Eventually, you get old enough to realize work is the thing you do to afford a life, not to create one. And I don't mind admitting that I'd also like a great grandchild before I die."

Milly smiles and places her hand over mine on the table. "Don't misunderstand me, I'm proud of him, and I'm glad he's helping you. I just wish he'd take more time for himself." She taps her fingers over mine and then lifts her hand. "There's something about seeing you with him, though. You keep him on his toes, I can tell."

She stands just as Lincoln reappears. "I'm gonna clean up. Why don't you and Keira go for a walk along the course before it gets dark."

I expect Lincoln to offer an excuse, but when Milly goes inside, he waves a hand toward the gate at the edge of the yard. "What do you say?"

As we walk down the golf cart path, the only sounds are our footsteps and the birds chirping. Palm trees dot the horizon, and the ninth hole stretches out before us. We have this entire amazing course to ourselves and it's breathtaking.

"Your grandmother is…" I smile as I try to think of the right adjective.

"Overbearing? Bossy?"

"I was going to say wonderful, but those things too."

"Yeah. She's great minus the setup attempts at every turn. Last week, a woman emailed me and asked about having me out for a clinic at her high school, and when I called her to get more details, she told me she'd gotten my number from Gram, and oh, by the way, she was the librarian."

"A librarian with a passion for sports…or maybe just the man playing the sport." I bump my shoulder against his and then remain close. "You're a catch."

He arches a brow. "My gram tell you that?"

"Me and every other woman in the state probably."

"Thank you for being so nice to her. She likes you."

"I like her too."

He steps away to pick up a water cup in the path and toss it into a nearby trash can. "You ready to get back?"

I nod. "Yeah, I should probably get started home."

We turn around and head the way we came, walking up the ninth hole. I step closer again and this time he doesn't try to put distance between us. The sleeve of his shirt and the warmth of his arm tickles me. "Why does your grandmother keep setting you up so she can, in her words, fix your issues?"

He groans. "Can we pretend she didn't tell you anything that would make our whole client-coach relationship inappropriate and awkward?"

"Definitely not. I mean…I yelled at you and then threw tequila on you. It's only fair I have dirt on you too."

His lips twitch at the corners.

"So? What happened?"

He makes a strangled sound and I think his pace speeds up as if he's trying to speed walk away from this conversation.

"Come on, tell me. It can't be that bad."

"I was married and things didn't work out."

I motion with a hand for him to keep going, which surprisingly, he does.

"Since the divorce, Gram has been on my case to get back out there. I keep telling her I'm fine, but she keeps pushing and setting me up on blind dates. I know she means well, but the woman refuses to accept that my life doesn't lend itself very well to relationships. I'm on the road a lot, and even when I'm not, I'm working or thinking about work. Anyway, now that you know entirely too much about me, what about you?"

"It's really just me and my dad. My parents are divorced, and my mom lives in Maryland with her new husband. Since my dad is as likely to set me up on dates as he is to cheer for the Cubs, I have far fewer dates than you."

"They aren't breaking down the door, making him clean his guns, or whatever the cliché dad jokes is?"

"Is that what you're going to do someday? Answer the door on your daughter's dates with a shotgun, blaring eighties rock, wearing jorts?"

He shakes his head. "I don't own jorts, and you're avoiding the question."

"I've dated, nothing serious since high school…if you can count that as serious."

"How come?"

"I don't know." I shrug. "There isn't a lot of time. Plus, guys aren't as into the whole standing on the sidelines and cheering on their significant other as chicks are."

"You're young, beautiful, and talented. I'm sure that's intimidating for some guys. Trust me, plenty of guys would love to be there to cheer you on."

My stomach flips, and I ask, "You really think so?"

His dark eyes meet mine, and those full lips pull into a wide smile. "I know so."

CHAPTER SEVENTEEN

Keira

The university golf course at Stanford is beautiful. Bright green colors set against the mountain landscape. In some ways, it isn't so different from home, but in all the ways it matters in relation to golf, it's completely different.

The elevation is different, for one, and then there's the turf. One bad bounce on our hard, dry ground in Arizona, and I'd be swinging at dust. The grass here is lush and more forgiving. Every shot from the fairway is like hitting off a tee.

"You looked good," Abby says as we're finishing our practice round. "All those extra hours of practice are showing. How'd it feel?"

"I don't know."

She laughs, but I'm serious. I don't think I felt my body the entire time. But now that I am focusing on it, a sinking feeling settles in my stomach. I'm so screwed.

"Come on, let's go back to the hotel, shower, and then watch

QVC before dinner."

"I don't think I'm gonna go to dinner."

"What? Why?"

"I think it'll just make me more nervous." The team dinner the night before a tournament is something that's supposed to be relaxing and uplifting, but it has the opposite effect on me. Maybe it's Coach Potter, maybe it's just me. Either way, I need to get my head right before tomorrow.

One thing is certain, if I screw this up, Coach Potter will make sure I never get another shot.

In our hotel room, I let Abby shower first and collapse onto the bed. I close my eyes and visualize the course. I see myself moving through each hole in best-case and worst-case scenarios.

Once it's my turn for the shower, I stand under the hot spray and let every negative thought or fear come to the surface, and then, one by one, I try to dismiss them. It's easier to let go of some than others.

"Are you sure you don't want to come? It might be good to get out and forget about tomorrow for a couple of hours," Abby asks as she grabs her purse.

I run a brush through my wet hair and pull the towel tighter around my body. "I'm sure."

"Do you want me to bring you back something?"

"Nah, I might order room service or walk downstairs to grab something from the market across the street."

"All right. See ya later."

I'm lounging on my bed in a T-shirt and jeans, watching the local weather channel, when my phone pings with a text.

Lincoln: How did your practice round go?

Me: Okay, I think. I shot one under.

Lincoln: Nice work. Eat a light dinner, drink lots of water, and get a good night's sleep.

Me: Does ordering pizza count as light?

Lincoln: Definitely not. Don't you have some sort of team dinner tonight?

Me: I didn't go.

Lincoln: Why not? You need to eat.

I roll my eyes but find myself smiling as the phone rings and Lincoln's name lights up the screen. "Hello?"

"What's wrong? Why aren't you eating with the team? Did Potter do something?"

The protective note in his tone makes me want to hug him simply for implying he'd be pissed if my coach had stepped out of line. "No, Coach Potter didn't do anything. Well, nothing out of the normal."

"Are you nervous for tomorrow?"

"Yes," I admit. "Terrified. What if I screw up?"

"You won't."

"You can't know that. I could go out there and bogey every hole. Or double bogey."

He laughs. "That's pretty unlikely."

"But I could!" I insist.

"Okay, fine. I'll play this game. Yes, you could go out tomorrow and double bogey every hole."

The sinking feeling grows in my stomach, making it hard to breathe.

"*Or* you could go out there and shoot sixty-two and let everyone know that you mean business. Either way, the plan remains the same."

"Coach Potter will never let me have another shot if I embarrass the team again."

"Fuck Potter," he clips and then his voice softens. "You're the best player on the team, Keira. Go out there tomorrow and act like it. Own that shit."

I'm nodding, that rush of excitement before a game finally thrumming through me. "Okay."

"Yeah?" He sounds surprised.

I nod again, more determined. "Yeah."

"Good luck tomorrow. Call me after and let me know how it goes."

A half hour after we get off the phone, my stomach is growling, and I'm considering moving from my spot on the bed to go find something to eat when there are three sharp knocks on my door. I look through the peephole and see a man carrying a tray of food.

I open it, prepared to tell him he has the wrong room, but then he smiles. "Room service for Miss Brooks."

"I didn't order anything."

He looks back at the paper in his hand. "Keira Brooks. Room three thirteen."

My stomach growls at the smell of something I can't place.

We're at an awkward standoff.

"Where would you like it?"

"On the bed, I guess." I go to my wallet so I can pay him.

"It's been taken care of."

"Like on a room charge?"

"No, it was paid for separately over the phone."

He leaves, and I remove the top off one of the plates. Salad.

I pop a crouton into my mouth, well aware of where the food came from now that I see the boring contents. The second plate has a grilled chicken sandwich with veggies. Still boring, but better.

Me: Thanks for dinner.

He doesn't respond, so I lift the top off the third plate. The smallest piece of chocolate cake I've ever seen makes me laugh. Such a complicated man.

I'M THE FIRST FROM VALLEY TO TEE OFF. WHILE I WARM UP ON THE driving range, Coach Potter stands back, arms crossed, and watches. It feels good, and my accuracy has improved, but I try not to get overly confident.

There is a tenfold stress difference between warm-ups and taking that first swing to start the tournament, and that difference is responsible for talented players falling out of competition by the end of day one. Myself included.

I hit my last ball and turn around for any parting wisdom from Coach.

"I think I'm ready," I say.

"No one is expecting much, so just go out there, do your best, and try to contribute to the overall team score. No matter what happens, keep your head. You represent us all when you're on that course. Understood?"

Anger vibrates under my skin, and a cool sweat makes me want to push up my sleeves even though it's barely fifty degrees. "Got it."

CHAPTER EIGHTEEN

Lincoln

If determination were ever personified by a look, Keira would be wearing it. Determined and pissed—at the ball or at life, I'm not sure which.

She's just off the fairway in the first cut rough about to take her second shot on this par five. It's her second round of the day, and I can tell she's in better condition than the other girls. While they're tiring, she still looks fresh.

Teddy, the coach from Stanford, spots me and weaves through the small crowd to where I'm standing in the back.

"Lincoln." He extends a hand, and we shake. "What are you doing here?"

"Watching." I nod toward Keira and one of his players, Wren Thompkins. "She's good."

He crosses his arms over his chest, and we stand shoulder to shoulder, watching as Keira takes her swing. It's long, and Keira's face shows her frustration.

Mine must show it too.

"That girl has power." He laughs as Keira shoves her club into her bag and shoulders it. "And spunk. Reminds me a little of you when you were fresh on the tour. Remember that time you almost took a swing at Johnson?"

I smile, but the memory makes me pissed all over again. He'd made a snide comment about Lacey and threw me off my whole game, which was exactly what he wanted. I should have punched him.

We walk behind the crowd as they move with the players. Thompkins looks indecisive as she tries to pick out the right club for her approach shot.

"Good to see you, Lincoln." He moves up to confer with his player, and I hang back because I'm fairly certain Keira hasn't spotted me yet.

I probably should have told her I was coming, but the truth is I didn't know I was until I found myself ordering her room service and then booking a plane ticket. Not being able to be here yesterday when she needed me ate away any concern of it being inappropriate.

We can practice every day, all day, but it's her ability to transfer that to competition that is important. She can do it, I know she can, but if she needs me to keep reminding her, I'll be here for those reassurances later.

Keira finds a rhythm on the back nine and ends the day one under and tied for fifth, though there are a lot of players who still have to finish. I find her in the clubhouse with one of her teammates.

The other girl elbows her when it's clear I'm headed toward them, and Keira's brown eyes fall to me. She does a double take and then a wide smile breaks out on her face.

"What are you doing here?" She steps forward and hugs me, taking me by surprise. She smells really good, and her body fits to mine a little too well. If I weren't her coach, I'd be all too happy to pull her against me and let her know I'm just as happy to see her.

"I came to watch you play, of course. Plus, my brother doesn't live far from here, so I wanted to stop in and see him." Kenton is in Seattle until tomorrow so it's unlikely I'll actually get to see him, but it makes me feel a little less weird about being here to add that tidbit.

Keira introduces me to Abby, or reintroduces me since we met once before, and then Abby excuses herself leaving Keira and me alone.

I motion for her to take a seat on a small bench next to the window and do the same.

"I can't believe you're here. I was just getting ready to text you."

"Yeah? What were you going to report?"

"One under." She makes a face that tells me it isn't as good as she hoped.

"How'd you feel out there?"

"Nervous, anxious, excited. By the second round, I was finally starting to calm down, but it's infuriating how good Wren Thompkins is. Her shots were chasing down the pin all day."

I chuckle. "You out drove her every single time."

She sits a little taller. "Yes, that I did." Her gaze turns to the window and out to the course. "I should probably get out there and watch, wanna come? Cassidy's on two."

I want to. I really do, but I know I have a dozen things I need to do, things I put off this morning to be here. "I can't. I need to do some work this afternoon. I'll check in later."

There's a hint of disappointment on her face that makes me seriously consider blowing off work, but she nods and stands to leave. "See ya later then."

I watch her go, each step she takes making the room feel a little less enjoyable.

"Keira," I call out before she's out of earshot.

She stops and turns her head, a hesitant smile on her lips. "Yeah?"

"Good job today."

That smile gets bigger, and she takes a step, still looking over her shoulder. "Thanks, Coach."

I'M ON THE PHONE WITH HEATH FOR OUR WEEKLY CHECK IN. ALL THE other employees check-in with the manager of their division because there's simply too many for me to oversee all of them, but I do Heath's one-on-one every week.

Really, I just want to make sure everything's good with him, but we do chat work for the first ten minutes and getting his take on things I might not see from my position, is always interesting.

I lean back in the single chair in my room while he tells me about the most entertaining client of his week, a woman who is trying to win her man back by learning hockey via barraging Heath with questions on terminology and breakdowns of games she's watched on television.

"Look at you, hockey guru and relationship counselor."

I can almost picture him flipping me off through the phone as he says, "Fuck off. I'm going pro after this year. Watch and see, old man. Then you'll have to find someone else to be your hockey guru."

"In the meantime, how about you stop procrastinating and

crack open a book. I have to make some other calls."

He mumbles something, but I'm distracted by the knock at my door.

I stand and speak as I cross the room, "Stay out of trouble. Call me if you need anything."

When I open the door, Keira holds up a bottle of wine in front of my face. I take it and open the heavy door wide so she can step in.

"How'd you find me?"

She walks in, taking in the space before sitting on the edge of the bed. "I asked. Nicely. And I might have batted my eyelashes at the cute guy at the front desk."

"Shameless." I put the wine on the dresser and lean my back against it, crossing one ankle over the other. "What's the plan for the night? Are you guys getting in some practice or taking the night off?"

"Night off. Coach was pleased with how things went today, and it was spitting rain as we left anyway, so . . . we have all night to prepare for the final round tomorrow."

"Is that right?"

She pulls her legs under her on my bed, and my thoughts go from golf to—fuck, I need a drink and to get out of this hotel room.

Keira and bed—two words I've already established don't need to be said or thought together. Seeing it, also real, reaaaal bad.

"Have you eaten?" I stand straight.

"Yeah." She bobs her head from side to side. "Well, sort of. I had a sandwich at the course."

"Come on, let's feed you something."

While Keira and I eat downstairs at the hotel restaurant, I give her a brief rundown of what I saw today. Then try to keep the conversation off golf so she can relax and have a few hours without stress.

I'm usually good at small talk, but I find myself struggling to say anything and simultaneously trying to keep it all inside. She doesn't need to know that I think it's beautiful how she lights up when she talks about golf or how I want to run my fingers along her smooth skin.

I'm on my third beer, which initially I thought was helping but now I'm wondering if sober state of mind was the way to go. A group of guys at the bar keep looking back at her. She's totally unaware and I'm not about to point it out to her.

Her phone vibrates on the table between us, and she glances at the screen. "I have to get upstairs. Curfew is in ten minutes." She lets out a long breath, all the nerves we chased away returning before my eyes. "Will I see you tomorrow?"

"I'll be there," I assure her. I've already paid our tab, so I down the rest of my beer and stand. "Let me walk you up."

She's quiet as we take the elevator up to her floor. I want to say or do something to make her feel confident. It's something I don't usually need to do with my clients because I build their self-confidence through months of training, but we've only been working together a short time, and she doesn't have that yet.

The doors open, and I step out with her.

"Thanks for dinner and for being here."

"No need for thanks. Does your dad make tournaments very often?"

"No. Don't get me wrong, he's my biggest fan, but he only comes to the home tournaments."

With my hands in my pocket, I linger in the hallway. "I have a call I can't miss tomorrow morning at eight, but I'll do my best to get to the course while you're warming up. Try to sleep tonight, I know how hard that is the night before the final day. No matter what happens tomorrow, you proved you belong out there today. They can't take that away from you."

"I don't want to just prove I belong; I want to win. I feel like I should stay up all night and visualize or practice my downswing. I can't just sleep when I could be doing something."

"I know." I free my hand from my pocket and take her fingers loosely in mine. It's only the lightest brush of skin, but I feel more connected by that small touch than I have felt fully naked with others. "Trust me when I tell you that the best thing you can do tonight is sleep. Tomorrow you can go back to conquering the world."

She nods, and I drop her hand and step back to the elevator. "'Night."

CHAPTER NINETEEN

Keira

Abby is on her bed texting Smith while I warm up with some light stretching in our hotel room. My alarm goes off, signaling the five-minute warning that the van is leaving.

"Ugh, I just want to lie here another hour," Abby says as she sits up.

It's still dark outside, but I don't understand why she isn't more excited. It's day two, the final day of this short tournament. Today we'll play our last round. Only eighteen holes to climb my way up the leaderboard.

"The guys say good luck." Abby stands and brushes her dark hair back into a neat ponytail and then grabs her visor and bag.

"Why are they up so early?"

"They have a special practice today to work on putting with another friend of Coach James'."

"Why am I not surprised?" I chuckle lightly. It doesn't bother me quite as much as it used to . . . probably because I know I've already snagged the best coach in the world.

Abby and I are the last to load up in the van.

"Morning," Erica chirps.

Kim and Cassidy wave from the backseat. Kim has her headphones on, and Cassidy goes back to staring out the window. We all have our own ways of prepping on tournament days.

"Everyone ready?" Coach Potter asks from the driver's seat. His sunglasses dangle from a black cord attached to either side so they hang around his neck.

On the ride to the course, I re-read the texts from my parents. Both sent early this morning, within minutes of each other, which makes me wonder if Dad texted Mom to remind her. Normally, I'd think it was Mom who'd have it neatly scheduled in, but there's no way Dad forgot. He may not know what to buy me at Christmas and think Hungry Man makes gourmet food, but when it comes to supporting me and my love for golf, he's never let me down.

Dad: Good luck today, sweet pea.

Mom: Good luck, sweetie!! I'm cheering you on from afar.

My mom included a picture of her and Bart wearing the Valley U golf T-shirts that I got them for Christmas. It's funny because I'd bet my dad is wearing his too.

My nerves kick in as we arrive at the course and exit the van. The sun is still rising, and the morning air is brisk, so I zip up my Valley jacket higher on my neck.

"I couldn't sleep last night," Erica whispers as we walk a step behind the rest of the team.

"Me either."

"At least you're in placing position. The top half of the leaderboard has to choke for me to come anywhere near the top three."

After all the groups finished yesterday, I'd been bumped to ninth place. It isn't great, but I'm still in it. Abby and Cassidy are in fifth and second respectively.

The team splits to warm up. Kim, Cassidy, and Abby start with chipping while Erica and I go to the putting area. Our easy conversation turns to silence as soon as our feet touch the green. Anxiety creeps up my body making my grip sweaty and my arms shaky.

A few minutes later, Coach walks over with Cassidy. The expression on his face and the way they both nod seriously tells me he's giving her last-minute pointers. He's putting all his efforts into her, which isn't a bad bet. She's really good and continually places top five. Still, I can't help but feel annoyed that he's never given me that type of coaching.

My high school coach used to say that when I stop yelling, that's when I stop caring. Coach Potter stopped yelling the day I threw my club in the water hazard and blew the tournament. Actually, he started and stopped that day. I know he doesn't believe in me, but in moments like this, a little boost of confidence, even from him, wouldn't hurt.

"Erica," Coach calls and waves her over. She glances at me, rolls her eyes so only I can see, and then heads over to them.

Closing my eyes for just a moment, I inhale and will my body to relax. All around me people are quietly talking and shuffling around, stretching, or pulling clubs from bags.

Players down the line swing and hit balls, the *ping* coming every few seconds. It's usually my favorite sound in the world, so I try to focus on it and ignore everything else. I search for that sound, among all hits, that perfect ping of the ball being hit on the sweet spot of the club.

A gruff voice, not much louder than a whisper, breaks my attention, and I turn to see Lincoln off to the side, away from the coaches and players.

Two bottom fingers wrapped around his coffee cup lift in a wave. The rhythm of my heart speeds up, but there's something soothing about his presence too. He's here for me. Just me.

I sneak a peek at Coach, who may as well not even know I exist, and walk toward Lincoln.

"Hey," I say when I reach him.

The smell of soap and coffee hangs on him. A white Under Armour hat covers his dark hair, and his face is smooth, as if he shaved only minutes ago. He fits right in with gray slacks and a black polo, but there's something about Lincoln that always stands out.

"Morning. How are you feeling?"

"Nervous."

His smile lifts. "Relax, have fun, and don't throw anything."

An unexpected chuckle slips from my lips, garnering the attention of those around us, including Coach Potter. If looks could kill, then I'd be squished like a bug under my coach's shoe.

"Shit," I mutter under my breath.

Coach Potter waits until he's close enough he doesn't have to raise his voice before he speaks. "Keira, get back in line and pretend like you want to be here, for heaven's sake."

My jaw drops, and I scramble for words to spit at him, but Lincoln's hazel eyes meet mine, and his head shakes ever so subtly from side to side.

I walk back and stand next to Abby.

"What was that?" she whispers.

"Coach being an ass like usual. God, I hate that man."

Lincoln and Coach exchange words, neither looking happy. Eventually Lincoln nods, glances over to me, and gives me one last reassuring smile before he walks away.

Coach turns, doesn't spare me so much as a cursory glance, and shakes his head in disgust.

I'm paired with Mia Arnold, a freshman standout, from New Mexico State. She struggled yesterday, but as she walks over to stand beside me to wait our turn, she looks confident and ready to go.

"Good luck today." She pulls her driver. The smile on her face seems to sit there so securely.

"You too." There is no smile on my face. I feel like I might throw up or pass out.

Hole one is a par five at five hundred and five yards. Yesterday, I parred it both rounds, but if I want a chance at placing, I need to do better.

Mia tees off first. A nice start with a drive around two hundred and fifty yards. Not all that long, but it left her in a good position on the fairway.

When my name is announced, I step up and position my teed ball just right of the center of the box. I do a quick glance for Coach, but don't find him. It shouldn't surprise me, but it still does. I bet he'll be here to watch the others tee off.

There isn't time to be disappointed or to wish things were different. This is my moment, my time to prove I don't just belong here, I'm here to win.

Lincoln lingers on the sideline with a few other spectators. His eyes bore into me, silently communicating everything I need to hear. *Relax, have fun, you can do this.*

I can do this.

The hole fits my strengths perfectly. It has a wide fairway and a gentle right to left dogleg. I take aim dead center with the intention of letting my draw move the ball toward the left edge of the fairway, which will setup a perfect approach. I take a breath and swing hard.

The ball screams down the center of the fairway with a hint of a draw. Holy crap.

I'm stunned for a moment as the crowd claps enthusiastically because not only did it go exactly where I wanted but also ended up sixty yards past Mia's.

CHAPTER TWENTY

Lincoln

The crowd at the fourteenth hole is twice as big as the one that was at the ninth hole. And it's all because of the amazing show Keira is putting on. With each hole, she finds a little more confidence, and people are getting to see the version of Keira that only I've been privy to. Well, me and her dickhead coach who wouldn't know talent if it slapped him upside the head.

Speaking of, Potter walks up from wherever the fuck he's been, a big, proud smile on his face. Hands on hips, he hangs back while Keira takes her turn. It's another beautiful shot on the short par four, putting her in a great position close to the pin and beating Mia Arnold's drive by a good thirty yards.

The crowd claps and starts to walk, but I hang back, watching as Potter approaches her. A hesitant smile pulls her lips apart like she's afraid to believe he's actually there and praising her.

They walk toward her ball together, all the while he's talking to her, waving his hands and suddenly super involved. Trying to temper my annoyance, I move with the rest of the spectators.

Mia Arnold's coach smiles reassuringly and gives her a few small claps to get her going. Keira's intimidated her, out driving her on every single hole and flying by her on the leaderboard as if she's on a do-or-die mission.

My girl is focused but relaxed, having fun and kicking ass. It's a real pleasure just to be watching. And the energy of the crowd tells me it isn't my own personal bias speaking.

I bring my index finger to my mouth and bite my knuckle while I wait for her turn. After Mia takes her second shot, Keira goes to grab her wedge. Potter stops her, talks to her for a second, and then backs away as she switches her club to a nine iron, looking a bit hesitant.

It isn't a good move. The hole sits on a slope. Keira is longer than the average female player, and if she goes long, she's not going to have any green to work with. No coach I know would play this hole like he's instructing Keira to do.

Shit. I don't wanna watch, but I do because if there's a chance Keira's going to look over for support, I need to make sure she sees whatever reassurance she needs on my face.

The crowd is none the wiser. They watch with hope that they're going to see her move up another spot on the scoreboard. She's six under par for the day putting her in third place overall, but at the rate she's dropping birdies, she has a shot to win the whole dang thing.

As she gets into position, her demeanor is less confident than it's been all day. She doesn't glance at the crowd or her coach before she draws back.

I can tell as soon as she gets to the top of her swing that it's going to be long. I tense as it sails through the air, and stop tracking the ball and watch her instead. She knows it too and her eyes fall to the ground at her feet.

The heartbroken sigh of the crowd puts a voice to the pain in my gut. Potter doesn't show any sign of understanding the magnitude of his fuck up. His face settles into a serious expression that gives nothing away. He should be kicking himself for his utter stupidity.

He gives Keira a nod and a go-ahead signal to take her next shot, clearly not sensing her mood. She's freaked. It may only be one mistake, but an unforced error like that can mess with your head. Lifting my hat, I rake my hands through my hair.

"Look at me, Keira. Look up. Come on," I mumble under my breath, willing her to look at me. "Take a breath. You're okay."

The guy next to me furrows his brow, and I feel him staring, but fuck if I can give him a second thought. If I thought it wouldn't throw her off more, I'd be shouting it to her. Screw the rules, screw the man holding the quiet sign.

Everything inside me screams that this is all wrong. She's off, spiraling inside, and I can't stop it.

I cross my arms and squeeze them into my body to keep myself still.

The next shot isn't awful, but it doesn't redeem her, and she ends up one over for bogey.

Coach Potter visibly withdraws from her and even the crowd senses the shift in their favorite new underdog. Still, they hang around through fifteen and part of sixteen. But with each shot, they lose a little more hope, and so does she.

Potter leaves her at the start of seventeen. She's in eighth place and solidly out of the running for placing today.

She doesn't so much as side-eye anyone on those last two holes. Retreating deeper into herself until all signs of the confident, capable woman I know are gone.

I wait for her in the clubhouse. Two of her teammates flank her on each side. They offer hugs and high-fives, but Keira's grim expression doesn't change.

When she finally approaches me, she looks completely broken. I rub at the sharp pain in the middle of my chest and force a pep in my step as I close the distance between us.

Instead of speaking, I wrap my arms around her and cradle her head against my chest. Any anger she was holding on to turns to sadness, and she buries her face into my shirt and cries. My hands tremble as I run my fingers down her hair and caress the back of her neck.

"Hey, you're good," I whisper so only she can hear. "I've got you."

Her hold on my waist tightens and her entire body leans into me like I'm the only thing keeping her upright. She's a fragile, beautiful thing in my arms and I've never felt more helpless or more needed.

"I've got you," I repeat. "I've got you."

KEIRA IS AT DINNER WITH THE TEAM, AND I'M IN MY HOTEL ROOM, shifting around my meetings for tomorrow morning. Originally, I planned to head out tonight, but there's no way I'm leaving now.

There will be other tournaments; she'll get more chances. I know it, she knows it, but that isn't the point.

It's after eight and my eyes are crossing from staring at financial reports when my phone pings.

> Keira: Thanks for coming today. We just got back from dinner, and I'm gonna crash. You're probably already on a plane back to Arizona. Anyway, I'm sure you have notes for me from today's performance. I know I fell into some of my bad habits at the end. I can fix it. Please don't give up on me yet.

Jesus. What the hell did Potter say to her? She spent the last three hours with her teammates and coach, I assumed that was for the best. They could girl talk or whatever, maybe Potter would have some encouraging words. She sounds just as defeated as when I left her.

> Me: I'm still here. Can you come down for a few minutes?
>
> Keira: You're still here?
>
> Me: Yes.

I'm holding my phone, waiting for her response, tapping my thumb against the device, when someone knocks lightly on my door.

I pull it open without checking, already figuring that it's her, and damn, maybe I should have. She looks every bit the young, beautiful college girl she is wearing cut-off denim shorts, a gray T-shirt, and orange flip-flops. Her hair is down, and her face is free of makeup. She steps inside and the door closes behind her.

The determination and focus she wears like armor on most days is totally stripped away. She walks to the center of the room and then turns to me. Her brown eyes glisten as if she's on the verge of tears. "If you're going to drop me as a client, just tell me now."

Um, what? My face contorts with confusion, but she doesn't allow me to get a word in.

"I get it. I screwed up today." She squeezes her eyes shut, and one tear slips from the corner. She swipes it away with the palm of her hand and then tilts her head up and bats her eyelashes as if she's annoyed that she's crying and trying to stop. "I embarrassed you, my team, my coa—"

My mouth is on hers, silencing the nonsense spilling out before I've decided I wanted to act. Though, it feels like the best decision I've made in a long time.

Her lips soften and mold to mine before responding. When she kisses me back, it's with her whole body. She steps against me and places her hands on my chest before breaking the kiss and looking up at me.

It's an unspoken question, a dare to do it again, or maybe a chance to change my mind. Fuck that. As hard as I've tried to keep her at arms-length, Keira has always been more than some client.

This time when I take her lips, there's no hesitation from either of us. My hands thread through her hair and tilt her head back. Deepening the kiss, my hands fall to her waist and around to cup her ass. She pulls her head back and peers up at me but doesn't break the contact of our bodies. I take a moment to drink her in. Lips wet, face flushed, her chest rises and falls with breathless excitement. She's stunning.

"You kissed me." Her voice hides none of the shock or want I can see on her face.

"Correction. I'm *kissing* you. I'm not even close to done."

CHAPTER TWENTY-ONE

Keira

"So, you aren't dropping me?" I ask, gliding my hands up and down his forearms, tracing the veins and enjoying his warmth and strength.

His back leans against the headboard, and I'm straddling him, knees bent underneath me.

A rough chuckle shakes his upper body, and he cradles my head and runs his hands down to rest lightly on my neck. "For what? You were amazing today."

One eyebrow cocks with disbelief. He can't be serious.

"Did you know you had the longest drive on every single hole today? Every single one. Not just against Mia, but in the entire tournament."

"I didn't, but even so, I lost. I totally fell apart. I should have placed."

"You stopped trusting yourself. You let Potter throw you off when he told you to switch to the nine, which was a garbage call, and then you couldn't recover. You should have trusted your instincts and smoked the wedge. You're comfortable playing power golf and when the situations get tight you need to play to your strength. Potter should know that. It's his whole job. Today's loss was a coaching catastrophe. You were the best player out there."

His words comfort me and light the fire of determination I lost earlier today. Lincoln has never fed me compliments when they weren't deserved.

"You mean that? It isn't just because you suddenly want to kiss me that you're saying that?"

"Suddenly?" His brows rise as a teasing smile plays on his lips. Slowly, he shakes his head. "I've thought about kissing you since you all but called me a creep and tossed tequila on me."

"Why didn't you?"

The playfulness falls away, and I wish I could suck in the question and keep it to myself.

"The business takes a hundred percent of my time and is my top priority. Yeah, I've thought about kissing you, but I also considered what that would mean for the relationship we've built. I don't want to mess with that or hurt you."

"I appreciate the honesty, but I just stopped plotting your death for making me run a thousand miles, so you can stop worrying. I'm not expecting anything. I have my own life."

Some of the tension in his body relaxes, but I can tell he isn't convinced. I look into his dark eyes. From far away, they look brown, but up close, they're more hazel. A myriad of beautiful, complicated colors that's fitting for this man.

I move my hands from his arms to his amazing pecs and the

steady thump of his heart under the cotton shirt to the nape of his neck. I curl my fingers into his thick hair. "Tell me again how good I was."

His teeth glide along his bottom lip before he smirks. Slowly, he inches closer until his mouth hovers over mine. His breath tickles and heats my skin as he says, "You really have no idea how good you are, do you?" He searches my face for an answer. "Watching you play is inspiring. Being your coach and watching you see the rewards of working your ass off . . . it's a privilege. You're the most incredible person I know, Keira Brooks."

I close my eyes and smile, letting those words and his nearness heal the embarrassment and frustration of my loss. They become my truth, and I cling to them.

Removing the millimeter of distance between us, I kiss him. I pour all the passion of my hopes and dreams into him, knowing that, whatever else happens between us, he'll be the protector of those things.

Large fingers wrap around my waist on both sides. His thumbs circle at the hem of my shirt and slip under so the calloused pads run along bare skin. Those full lips leave mine only to find my neck and collarbone. His touch brings goose bumps to the surface, and we make out like two people who need connection more than air.

Moaning and tilting my head to give him better access, I'm not prepared for his words. "We should stop."

"What?" My eyes fly open. "Why?"

"Because I don't want to wreck what we have. I like you." His head rises slowly, kissing the sensitive skin on the way, as if he's convincing himself with his own words while enjoying a final taste.

"Turning down sex because you like me? Well, that's a first."

He lifts me from his lap with a groan and places me next to him where our legs still rest against each other. "I meant what I said earlier. That wasn't me feeding you a line or giving some bullshit excuse. I don't have a lot to offer. I can't be a boyfriend or even promise to be what you need tomorrow. I like and respect you too much to lead you on. I enjoy helping you and being around you. I'm not going anywhere, but there are limits to what I have to give outside of coaching."

"I get it," I reaffirm him. "But it's really cruel to offer all this up"—I gesture to him and his hotness—"and then take it away. Will you at least take your shirt off?"

He chuckles and brushes my hair back from my face. I can see his resolve to take this back to G-rated. No matter what he says, I know the lines he just drew are about him, not me. I'm perfectly capable of separating sex with Lincoln from our working relationship. But fine. I mean there are lots of things Lincoln and I can do fully clothed and not touching.

I enjoy him. Our connection with golf and our desire to push ourselves gives us a lot to talk about. Though talking naked is obviously my preference.

"Fine, but can I stay in here tonight?"

He tilts his head, and I raise both hands innocently. "I only want to talk golf. I'll keep my hands to myself."

And I do. Mostly.

I barrage him with questions. Silly things that don't touch on serious topics because tonight is about pulling back the curtain, getting to know him in a way that he's kept off-limits.

His favorite color is green, favorite food is tamales followed closely by Chicago style pizza, he doesn't care for sweets, he still uses a putter his grandfather gave him for his high school graduation, and so many more things that I file away for safekeeping. I know I'll never forget a single thing he tells me, no matter how small or insignificant he thinks it might be.

He lies on his back, an arm around me as I snuggle into his side. My head rests on his chest and I run my fingers across his stomach. Even through the soft material of his shirt I can make out the lines and dips of muscle.

My eyes are heavy from the physical and emotional toll of the past few days. I fight to keep them open so I can savor this moment. In his arms I feel invincible.

"Got any Red Bull?" I ask, stifling a yawn.

"For what?"

"To keep me awake."

His chest shakes with a silent laugh. "Go to sleep. It's been a long day."

"I don't want to sleep." I'm bolder with my exploration of his body this time and dip my hand lower on his stomach.

He makes a strangled groan of a sound, captures my hand in his, and rests them on his chest. "Sleep."

I try to keep my eyes open despite his bossy command, but his thumb moves in a slow circle on the top of my hand, and my lids droop.

"I'm staying up all night," I threaten, but even as I say it, I start drifting off.

The next morning as I'm getting ready to leave his room to catch the team van to the airport, Lincoln brushes his teeth in the open bathroom. He slept in a T-shirt and gym shorts, but that shirt is gone now, and I'm not shy about getting a good look at his chiseled upper body while he's showing it off.

He has a great chest. Not so muscular that he's beefy, but defined enough that it lifts and falls in all the right places, a light smattering of dark hair trimmed close.

"Talk to you later?"

He nods, leans over the sink, spits, and rinses his mouth out before standing and wiping his face with a towel. I watch the whole thing completely entranced. He's so comfortable in his skin, and that skin... well, it's sensational.

"Yeah, I'll update your training plan sometime today. I have a few meetings first."

"Okay."

A beat of awkwardness plays out between us before he strides forward and places a hand at my hip. The warmth and strength of his grip makes my breath catch. I want to go back to twenty minutes ago when we were in bed, every inch of my body touching him in some way, and stay there all day.

"What do you think about doing the sectional qualifier in April?"

"You mean the *Open* qualifier?" My voice quivers with excitement or maybe disbelief.

"Yeah." He pulls me against him. "That gives us a couple of months to work your swing out, and then you can go show everyone what you're capable of."

"You think I'm ready?" I hate the way my voice wavers with my lack of confidence.

"I think I'll make sure you are. You might hate me again. It's going to mean working twice as hard as before. More running and weights and—"

I stop him by pushing up onto my tiptoes and kissing him. When I step back, the excitement in his eyes matches mine. "Bring it on."

CHAPTER TWENTY-TWO

Keira

We have a rare day off practice Tuesday, so I use the time to check on Dad. Over a sausage pizza, he grills me about the tournament.

Normally I'd be all too eager to talk golf, but I'm blushing and squirming in my seat as if Dad can tell by looking at me that I spent the night with my hottie swing coach. So, I give him a lightning speed overview and then ask about his scheduled doctor appointments and physical therapy this week.

He should be cleared to drive at this appointment, and I'm both looking forward to him regaining his independence and already missing the time together.

Dad retires to his chair and puts on the game, so I take that as my cue to head back to the dorm.

"Hey you." I nearly run into Abby as she opens the door to our dorm before I can.

"Hey." She smiles and backtracks into the room.

"Headed to Smiths?"

"Study group then Smith's." She points to a box next to my bed. "That came for you."

"To the room?"

"Yeah, they brought it straight up because it was taking up too much space in the mail area downstairs." She raises a brow and looks to me, expecting answers. "What in the world did you order?"

"I didn't." I try to lift the box, but it's heavy. Really heavy.

"All right, well the suspense is killing me, but I have to go." Abby heads to the door. "Text me later."

"I will. Bye," I call over my shoulder as I search for my scissors.

Once I find them, I sit on the floor next to the box, cut the tape, and peel back the flaps. I find a piece of plain, white copy paper on top.

For your dorm. Let me know if you need anything else.

Lincoln

I set his note on the floor and dig through the contents of the box. Foam golf balls, a chipping net, a hitting net, a small putting mat, and a much larger hitting mat. A nice one. It's way nicer than the one at my dad's. There's even a pair of ear plugs that I'm guessing are supposed to be for Abby. He thought of everything, because of course he did.

He calls as I'm working on a new trick shot. I place the phone on my desk so I can show him before grabbing my wedge and a ball. "Prepare to be amazed."

"What is it you're trying to do exactly?" Lincoln asks, dark brows raised and a smirk on his lips. Those lips...now that I know what they feel like against mine, I can't look at him without doing an instant replay of our make-out session.

"No look into the cup."

"I can't see the cup," he says.

"It's on the floor by the wall," I say as I bounce the ball off the clubface and turn so that my back is to the cup. I tap it into the air, flip the club, and hit it over my shoulder. I turn in time to see the ball hit the rim of the cup and bounce away. "If you didn't see it, I guess I can pretend that went in."

The ball continues to bounce around the room noisily, and we both laugh.

"I just need a little more practice." I grab the phone and my laptop. "You want me to log into the site?"

"Nah, it's fine as long as I can see you. I'm reviewing the videos you sent this morning now."

"Check out my new setup." I angle the phone so he can see how I've pushed my and Abby's beds farther apart and put the net between them. My mat is on the floor in the open space.

"I have just enough room to swing my club." I move the phone again so I can show him where I put the putting mat and chipping net. "Thank you. This is ridiculous, but I love it."

"Don't thank me yet. Now that you have a decent setup in your room, I'm going to up the intensity."

"Do your worst."

Lincoln shakes his head and laughs before going back to analyzing my swing videos from earlier. "Swing looks pretty good. I see what you're talking about with your arms not being at full extension past impact. Let me see it. Can you position the camera so I can see your swing from the front?"

I spend the next hour taking swings in my new makeshift training area while Lincoln coaches me. He tweaks and nitpicks, but he's encouraging as he does it.

"We have our home tournament in two weeks."

"Good. You could use another competition to work on playing under pressure."

He's in his living room. The computer sets in his lap, phone resting on the couch beside him. His brow's furrow, legs are kicked up on the coffee table.

We finished our training session fifteen minutes ago, and he's moved on to checking email while I force him into conversation. He is a willing, if a bit distracted, participant.

"Will you come?"

"Hmm?" He briefly glances at me and nods. "What days? Saturday and Sunday?"

"Yeah."

"I'll try. I'm supposed to fly out to L.A. to watch Kenton play on Friday. My parents are coming in from New York, so I can't skip it, but I'll see if I can get a flight back Saturday."

He says it casually, as if everyone jets off to amazing sporting events on the regular.

"Fair enough. I'd choose the Stars over me too."

He sets his phone down on his thigh. "You like soccer?"

"It's okay. My dad loves sports, so I spent a lot of time fighting over the television with him. Soccer and basketball I didn't mind so much."

"You guys ever been to a pro game? Soccer or basketball? Football?"

"No. My dad is pretty much a homebody. Always has been, but

especially after the divorce and now that he's injured—forget about it."

He nods thoughtfully. "What does he do?"

"He is a roofer, but he's on leave until they clear him to go back."

We're quiet for a moment, him on his computer and me thinking about my dad.

"How long was it after your divorce before you started dating again?"

Lincoln pauses, and his eyes meet mine.

I pull my unicorn scrunchie out of my hair and slide it onto my wrist before combing my fingers through the tangled strands. "It's just that it's been years since my parents split, and as far as I know, my dad hasn't dated at all. I worry about him. When I graduate, he's going to be all alone, eating frozen dinners and watching the game in his old chair."

He rubs his jaw and sighs. "That sounds pretty good to me." I think that's all he's going to say, but then he adds, "It was nine months, but to be honest, every date I've been on since has been a Gram setup. I am perfectly content to sit in my chair and eat meals by myself."

"Really? Forever? Isn't that, I dunno, lonely?"

"I don't have time to be lonely. Plus, I have months of entertainment to look forward to with you while we get that swing of yours right." He winks.

"You'll never be lonely with me around."

"Definitely not."

Thursday night, Keith and I get permission from Professor

Teague to do next week's lab early since Keith is travelling with the boys' team for a tournament in Texas and won't be back for our Monday night class. I show up to lab with a Pop-Tart in one hand and an energy drink in the other, still sweaty from weight training. There's another lab going on, but I find Keith set up in the back.

I fan my sticky shirt away from my body, and Keith gives me a questioning glance.

"Sorry, I came straight from the gym."

"Your coach lets you eat junk like that?" He motions toward my dinner.

I know he means Potter, but I think of Lincoln. "What he doesn't know won't hurt him. Besides, I had a protein drink on the way over. This is my dessert."

Professor Teague comes over to our table and gives us brief instructions before he starts his class. Keith and I fall into the work silently. I'm not sure how long we've been working before my phone starts vibrating in my pocket. As discretely as I can, I take it out and glance at the screen and then answer.

"Hey," I whisper. The only person who notices is Keith, and his brows pull down in disapproval.

Lincoln's serious expression slowly drags into a big grin. "What are you doing?"

Lifting the goggles off my eyes, I answer. "I'm in lab."

"Why the hell did you answer?"

Because it's him. Because I haven't talked to him all day and it's becoming my favorite part of the day. "What do you need?"

Behind him, it's dark, the sun setting on the golf course at his grandmother's house. "Are you trying to escape another blind date?"

He chuckles. "Nope. Just me and Gram tonight. Those goggles

are charming as hell. You have adorable raccoon eyes."

I rub at my eyes in a weak attempt to make the marks go away. "Maybe you've already turned down every eligible bachelorette she knows."

He laughs. "I doubt it. Anyway, I called because I'm teaching a golf clinic tomorrow and I have to go to the Suns game tomorrow night, but I'm free between and was thinking of playing a round."

"Your life is bizarre."

A grin tugs up one side of his mouth. "But awesome, right? Come with me."

"What?" Did I just hear him right? Because it sounded like he invited me up to see him.

"The course here is tougher than the one you play at Valley. I think it'll be a good challenge for you."

I mull it over, though it really isn't a matter of if I want to go but rather if I can work it into my schedule. "What time?"

"Miss Brooks," Professor Teague addresses me from the front of the class.

"I gotta go," I say quickly and hang up on Lincoln's amused face before shooting my professor a sheepish smile. "Sorry."

Keith shakes his head, and I shrug. As I go to put my phone in my backpack, I get a text.

Lincoln: Sexy scientist, I dig it. ;)

After lab, I head back to the dorm. Abby sits on her bed facing Cassidy and Erica, who are on mine.

"Hey, what are you guys doing here?" I ask as I drop my backpack to the floor.

"Well, since you won't come to us, we decided to come to you."

Cassidy smiles with her elbows resting on her knees and her chin perched on her palm.

"I just saw you guys at practice a few hours ago."

"Not the same and you know it," Erica says. "Get ready and let's go out. Wherever you want."

"Where's Smith?" I drop onto Abby's bed next to her.

"He's at the library. Thought I might try sleeping in my own bed for a change." She elbows me gently.

"Novel concept."

"We miss you," Cass says. "You haven't been out with us in weeks."

"I miss you guys too, but I'm exhausted. I don't feel like going anywhere tonight. Maybe this weekend?"

My phone pings, and Abby narrows her gaze. "Or maybe you'd rather spend the night talking to Lincoln. I mean, look what he did to this room?" She gestures to all my golf stuff.

"I'm sorry. I've been training nonstop."

"Hey, no need to apologize. He's seriously fine. I'd be glued to my phone too."

My face warms, and I shift in my seat. I haven't told anyone except Abby about staying with him last weekend. It isn't that I'm embarrassed or anything, but telling them leaves it open to scrutiny and I want to keep whatever is between Lincoln and me in a bubble.

"Oh my God. You're blushing, Keira." Erica tosses my pillow at me. "You absolutely slept with him!"

"What?" Cassidy screeches. "You had sex with Lincoln Reeves?"

"No." I toss the pillow back at Erica. "I didn't."

She catches it easily and holds it up as if she might toss it back. "I don't believe you. Your face is so red."

"We kissed. That's all."

Erica and Cassidy scream and laugh. They high-five, which I find particularly amusing.

"It isn't a big deal," I try to say, but they aren't listening.

"Tell me everything," Erica says when she's settled down. "It's been so long since I've kissed a guy. What were his lips like? Where did he put his hands? Have you seen his penis?"

"Oh my God." I laugh. "Let's talk about why you are on a self-imposed sex hiatus instead?"

"It isn't self-imposed, there's just a serious lack of options."

"What about Chapman or Han? Or Keith, he's sweet."

Erica shakes her head. "Does Lincoln have any hot, single friends?"

"Uh, I don't actually know. I get the feeling he doesn't do a lot of hanging if it isn't work-related. He does have an in with several pro sports teams, though, so I'd say the odds are good at least one of them fits your criteria."

She claps excitedly. "Let's go to The Hideout and snag a corner booth and you can tell us every detail over cocktails."

"I have to get up early, and I don't really feel like changing out of comfy clothes." I've been living in leggings and golf skirts for weeks.

Abby stands and disappears into our closet only to pop out a couple of seconds later with a bottle of RumChata. "Fine. Then we'll just drink here. I've had this bottle stashed since before winter break and have been waiting for the perfect time to break it out." More than two months have passed. Between golf and school . . ."

"And you basically living at Smith's," I add.

"And that." She nods. "But, seriously, how many more opportunities are we going to have before Erica and Cassidy graduate?"

I look between my friends. Their faces are a mixture of excitement and sadness. I know they're right, and I do want to spend time with them.

Finding a balance has been hard, and okay, maybe spending every night working with Lincoln hasn't been the biggest burden. The man is seriously hot and smart, and being coached by him is probably the single most exciting thing that's ever happened to me. Still, putting in all this hard work won't mean much if I've alienated everyone along the way.

"Hand it over," I say finally.

CHAPTER TWENTY-THREE

Lincoln

I fumble for my phone on the nightstand and bring it to my ear, eyes closed and only vaguely aware of what I'm doing.

"Hello?" It comes out in a croak. My voice is groggy, and my throat feels like sandpaper, so I clear it a couple of times and try again. "Hello?"

"Hi!" Keira's bubbly sweet voice answers. "Did I wake you? What time is it?"

"I'm not sure." I bring my free hand to my forehead and rub it absently.

"You aren't sure if I woke you or of what time it is?"

"Both."

Her sweet giggles filter into my ear, and I hold the phone out so I can check the time.

"What are you doing up so late?" I ask, placing the phone back to my ear.

"I was hanging out with the girls."

"Oh, yeah? What was on the agenda tonight?"

"Boy talk, junk food, and now drunk dialing."

"*Mmmm*. Sounds fun."

"It was, but now that I'm in bed, I'm fading fast." She yawns. "Is the offer to come up tomorrow still good?"

"Yeah, of course. I checked the weather it's supposed to be really nice and—" I'm about to add to the list of reasons she should come, but she interrupts me.

"You should send me a picture?"

"Uh, what?"

"A picture."

"A picture of what?" I play back our conversation in my head. "The golf course?"

"Of you. Duh. What do you sleep in?"

I'm smiling as I answer, "Boxers, sometimes shorts or sweats."

"No shirt?"

"Not usually, no. Why?"

"I knew it!" she shouts, and I pull the phone from my ear for a second.

"What did you know?" Following this conversation is hard, and I don't know if it's because I'm half asleep or because she's tipsy. Either way, I like that it's me she's drunk dialing.

"The night at the hotel you slept with your T-shirt on. I got totally cheated. Show me."

"I'm not taking a picture of my chest."

"You're no fun."

I try to picture her on the other end of the phone. Smiling and face flushed from alcohol.

"What time will you be here?"

She yawns again. "We don't have formal practice tomorrow. I just need to get in eighteen holes with my group. We're meeting at eight. I'll call you on my way up."

"I was thinking, can you stay the night and go back Saturday morning?"

"Like stay at your place?" Her voice slows and the pitch goes up at the end of her question.

"Or I can get you a room at a hotel if you're more comfortable. I'd like to take you to the game, but it might be kind of late by the time we get back."

She's quiet for a second, and I wonder if she's trying to find a nice way to turn me down or maybe she passed out.

"Keira?"

"Will you sleep with your shirt off this time?"

IT'S JUST AS BEAUTIFUL AS THE WEATHERMAN PREDICTED. THE SKY IS A brilliant blue, the few clouds look as if they were painted on, and there is just enough of a breeze to need long sleeves. I do a lot of small clinics at my home course, and today, I'm teaching a bunch of Pop's old friends and students how to adjust their putting speed.

This kind of thing is far more laid back since most of the guys have known me since I was a kid following Pop around. The country club was my daycare and my playground far before it became my office, and these guys will never let me forget it.

"Hey, Linc, the wife said you turned down our Franny." Darrell raises his head to see my reaction before he takes another putt. "My granddaughter not good enough for you?"

"My Angel, too," Lance pipes in. "Something wrong with your equipment, son?" He uses the end of his putter to point toward my crotch.

"The wife says he's *brooding* after the divorce."

"I'm not brooding, and my equipment is just fine. Your lag putting, on the other hand, is shit. Focus on that, Darrell."

The guys snicker, and I shake my head.

As we are finishing, Keira arrives wearing a black skirt that shows off her toned legs and a blue zip-up that's skin-tight, highlighting her athletic curves without revealing any skin.

Her sunglasses sit on top of her head, hair still down, though I know from the many times I've watched her play or practice, she'll take the unicorn scrunchie from her right wrist and secure it back before she starts.

"Hey," she greets me and glances over at the guys and gives them a shy wave. They've all stopped what they were doing to check her out. Our clientele is very strongly in the sixty-plus age bracket, so they aren't shy about their interest in her. "I thought I'd hit the driving range if you're still working."

"It's all right. We're done here," I say loudly enough that the guys can hear me. "Nice work today, guys. See ya next time."

With a wave and a few personal goodbyes, I collect my stuff, and Keira and I head toward my golf cart. "Do you still want to hit a few balls or are you ready to go out?"

"I actually already hit a small bucket. I got here early and didn't want to disturb you," she says as she slides into the passenger side.

While we wait to tee off at the first hole, Keira takes a long drink from her water bottle.

"Hung over?"

She gives me a small, rueful grin. "A little. Sorry for the late-night call."

"Don't be. You can always call me. Besides, you're a funny drunk. What was the occasion anyway?"

"Just some girl time. Seems like I have less and less time every week. Not that I'm complaining," she adds quickly and then elbows me. "My coach is a real hard ass."

"Yeah?"

The wind blows her hair around her face, and I push it back with my fingers, resting my thumb on her cheek. When she leans into the touch, it answers the question I've had all week on whether or not I imagined the chemistry between us last weekend. Her eyes fall to my lips.

Another cart pulls up behind us at the tee box, and I let my hand fall away.

Forcing myself from the cart, I stand and grab my driver from my bag in the back, and then toss her a cocky smirk. "Your hard ass coach is about to kick yours."

We zip through the course, playing through other groups. I can't remember the last time I had so much fun. I don't coach her unless she asks for specific feedback, and instead, we take turns launching bombs down the fairway and enjoy being on the course together.

As we finish on eighteen and head into the clubhouse, Darrell and Lance are standing behind their cars while the kid from the pro shop puts their bags in their respective trunks for them.

"Well, look who it is," Lance says. He smiles at Keira. "Lovely day for golf."

"It was." She smiles back at them, sun-kissed skin alive with excitement.

"What about you, Linc? Did you have a good time?" Lance asks, a hint of humor in his tone. He places his white golf glove in his back pocket.

Darrell smirks. "Guess it wasn't your equipment after all, just reserved for someone else?"

I shake my head. "See you guys later."

"OH MY GOSH!" KEIRA'S EYES ARE WIDE WITH EXCITEMENT AS I GUIDE her through the arena. "I feel like I should have changed or put on some fresh deodorant or something." She smooths a hand over her hair.

She looks beautiful in a golf skirt and spandex shirt. Her face is free of makeup but painted with a glow from the sun.

"I have you covered," I say and point to a table of Suns merchandise.

She looks over every item before she narrows it down between a hat and a T-shirt each with the team logo.

"She'll take both," I tell the guy and hand him the money for it.

"Thank you." She pulls on the T-shirt over the one she was wearing and then places both hands on her hips. "What do you think?"

I set the hat on her head. It's too big and nearly covers her eyes. "Perfect."

Stepping closer, I adjust the cap, tuck her hair behind one ear, and let my hand linger at her neck. She leans into my fingers, and the day of being around her with only small touches and no kissing has officially become too much. I've been itching to feel more of her, brush my lips against hers.

The thing is, I knew it'd be just like this once I gave in—an obsessive desire to touch her all the time. And as super as that sounds, Keira isn't just some girl I'm seeing. Lines have blurred, for sure, but I still have a job to do. And right now that job is to reward her for all her hard work.

"Come on, stinky." I let my hand fall away and take hold of hers, interlocking our fingers.

Seeing Keira's excitement as we sit behind the team is worth everything I own and then some. The team is still warming up, and Keira perches on the edge of her chair, one hand squeezing my thigh as she takes it all in. Zeke Sweets, the team's rising star, waves and walks over when he spots me.

"Hey, Zeke, how are you?" I stand and shake his hand.

"Good, good. Nice to see you." He glances at Keira and smiles timidly. For all his stardom, he's a pretty quiet guy.

"Zeke, this is Keira. Keira, this is—"

She stands. "Zeke Sweets, I know. You went to Valley, too. My dad and I have been following your career. You're amazing. Incredible. Really, I'm a big fan."

The big guy smiles for real at her cute rambling. "Thank you."

"Keira plays golf at Valley," I tell him and watch her face pink. She's freaking adorable all flustered in front of Zeke.

"That's great. I hear the team's pretty good." He holds the basketball at his side, giving Keira his full attention.

"You follow golf?" Her jaw drops, and I can't resist chuckling at how awestruck she is.

"I keep an eye on all the Valley teams. Gotta rep the alma mater." He glances over his shoulder. "I should get back out there. Good to see you, Linc." He smiles at Keira. "Really nice to meet you. Good luck on the rest of the season."

Keira turns to me when Zeke walks away, opens her mouth, and lets out a long, quiet scream. "I can't believe I just met Zeke Sweets. Your life really is awesome."

I nod and drape an arm around her shoulders. "It really is."

I PULL INTO THE GARAGE, KILL THE ENGINE, AND TURN TO KEIRA, WHO slept almost the whole way back to my place.

"Rise and shine, beautiful."

She lifts her head slowly from the headrest and looks around. "Where are we?"

"My place," I say before sliding from the car.

She's unbuckled and sitting up by the time I get around the vehicle to open her door. When she places her hand in mine and I start to lead her inside, a weird sensation pulses through my body. It takes me a second to decode the feeling. I'm nervous.

My apartment isn't big. Kitchen, living-dining room combo, two bedrooms, two bathrooms, and it's sparsely decorated. I'm sure it screams divorced, single man, but Keira walks into the middle of the living room and turns a circle. When her brown eyes land back on me, there's nothing but delight on her face.

"I love it. It's exactly how I pictured it. The space is great."

I chuckle and walk to her, wrap my arms around her waist. "I forget you've already seen most of my place."

"Only in pieces. Plus, I was distracted by you."

She tips up onto her toes, and I lean down to take her lips in a quick kiss.

"I'm not here often, but it's on the course and near Gram." It's on the tip of my tongue to tell her most my stuff is in storage, make excuses for how bland it is, but then that makes me think of Lacey and how I still haven't called her back.

"I like it. Honest. It suits you."

I'm not sure what that says about me, but I don't think on it too hard.

She goes to the couch and sits, making a big show of crossing her arms over her chest, leaning back, and putting her feet on my coffee table. Forcing a frown, she asks, "Who am I?" Her voice deepens in a shit impersonation of me. "One hundred more reps. Do it until you get it right, and then do it until you can't do it wrong. No, no, no. That's garbage! Who taught you how to swing a club?"

"I don't sound like that, smartass." I fall onto the cushion beside her and pull her onto my lap, remove my hat and toss it onto the table, then run a hand over my matted down hair. Her eyes follow the movement and then her fingers come up to take over, gently threading through the strands.

My scalp pricks at her touch, and a pleasant warmth spreads through my body. "That feels good."

She scoots farther onto my lap, knees inching toward the back of the couch. The black skirt she's wearing lays flat, so I'm not getting a show, but the position and all the ways our bodies are touching is almost as good. My eyes fall closed, and I relax into the leather as she continues to comb through my hair with her fingers.

I bring my hands to her thighs and run my thumb along the hem of her skirt. Her skin is smooth and taut, and even though I'm not looking, I can recall her legs in vivid detail from the hundreds of times I've seen them on video.

I'm tired. A bone-deep exhaustion that has nothing to do with lack of sleep and everything to do with the restraint I've been holding on to all day. There are a million really good reasons I should stop whatever this is between us, send her on her way, rub one out, and go to bed alone.

I don't have any delusions of this ending any way other than with Keira eventually finding her swing and us going our separate ways. Maybe we'll run into one another again or maybe I'll be at a pro tournament and get to watch her dominate, like I know she will, but we aren't skipping into the sunset holding hands after tonight.

I know this. She does too. Yet, here we are anyway.

"I love your hair." She tugs gently. "It's so soft and thick." Her voice is quiet and husky, straight-up phone-sex-operator style; though, I know it isn't intentional.

Weeks of foreplay, of staring at one another through a screen but not being able to reach out and feel the person on the other side, makes everything more intense than it would have been had tonight been a real first date.

I groan a reply, and her hands still. When I open my eyes, she's staring at me, tongue between her teeth in concentration.

"What?" I ask, suddenly a little self-conscious as her beautiful brown eyes dance slowly over my features.

Instead of answering, she brings her mouth down and presses her lips softly against mine. It's torture as I let her run the pace. Her nails sweep over the stubble along my jaw as she kisses me.

I hold out on taking control for as long as I can, but when she moves closer so that her sweet heat presses against my dick, I grip her hips and draw her hard against me.

We're a tangle of tongues and a clash of teeth as we press together as tightly as our clothing will allow. Her tits crush against my chest so that I can feel the rise and fall from her labored breathing. I bring my hands around her back and fist a handful of hair so that her face tilts up and I can reach her neck.

She tastes sweet, the slightest tinge of salt from a day golfing in the sun. A low moan escapes from her as I nip at the sensitive flesh.

"Lincoln." She says my name in a way that no one has in so long. As if she enjoys being with me. As if she wants me. As if right now is enough.

When I don't answer her, she pulls back until I look at her.

I lean forward and kiss her collarbone and then retreat so I can see her stunning face again. "Yeah, baby?"

She bites the corner of her lip and smiles. Her hands fist my shirt on either side, and she raises the material an inch. I love that she's so excited to see my body because that's a mutual desire. I sit forward and allow her to peel my shirt off for me. She holds it in her hands as her eyes greedily take in my chest.

I work out most days and have stayed in shape since I quit the pro tour because it keeps me in a good place mentally, but right now, it feels as if it were for this moment—for that look on her face.

She traces the lines in my upper body, flattens her palms and glides across my pecs and abs. Finally, after she's thoroughly explored my bare chest, her hands move down to the top of my belt.

That side of her lip goes between her teeth again as she seems to contemplate removing my pants. I move to stand, and she squeals and throws her arms around my neck so that she doesn't fall back.

I kiss her hard as I walk toward my bedroom. I don't bother turning on the lights, but she still gives a quick glance around the darkened space as I set her on the bed.

"A room I haven't seen before."

"I don't work in here."

"No?" she questions and removes her shirt and tosses it.

Black lace wraps around her, lifting her tits and teasing the shit out of me. I place a knee on the bed, forcing her onto her back. Bracing over her, I drop my mouth to one bra-covered nipple and gently bite.

"Separation of church and state."

She giggles, the sweet sound eliciting a smile from me as well. More clothes come off and are tossed to the floor between smiles and laughter. Getting naked with Keira is fun in a way I never knew it could be. I'm of two minds: wanting to worship and take my time with her and needing her quickly so I can finally take a real breath again.

It isn't until I'm grabbing a condom from the nightstand and covering myself, staring down at her gorgeous body, that the air shifts between us. All playfulness fades to hot desire.

"Are you sure you wanna do this? We can go back to making out or watch a movie, talk golf. I'll even keep my shirt off."

"Don't you dare try to talk me out of this." She reaches for me. Her fingers wrap around my throbbing dick and she strokes me slowly, hand gliding down until the girl literally has me by the balls. "I know what this is, and I still want you."

Nodding, my pulse races as she brings my dick to her wet entrance. Brown eyes lock on mine as I push inside. Her mouth drops open, and I can see the effort her breathing takes, the flush of her skin and the sheen of sweat from desire.

As I stare down at her, heart in my throat, I can't help but think that she might know what this is, but I'm not sure I do anymore.

CHAPTER TWENTY-FOUR

Keira

It's still dark out when I wake up in Lincoln's bed alone. I check the time on my phone as I swing my legs over the side and place my feet on the cool, hard wood. I find my panties and new Suns T-shirt Lincoln bought me and pull them on before padding out of the room to find him.

The apartment is set up with the bedrooms on either side of the kitchen and living area. Light seeps out from the spare bedroom and a familiar sound draws me toward it.

Standing in the doorway, I lean against it and watch a shirtless Lincoln swing the golf club. He has quite a setup in here. There is a large floor-to-ceiling net that spans the better part of a wall, and a golf mat that matches the one he sent me.

A desk is pushed to one corner, his laptop, a shoebox, and some other random things spread across the top of it.

His muscles flex and turn as he takes another shot. He's focused and completely oblivious to everything else. I let him hit a half dozen more before I speak.

"Nice swing, Coach."

He hangs in the follow through a second longer before turning to look at me. "Morning." He leans his club against the wall and grabs his water bottle. "Did I wake you?"

"No, I slept like the dead." I walk fully into the room, checking it out. "This is amazing. Is that a simulator?"

He nods, picks up a remote, and an image of a golf course is projected onto the net with amazingly life-like details.

"Oh my God, you never need to leave your apartment."

He shrugs. "I don't use it much anymore, but when I was touring, it was nice to be able to get reps in at home."

"What was it like touring and getting paid to play golf?" I pick up his club. It's heavier than mine, grip still warm from his hands.

"It was hard, time-consuming, and stressful. I gave everything to it, and some days, it gave very little back."

As he talks, I take a few practice swings, stretching out my sore muscles. I get in position and then feel his body press up against me. Even after being in his arms all night, the feel of him this close is exhilarating.

His hands guide me slowly through the swing twice before he says, "But when it gave back, they were some of the happiest times of my life." He kisses my shoulder and his hands fall to my waist. "You'll see."

"How can you be so sure I have what it takes to make it?" I turn so I can face him. No one has ever believed in me the way he does, except maybe my dad, and that's mostly parental love bias.

"I've been watching people swing golf clubs my entire life, and you remind me a lot of myself when I was starting out. Hot headed and passionate with an incredible work ethic. Very few people are willing to do everything that's asked of them." He brushes my hair away from my face. "And you do it and then ask for more."

"Maybe it's just you who I'm good at pleasing."

His mouth pulls up into a smile. "That you are."

"You've never said why you gave it up."

"Not a lot to tell. I quit so I could coach and build my own business."

"Do you miss it?"

"I miss the pursuit, working toward a goal and then moving the bar higher. But, no, I don't miss touring. Getting hurt was a blessing. It made me realize it wasn't being out on the course that made me happy, it was the work I put in to get there. I spent an entire year training so hard to get back and then when it was time." He shrugs. "It didn't sound as appealing as what I'd been doing in the gym. And giving that to other people, the same way my Pop did, it's like I can feel him smiling down at me."

I'm nuzzling into him, enjoying the heat of his skin and the touch of his body, thinking about his words and how amazing he is, when he steps away. "I gotta hop in the shower before a call. I made oatmeal, and there's fruit in the fridge."

The grimace that turns my lips down makes him chuckle. "There are also Pop-Tarts. I couldn't remember if you said you preferred s'mores or brown sugar cinnamon." Now it's his turn to make a face. "I got both."

"Oh my God, you do listen when I talk."

He smacks my ass as he starts to the door. "Hmm? What'd you say?"

I'm still half-dressed and still playing with his toys when Lincoln returns, smelling of soap and dressed in slacks and a green polo. The ends of his black hair are wet, and he runs a hand through it. I'm not sure why I expected him to spend the day lounging in gym shorts and a ratty T-shirt since he's worked every Saturday since I've known him, and I'm disappointed as he takes a seat behind his desk like he's ready to settle in for the day.

"This thing is amazing. If they had these in arcades while I was growing up, I never would have left."

He smirks and opens his laptop.

"What do you have today? Jetting off to an NFL game? Calling up your Stanley Cup winner friends?"

"Lots of emails, checking in with my other clients, phone calls with . . ." He stops and raises his brows. "You really want to hear the details?"

I scrunch my nose and shake my head. "All day?"

He must read the disappointment on my face. "Yeah. I figured you'd need to head back to Valley this morning. You're welcome to stay as long as you want. I can take calls in the living room so you can hit balls in here or you can take the cart to the course."

I fake a smile as he goes back to his laptop. I leave the spare room, grab a Pop-Tart from the kitchen, and wander around his apartment while I eat.

His office is the only room that looks lived in. The living room is sparse—coffee table, couch, and television. He's tidier than I am, which isn't exactly a large feat, and there are no water rings on the coffee table or stacks of papers.

In his bedroom, I close my eyes and inhale his scent. It lingers from the open bathroom. He's made the bed, which earns a chuckle from me. Of course, he makes his bed every morning. I shower and get dressed, pack up the few things I brought, and then head back into his office.

He's on the phone, leaned back in his chair, brows furrowed, and the end of a pen between his teeth. I hang back until he sees me and motions me in.

I grab his club again and take a few swings in front of the simulator without a ball. His eyes track my swing, always dissecting and coaching. I half expect him to pass me a notebook filled with critiques, but he only watches until I give up and go to him.

Facing him, I sit on the edge of the desk. I don't touch him or speak; I just want to be near him.

His free hand palms my thigh, and his long fingers run absently across my skin. He doesn't look at me or acknowledge me in any way but with his touch. And he doesn't freaking skip a beat on the phone. He's all tech talk about maintenance times and backups. Still, it's pretty hot watching him be the boss man.

When he's finally done with his call, he blows out a breath, drops his phone onto the desk, and then puts a hand on either side of my legs. "I thought you were practicing."

"I am. I'm visualizing."

He smirks before his lips twist into a regretful frown. "I have to send feedback to a client and then hop onto another call."

"I know. I don't want to get in the way. I should head back soon anyway."

He tugs me down onto his lap, and his thumb holds my chin steady as he brings his beautiful, full lips to mine. His touch is soft, but his kiss is demanding. No warm up or interlude, just greedy desire to take what he can with the moments he has.

I don't know how we get there so fast, but I'm grinding into him and he's got both hands under my shirt when he mutters a string of curses. I'm breathless when he pulls back. It's only then I realize his phone is ringing.

He answers, sounding totally normal while I can barely form a thought in my lust-addled head. I start to stand to give him privacy, but he holds me in place.

"Sorry about that," he says when he hangs up a minute later.

"Is that a yo-yo?" I point to the open shoebox on his desk. His long fingers splay out over my ribs and he nods as his mouth covers mine.

His phone rings again, and he hums an annoyed sound as he inches back. His expression is apologetic but also resolved like he wants—or maybe needs—to answer it. I stand and step away. He doesn't let go of my hand like I expect him to, and I'm stuck an arms-length away. "Thanks for yesterday. Go be awesome, Coach."

"Your swings from the driving range looked pretty good. You still aren't releasing your hands at impact, though."

I nod and slowly rotate through my swing, focusing on keeping my right side from overpowering my left. Practice tonight has been beyond frustrating, and the tension, even through the screen, fills my room.

"I'm not seeing it with the foam balls. You have it here, but you gotta translate it to the range and course. There are more distractions out there, more pressure during a tournament." His serious tone and the furrow of his brow make me want to work harder, but I'm already working hard, and I still can't seem to get it.

I blow out a breath of irritation.

"Take a break. You have to give your brain time to piece it all together. We've thrown a lot at it. It's just time and reps."

"Time I don't have," I say and take another swing.

He lets me swing a dozen more times before saying, "Show me some of your fancy club work."

"Why?"

He shrugs and leans back in his chair. "I think it's cool. Come on, show off for me."

I think for a moment before I go into one.

Tap. Tap. Tap.

I fall into the rhythm easily and allow my breaths to even out as everything else falls away.

Tap. Tap. Tap.

On the last bounce, I push the ball higher into the air and then catch it, pause with it on the face of the club, and turn a quick circle, arm straight. I end with bouncing it a few more times on the clubface and then catching it behind my back.

I do a mock curtsy at the end, a little annoyed but not exactly at him. I can do tricks all day, but it won't fix my swing issues.

"That was awesome." The proud smile on his lips erases some of my frustration. "Wanna see one of mine?"

When I nod, he grabs the yo-yo that was on his desk last weekend. He stands and adjusts the screen so I can see him. With a wink in my direction, he loops his finger through the slipknot and begins. He's laser focused as he gets into it like he's remembering the feel.

After a few times up and down, he looks at me. "This one is called the sleeper." He tosses the yo-yo to the ground and keeps it there, allowing it to spin for several long seconds before snapping it back up to his hand.

"Walk the dog." He throws it back down and somehow moves it along the floor. "Around the corner. And . . . take the elevator." He finishes with some fancy handwork and a big, boyish grin.

"Wow. That is the nerdiest thing I've ever seen." Also, the hottest. Who knew yo-yoing was hot?

"Don't pretend you aren't impressed."

I fake a yawn and look away from the screen. "Eh."

When I glance back, he's pulling his shirt over his head.

I sit forward, and he grins. "More interested now, huh?"

"Show them to me again."

He does, and this time, at the end of them, he adds another, something he calls man on the flying trapeze.

"Why do you know all these?"

"My pop taught me. He kept it in his truck, and when I'd go with him to the golf course, he'd teach me a trick and then tell me to master it before I did anything else. Mostly, I think he was just trying to get me out of his hair for a while. A bucket of balls only kept me occupied for so long, and he spent four or five hours at a time with clients." He stops and looks at the yo-yo in his hand. "I'd actually forgotten about this thing until I found it in some of his stuff."

"Well, I never thought I'd say this about yo-yoing, but that was hot. Take your pants off and do it again."

He shakes his head, and a deep chuckle makes my insides turn to mush. Lincoln happy and laughing makes everything seem better. Well, almost everything.

He must sense my mood shifting back because his voice changes. "Get some sleep, Keira. You worked hard today. Tomorrow will be better."

CHAPTER TWENTY-FIVE

Keira

It rains on and off all week. Practices are inside, and by Thursday, we're all sick of being cooped up inside the small, indoor practice room and ready to get outside and take some real swings outside.

Coach dismisses us, telling us to get over to the driving range either tonight or early in the morning. Teams will begin showing up tomorrow afternoon for our weekend tournament.

"Are you going over?" Abby asks at the same time Coach says my name.

"Not sure. Go ahead. I'll text you when I'm done."

Coach talks to Brittany, and I approach slowly. He and I have been getting along just fine since he mostly ignores me, sometimes muttering under his breath when I do things to annoy him, but I've stopped letting him rile me. He isn't worth it, and I don't need him now that I have Lincoln.

"You wanted to see me?" I ask when I reach him.

He nods, and Brittany opens her stance to include me instead of leaving. My gut twists with the look of apprehension on her face.

She drops her eyes to the ground as Coach speaks. "Brittany's been cleared to play at the tournament this weekend."

"But—" I glance between them. "How?"

"My wrist is better." She lifts her arm and smiles.

"But she hasn't practiced in weeks. I'm a better choice to play this weekend." I look to Brittany with what I hope is an apologetic smile. "I'm sorry, but it's true."

"You don't get to make the decision." Coach Potter yanks at his belt, hitching it higher on his hip. "I make the call, and I'm including Brittany in the lineup. I'm sorry, Keira. You're just not consistent enough in your tournament play."

I ball my fists in irritation. I don't know if I'm angrier with him or myself. I text Abby that I'm not going to the driving range, and I do something I haven't done in a long time, I crawl into bed before dark.

Lincoln texts around our usual time, but I tell him I'm exhausted and going to sleep early and turn off my phone. I need to tell him that I'm not playing this weekend so he doesn't bother trying to make it, but I don't want his, or anyone else's, pity or empty words of encouragement. I want to wallow.

I'm surprised when Abby shows up at our dorm, but one look at her face tells me it's solely for my benefit.

"You heard?"

She nods. "Brittany was over at the guys' house. Why didn't you tell me?"

"I just wanted to be alone."

She picks up an empty Pop-Tart wrapper and raises a brow.

"No judgment. I'm eating my feelings."

"Well, stop because you're playing this weekend." Abby sits on the edge of my bed.

"No, I'm not. Coach made it very clear that I was not in the lineup."

"That was before I quit."

She smiles at my reaction–jaw dropped and eyes wide. "What? Why?"

"I've been thinking about it for a while." She shrugs.

"But you're playing so well. Don't quit just because of me. You've earned that spot."

"I know I did. To be honest, standing up for you is only part of the reason I did it. Golf isn't fun anymore. It's become just part of my routine. I spend practices wishing I were doing just about anything else. Seeing how much you love it, I don't know, it made me realize how much I don't. I want to enjoy my last year of college without running to practice every afternoon or travelling to tournaments I don't want to play in."

"You could see the season out. Quit before fall semester."

"I could, but it felt much sweeter to do it this way."

"I don't know what to say."

"Say that you'll spend tonight hanging out with me, watching cheesy romantic comedies, eating Pop-Tarts or whatever other junk food you have stashed, and tomorrow morning, you'll get up and be ready to kick some ass in that tournament. Unicorn-scrunchie-wearing badass, remember?"

I laugh and glance down at my wrist. "Deal."

On Friday, the sun finally comes out from behind the clouds, drying out the course as teams start to arrive. Lincoln calls as I'm leaving my dorm to head over to the course.

"Hey," I answer with the phone between my shoulder and ear.

"Did I wake you?"

"No, I'm on my way out now. I want to get some extra swings in this morning."

"Don't tire yourself out before it starts," he warns. "Go through your usual routine, and if you still feel like you need more time, do some visualization and drills without the club."

"Okay."

He chuckles. "I'm serious. There's such a thing as being over prepared, and it usually goes hand in hand with too little rest. Remember, it's supposed to be fun."

"It'll be fun when I'm on the leaderboard."

We continue to talk as I drive over, and when I pull into a parking spot, I linger in my car because I'm not ready to say bye to Lincoln yet. Even though he's always miles away, it feels weird knowing he's boarding a plane and won't be within driving distance.

"When do you fly to Los Angeles?"

"This afternoon. I land around five, but text me when you're done with the practice round and let me know how hard you kicked ass today, all right?"

"Yeah, okay." I inhale a deep breath and let it out. "Will you be back tomorrow or Sunday?"

"I'm not sure yet what Kenton and my parents have planned for me this weekend. I'll do my best. Listen, I gotta go, my IT guy is calling. Give 'em hell today."

The first eighteen holes are a blur. I'm in a zone. A mixture of determination and anger. I only get a short break before I'm teeing off for my second round.

Coach Potter waits at the first par three, but his words don't even register. Part of not letting him negatively impact me anymore means I can't let him positively impact me either. So, I tune him out and focus on everything Lincoln's been telling me for weeks.

On the tenth hole, I hit a beautiful stinger that gets a lot of cheers. The girl I'm paired with steps up to take her turn, obviously shaken and in her head. I'm intimidating, who knew?

My heart beats wildly, and every step closer to the final hole feels a little more like I'm walking on a cloud. As I walk to eighteen, the crowd follows alongside me, and it sinks in. I'm leading. It's early, there are still a few groups to finish today and I have to get through tomorrow, but I'm freaking on top. By *five*.

A pang of something hits me. Lincoln. Lincoln knew. I glance over at the sidelines, hoping to see his dark head among the spectators. It's silly. I know he isn't here, but I wish he were anyway.

Abby catches my eye and waves. Her other hand is linked with Smith's, and they are wearing matching smiles that tell me they're proud of me. Keith and the rest of the guys are here too. I wait for it to fill me with the same burst of pride I get when Lincoln smiles at me, but it doesn't come.

It isn't just because of how much I respect him; though, that certainly helps, it's because I know he gets it. This hunger inside me to succeed. He's been in my shoes, and he knows what this feels like and what it's going to take to make it.

With my final putt on eighteen, I stand, ball in hand, and wave. Coach Potter grins like he's suddenly a proud and involved member of my success. I walk right past him and hug Abby hard. If it weren't for her, I wouldn't have this moment. We may not want the same things, but she's here and she believes in me.

My dad didn't want to try to crutch his way through so it's a little bittersweet playing in Valley without him here, but I know he'll be proud too.

"Oh my God, that was amazing." Abby refuses to let me go, squeezing me so hard I have to hold my breath.

"All right, babe, let her go, she's gonna pass out from lack of oxygen," Smith says.

"Sorry." She steps back. "I'm so proud of you."

"Thank you." I'm grinning so widely that my cheeks hurt.

"Congrats," Keith says and offers his fist for me to bump. The rest of the guys offer their similar praise.

"Thanks, guys."

Abby links her arm through mine. "Celebratory dinner, or are you planning to go back to the room to work with your hottie swing coach all night?"

"Hottie?" Smith questions with enough jealousy in his tone that we all laugh.

"We'll celebrate tomorrow *if* I win," I say, nerves already ramping back up. "I wanna swing by my dad's and tell him all about it. I'm sure he's going crazy not being here."

Abby hugs me one last time, and I say bye to the guys and thank them all for coming. I text Lincoln when I get to my car, but by the time I get a pizza and take it to dad's house, he still hasn't responded.

"Nice job, sweet pea." Dad hugs me in the doorway with one

arm, the other holding on to his cane. He's getting around better, but I can tell by the way he hobbles that his knee still bugs him.

I babble on through an entire pizza, excitedly telling him every detail. He listens intently, smiling proudly.

"Did you call your mom? She'll be dying to hear all about it too."

"No, not yet. I came straight here. I haven't even showered yet."

"I thought I smelled something." He winks. "Go, call her, and then get some rest. Tomorrow is a big day."

"Thanks for reminding me. No pressure, right?"

He chuckles softly as I kiss him on the cheek. "Good luck tomorrow, kiddo, not that you need it."

CHAPTER TWENTY-SIX

Lincoln

"It was amazing. I was in a zone like I've never been before. I hope I didn't use all my awesomeness today."

I smile as I lie back on the bed in Kenton's spare room while Keira tells me about her day. She holds the phone out in front of her face, free hand waving wildly and smile so big it's contagious. Getting to listen as she relives it is almost as good as it would have been to be there. Almost.

"Did your dad go?"

"No." Her smile falls only slightly. "He still isn't getting around that well, but I went by and told him about it after."

She's quiet for a second and then goes back to telling me about the tournament. "Oh, and you should have heard Coach this afternoon. One of the local news stations was there, and Potter walked up in the middle of my interview like he was my number-one fan. He told them, and I quote, 'Keira's made a lot of really solid improvements this season, and our hard work is finally paying off.' *Our* hard work, like he had any part of it."

"Potter's a prick. He's going to take every opportunity he can to make it about him. You did this. Not him."

"*We* did this. You and me."

"No. This was all you. No one made you get up day after day and put in the work. I've coached a lot of people, especially when I was just starting out. They'd tell me how bad they wanted it, they'd fork over thousands of dollars for lessons, but when push came to shove, they wouldn't put in the work. So, no, *we* didn't do this. It was all you. Own it. Enjoy it."

She flops onto her bed, still holding the phone out so I can see her face. "Tell me about your day."

"Spent it with my parents, got to watch Kenton play, and then he had a few people over after the game."

"Did his team win?"

"Yep, it was a good day for both of you."

She settles back against her headboard. "What are your parents like?"

"They're cool. Dad was a high school history teacher and golf coach, and my mother worked in advertising. They retired a couple of years ago and primarily live in upstate New York. That's where my mother's from originally. I have a bunch of aunts and uncles out there."

"Do you see them often?"

"They come back to Scottsdale every few months, and Kenton and I go up there for Christmas every year. It's cold as fuck." She covers a yawn as I talk. "I should let you get some sleep."

"Fat chance of me sleeping tonight." She yawns again. "Are you coming back early tomorrow?"

"No. Kenton has another game tomorrow, so we're staying until just after it. I should be back to Arizona about the time you're finishing the tournament. I'm sorry I'm gonna miss you kicking ass."

"I understand." The tone of her voice says that may not be entirely true.

"All right, baby, get some sleep."

"Uh-uh. I wanna keep talking to you."

"Close your eyes."

Her brown, tired eyes widen in defiance.

"Just do it."

She gets up from the bed and walks across her room. A second later, it darkens. "Fine, but if I fall asleep, promise me that you'll hang up immediately. I don't want you watching me drool or snore." She makes a horrified face as she climbs back into bed and lies down, but then her long lashes flutter closed and fan out against her fair skin.

I turn on the television in my room to the sports channel and turn off the lamp on the nightstand.

"Are you going to tell me a bedtime story?"

I chuckle quietly. "Will it help you fall asleep?"

"Maybe." She turns onto her side and opens her eyes briefly to position the phone on the bed next to her. The angle has the top of her head cut off but gives me an eyeful of the cleavage popping out of her tank top—a darkened eyeful, but still an eyeful. "Tell me about your first pro tournament."

"You wanna talk golf right now?" I swear this girl never gets sick of the topic. She's more hardcore than I am.

"Well, I'm too tired for phone sex, and golf is the next best thing." Eyes still closed, her mouth tips into a sleepy smile.

Just the mention of sex makes my dick twitch, pleading with me to make her reconsider, sleep be damned. Ignoring the semi, I adjust myself with one hand and think back to my pro debut. "It was in Milwaukee. I'm sure I was scared shitless, but the only thing I can remember is how excited I was to be in the same place as guys I'd looked up to for so long—some my entire life."

"You don't look nervous in the videos and pictures online."

Her having watched the footage makes me smile, but I'm not really surprised. I looked her up the same way.

"I don't know. Maybe I was too dumb to be nervous. I don't really think it struck me how big of a deal it was until after. It took years of effort to get to that point, and once I was there, all I could think about was proving myself. That need and desire to get to the next level never really goes away. The goalpost moves every time, and you have to learn to celebrate the small wins. Like today for you. No matter what happens tomorrow, today you proved to yourself that you can do it."

"I really want to win tomorrow."

"I know." I close my eyes too. "Did you see that putt where I almost choked on the tap in?" I ask, still reminiscing about my debut tournament.

"*Mm-hmm.*" Her response comes on a hum.

"God, my heart was in my throat. It took three holes to calm down."

"I couldn't tell."

"Well, I knew I couldn't blow up and make a scene on my first day."

"I also saw the tournament where you broke your driver over your knee."

I groan. "Ah, man, I was really hoping you'd never know about that one."

"It's probably my favorite of all the videos I've watched of you."

"Really? Why? It's one of my worst rounds of golf ever."

"Because I can see the passion on your face. People who aren't dropping f-bombs or thinking of breaking their club while playing a round of golf are either having an incredible day or don't care enough. That video shows how much you care. You were frustrated and you let it show, but then you pulled it together and had an incredible round the next day."

"I had to after that."

"Golf is a lot like love, I think. If it isn't making you a little nuts, is it even real? Passion—good or bad, is how you can gauge what's really important to people."

We both fall silent, and I contemplate her words. It isn't an uncomfortable silence since the voices of the television provide white noise so we aren't listening to each other breathe. Still, doing shit like this with anyone but Keira would be weird, but with her, everything feels normal.

I'm just about to drift off when I can sense she's fallen asleep. I open my eyes to verify. There's an ache in my chest as I stare at her parted lips and the soft rise and fall of her chest as she breathes. After a few long moments, I move to end the call. "'Night, baby."

THE LAST UPDATE I GOT ON THE VALLEY TOURNAMENT WAS AN HOUR ago, and Keira had a two-stroke lead with four holes left.

Pacing back and forth at my flight gate, I'm refreshing the website for the millionth time for final scores when my boarding group is called. I head down the jet bridge with my overnight bag, phone still in hand. After I take my seat, I continue hitting refresh.

"I'm just there." A man stands in the aisle and points to the empty window seat beside me. I stand, annoyed for the interference of hitting refresh, no matter how irrational it is, and let him pass.

The boarding process takes forever and every second delay in getting back to Arizona makes me more restless. I know I'm too late to make the tournament but I need to be back in the same state where I can comfort her, if needed.

I pray to God she won today, but if she didn't, she's going to need to talk it out. After the high of yesterday, a loss today would be brutal.

As the plane taxies down the runway, the flight attendant starts in on the in-flight safety procedures. I tune her out, hit refresh again, and freeze when the final tournament results load on my screen.

"She won," I whisper. I stare at her name at the top of the final leaderboard. Pride fills my whole body. I look over to the guy next to me and repeat it. "She won."

He smiles politely, clearly having no idea what I'm talking about. I show him my phone, and he humors me with a quick glance. "Keira, I mean my client won a golf tournament."

"Congratulations."

"Thanks." I tip my head back against the seat and shake it from side to side in astonishment. She did it. She freaking won.

There's a strange feeling as I sit there, heading up into the sky and a few hundred miles away from Keira. I'm so damn proud of her. Happiness tinged with regret for not being there to see the look on her face when she realized she'd done it. Not being the person she shared all of it with.

My life, my job, has always meant more to me than single moments like this. Even big moments. Hell, aside from the actual day my ex and I exchanged vows, I spent most of the days surrounding my wedding wondering why there had to be so many small celebrations involved. An engagement party, a bachelor party, dinner with the two families, a bridal shower, a rehearsal dinner, and on and on.

My job was always a point of contention with Lacey. The honest truth is that I worked harder at golf and then the business than I did at being a good husband. And while I have my regrets, I think I always knew that she and I would never work.

Selfish men don't get a happily ever after. They might get a significant other who deals with always being second priority, but that knowledge comes at a price. Lacey wasn't willing to pay it, not that I blame her, and I'm not willing to put anyone through that again. No one deserves that. Not Lacey and certainly not Keira.

I smile at the thought of Keira letting anyone put her second to anything. And then there's that pang in my chest again because, for the first time, I realize it isn't going to be me who walks away from Keira when we're done working together, it'll be her walking away from me. Because she deserves better, and she knows it.

CHAPTER TWENTY-SEVEN

Keira

Coming down off the high of my win today, I sit on my bed eating frosted animal crackers and watching Abby pack an overnight bag. Nothing like a post-celebration with a little sugar and bed crumbs.

"I'm heading to Smith's," she says, zipping her backpack and slinging it over one shoulder.

"Thanks for hanging out tonight."

After the tournament, she and the guys took me to The Hideout to celebrate. I'd been too amped up to eat then, but now I'm starving. I'm also a little tipsy, which probably isn't helping.

"Are you kidding me? There is no way I would have missed tonight. I'm so freaking proud of you."

"Thank you."

She points to the pile of clothes between our beds. "Can that disappear before I return?"

"I can't do laundry when I'm celebrating."

She laughs. "Well, then, at least move it to the other side where I don't see it. Out of sight, out of mind."

"Okay, Mom." I smirk.

She waves and heads out, shutting the door behind her. Silence floods the room and washes away the adrenaline from today.

I unlock my phone and open my texts. I haven't heard from Lincoln since the good luck message he sent this morning, and I'm desperately trying not to be upset that he hasn't checked in yet. It isn't like I expected him to be glued to his phone waiting for updates, but I thought he'd be more anxious to hear how it went. Even my mom has called to say congratulations.

I flip through Netflix for something to watch, but I'm too antsy or tired or some weird combination of both, so I give up and get out of bed to grab my wedge and a ball. The door to my dorm opens before I reach my bag, and I look up, pleasantly surprised to see Abby again.

"Hey, you're back. Thank God, I just realized, I have no idea what to do when I'm not—"

Lincoln steps in behind her, silencing me with his presence.

"Look who I found," Abby says around a grin. While Lincoln isn't looking in her direction, she mouths *oh my God* and fans her face.

I laugh, and Lincoln turns to see what's so funny.

Abby uses the hand she was fanning herself with to wave. "See you two later."

Once she's gone, he walks toward me slowly, offering a quiet, "Hey."

"What are you doing here?"

"I wanted to surprise you."

"Well, you succeeded."

I close the space between us with two skips and throw my arms around his neck. "I can't believe it. Seriously, not complaining, but why are you here? I thought you'd call."

He waits until I pull back. His hands frame my face, and the pad of his right thumb runs along my cheek. "You won today."

Three simple words that make pride and happiness swell inside me. "I did."

"So damn proud of you." His lips meet mine in a caress, and when he speaks again, his words drift to me softly. "I'm sorry I missed it."

"You're here now."

I make the move this time, smashing my lips against his. It feels better than any victory. Electricity courses through me as his hands fall to my hips and then swoop under my ass to pick me up. My legs wrap around his waist as my fingers sink into the dark hair at the nape of his neck.

Lincoln's lips pull into a smile against my mouth before he says, "Let me guess, yours is the unmade bed?"

"I was busy today. Hello, Valley Invitational tournament winner."

I kiss him again, so he doesn't look around at the rest of the mess.

He lays me on the bed and stands beside it staring down at me. "You're beautiful." He tosses a shirt off the foot of the bed and then a tube of mascara follows. "Messy as hell, but beautiful."

His sexy smirk stays in place until I sit up and take my shirt off. I toss it in the same direction as the others. That moves him to action. With one hand at the nape of my neck, he guides me back and then settles on top of me.

My hands go to the hem of his shirt and tug. We break apart only long enough to remove it and then he's back at my lips, tasting and teasing.

I yank at his thick, dark hair as his expert mouth explores mine and then lowers to my chest. He palms one breast and nips at the other as I arch into his touch.

He takes his time even as I trail my hands down and try to cop a feel by squeezing my hands inside his pants.

"Pants. Off," I finally mutter.

"I'm celebrating up here." His tongue circles my nipple and then his teeth clamp down on it.

"Can you celebrate with your penis inside me?"

He chuckles but doesn't relent. My orgasm is on a hair trigger when he finally kisses down my stomach and pushes my shorts and panties down past my hips. Every inch of my stomach gets kissed or licked or nipped before he finally removes my clothes completely and his lips descend to my pussy. He kisses it, and the small amount of friction pulls a long moan from me.

He settles between my legs and looks up at me. His dark eyes shine with mischief and my heart thumps wildly.

Finally, he pushes my legs apart wider and licks me. One long swipe of his tongue that makes me feel drunk and desperate.

"Lincoln," I pant as he presses a thumb to my clit and moves it in slow circles as he tastes me.

My body quakes, and the noises that pour out of me are porn-star worthy. He's porn-star worthy. I want him to stop and to never stop. The orgasm that builds is so powerful I'm sure it'll break me into a million pieces.

Stars dance behind my eyelids while he moans as if my pleasure is getting him off as much as it is me. My eyes fly open as I come. Our stares collide, and my heart squeezes as so many things I can't or won't say pass between us.

As I'm panting and trying to get my world to stop spinning, he undresses and grabs a condom. His fingertips slide across my cheek and tuck my hair behind my ear before he tears the foil opens and sheaths himself. He positions himself at my sensitive core and slowly eases inside.

The walls of my pussy squeeze him, and he hisses a breath as he buries himself completely. The rhythm is slower than the last time, and something about it makes my body soar faster.

This unhurried pace and the look in his eyes as he stares down at me seems to blur the lines we've drawn and all the rules we've set. Not that we set them exactly. He told me he couldn't be a boyfriend, and I accepted that. But tonight, I feel as if he's giving me more of himself, and I cling to it, taking it, savoring it, hoping for more.

I close my eyes, letting his touch be the sensation that overpowers all others.

"Look at me," he says, stilling until I comply. His lips hover over mine as he whispers, "Congratulations, baby."

He takes my mouth in a bruising kiss and pumps into me faster. Raking my hands along his back and lifting my hips to meet each thrust, I use my body instead of words to thank him for being here, for seeing something in me that no one else has, and for breaking the rules—whether he realizes he's breaking them or not.

LINCOLN PUTS ON HIS BOXERS AND JEANS WHILE I LIE NAKED IN BED watching him. I grab his hand. "Stay."

I try to fight the yawn, but it's been a very long day and my body is like putty. "I missed you. Don't go."

"I don't think there's room in that bed for two of us." He turns his shirt right side out and puts it on before sitting on the edge of the bed. "I don't want to, but I have to get up early for work."

"You can work here." I motion to my desk, which is currently covered by books and clothes. Luckily, he doesn't actually look at the place I'm suggesting as his workspace.

"You brought your laptop, right?" I ask, knowing he never goes anywhere without it.

I sit up and wrap my arms around him and he lets me wrestle him flat on his back while he wears an amused grin at my insistence. Lying on top of him, I pull the comforter around us. I don't expect him to give in, but when I wake up a few hours later, I'm still wrapped tightly in his arms.

CHAPTER TWENTY-EIGHT

Lincoln

"I'm not wearing that."

Keira looks from the button in her outstretched palm to me and back again. "Why not? Everyone else is wearing them."

When I still don't make a move to take it, she rolls her eyes and extends the poster board in her other hand to me. "Then you're holding this."

The Valley U hockey team takes the ice and the crowd stands and cheers. It's the last home game of the season—family night.

"It's a bummer Heath's family couldn't make it." She pins the button with Heath's face on it to her shirt and an irrational flash of jealousy surges through me.

"I don't like it."

"They probably don't either, but at least you're here. You're a pretty good guy, Lincoln Reeves."

"I meant I don't like other dudes touching your boobs." I cover the button with my fingers, so Heath's cocky smirk isn't staring at me and also because it's placed in just the right spot for me to be able to cop a feel.

She bats my hand away. "Look, there he is. Hold up the sign."

I groan but lift the "Feel the PAYNE" sign Keira made and insisted we bring. If Heath sees me holding this, he'll never let me live it down.

I'm only slightly relieved when I'm able to sit and put the sign at my feet. We're touching shoulder to knee in this packed arena, reminding me I haven't had sex in a week. Before Keira, I went... well, way too damn long without. But now, even a day of not being inside her, is a day too many.

For the past month, we've alternated driving back and forth between Valley and Scottsdale. Sex, golf, repeat. Life is great.

"He's really good," she says, leaning in so I can hear her and putting more of her soft curves against me.

"*Mm-hmm.*" I slide my hand up her thigh an inch or two.

"Is he really good enough to go pro? He told me he was, but I don't really know anything about hockey."

Another inch. "Sure."

"Hockey players are hot, don't you agree?"

"Yes."

"So, what position does Heath play? Quarterback? Outfielder? Point guard?"

"Yeah." Another inch.

"Lincoln!" She grabs my fingers and twists.

"Ouch. Shit."

"You aren't even listening to me."

"Yeah, I was. Heath's good, yada yada."

"I mixed in terminology for three different sports, but you didn't even notice."

"I noticed. It wasn't important."

Not the right thing to say when she still has my hand in a death grip.

"Ow. Ow." I pull free. "What I meant was that it wasn't as important as being here with you."

"Awww." Her face softens and then she rolls her eyes.

"I mean it." I duck my head to press my mouth to hers as I drop my hand back to her upper thigh. "I missed the hell out of you. Touching you, kissing you…"

She hums a little needy sound. "You're vibrating."

"Damn right I am."

Her lips curve into a smile. "I meant your pocket."

She pulls away, taking all her soft, warm awesomeness with her, and stands with the rest of the crowd, which is now screaming, waiting for the puck drop.

My phone keeps vibrating, and I take it out to read through my messages. Nathan thanked me for being at the game and asked me to get a couple shots of Heath playing, Kenton sent a picture of the new ninety-eight-inch television he bought for his place, a couple work-related messages, and one from Lacey.

I wait to open hers last, already knowing what it will say. She's politely reminded me twice about the storage unit, but I can't ever seem to find the time to meet up. And okay, fine, I might be avoiding it.

I'm pocketing my phone as Keira takes her seat. Her expression morphs from happy to concern when she sees my scowl.

"Everything okay?"

"Yeah, just something I need to take care of tomorrow."

"Ominous."

"I have some stuff in storage I need to get."

"That's why your apartment is so bare. Need any help?" she asks, facing forward and following the action on the ice.

"No thanks, I've seen your hobo style. It isn't for me."

I get a playful glare before she's back to watching Heath. "Help cleaning out the storage unit, smartass."

"I thought you were going with your dad to an appointment tomorrow."

"I am, but I could come up after."

"How about I clean it out while you're with your dad so when you get to my place, we can just focus on getting naked?"

Finally, I get her full attention, and she crowds my space. Her eyes go to my lips—girl really likes my lips. She might have more restraint than I do, but I know she feels it too. This crazy chemistry and insatiable sexual desire between us.

Sex with Keira is awesome, obviously, but I've had awesome sex before and not been this . . . addicted. I don't think I'll ever get enough.

"Deal," she says, pressing her chest (and Heath's face) into mine.

I pull back suddenly. "Wait, did you say hockey players are hot?"

The next day, I pull up outside of the storage unit and kill the engine. Lacey waves from the open doorway, an apprehensive look on her face.

"Hey," I say as I approach her. "Good to see you."

"Yeah, you too."

Well, this is as awkward as I imagined. Seeing Lacey and the hurt I caused her never gets easier. The girl who used to look at me as if I hung the moon, can now barely stand to look at me.

Maybe we were always doomed to fail. We married young without really talking about what kind of life we wanted together. But regardless of the reasons, I feel a deep sense of responsibility for the way it all ended.

"I'm sorry it took me so long to get out here."

"It's fine."

"All right. Should we get started?" I'm starting to sweat under my shirt.

"I already grabbed my things." She nods to her car and the packed back seat and then hands me the keys to our unit. "It's all yours. Just turn those in at the front desk when you're done. If no one is there, they have a drop box."

"Oh, okay. Thanks. Do you need any help unloading? I could follow you."

"No thank you. I've got it," she says and nods curtly.

The thing about divorce is you're either fighting or being too polite to one another. I'm not an asshole that wants to yell and scream, but her anger was easier to live with.

She takes a step toward her car and I call after her, "Lace."

She turns slowly, shoulders tensing as her guard goes up. "Yeah?"

"I really am sorry. For not taking care of this sooner and for… everything really."

She stares at me for a moment as if she's gauging my sincerity.

"I know that I've apologized before, and I don't know if you believed it then or if you'll believe it now, but not a day has gone by that I haven't been sorry for how things ended. You deserved so much more. I hope you find it."

"Thank you." A tight smile lifts her lips. Maybe she believes me, maybe she doesn't. Maybe the wound is too deep for my apology to make a difference either way. I don't think I'll ever know the answer, and I guess that's my punishment. "See you around, Lincoln."

I force myself to watch her go, waving as she pulls out of sight, and then with a deep breath, I turn toward the storage unit that holds my previous life. One side is empty where Lacey already grabbed her things, and the other contains boxes and colorful tubs, a few pieces of small furniture.

I load it all into my SUV, each item adding weight to the light feeling I walked in here with.

Since Keira came into my life, I've allowed myself small, indulgent thoughts. Not about the future exactly, but glimpses of what it might have been like with her instead.

But here, all around me, are the reminders that I can't change the past or escape the baggage I carry from it. The best I can do is shove it, like these boxes, from one dark corner to another so it doesn't touch what Keira and I have.

CHAPTER TWENTY-NINE

Keira

I head up to Lincoln's the weekend before the sectional qualifier to play a round on the course and attempt to settle my nerves. He answers the door with his phone glued to his ear.

"I hate Friday night traffic," I mumble.

Smiling as he talks to the person on the phone, he drops a quick kiss on my lips and then takes my bag from me and disappears toward his bedroom with it. He returns a second later, heading across the apartment to his office, talking on the phone the entire time.

I follow along behind him. Exhaustion from the long hours I've put in over the past few weeks mixed with excited anticipation makes me too frazzled to do anything else.

Lincoln takes a seat, and I climb onto his lap and wrap myself around him, hugging him tightly and breathing in his clean, familiar scent. We've seen each other almost every weekend over the past two months, and each time I miss him more between visits.

As he speaks, his chest vibrates under me. He scoots his chair closer to the desk, puts his phone on speaker, and sets it next to the keyboard. His arms circle around my waist so he can reach his keyboard behind me. I should probably move and let him work, but he doesn't ask, so I melt into him.

The man on the phone gives Lincoln numbers—stats on total registered members for the website broken down by area of interest. It hits me in a way that it hasn't before, how massive his company is and how much of a sacrifice he made when he agreed to coach me.

I lift my head and kiss his neck. Goose bumps pebble under my lips, and a thrill runs through me. Lincoln talks on, seemingly unaffected, but those little raised dots give him away.

I kiss my way up to his jaw, and he dips his head to take my lips. I smile into him as our mouths lazily linger and play.

The guy on the phone asks Lincoln a question, and he raises his head to respond. I nuzzle into him again, fully prepared to continue my seduction as soon as he's off the phone, but I must fall asleep because, the next thing I know, I'm being carried through the dark apartment to his room.

"What time is it?" My voice is raspy.

"After one in the morning."

"You let me sleep on you that long?"

He chuckles. "I was on the phone for most of it, but yeah. I could get used to working with an adorable sleeping woman on my lap, even if it makes simple things like using a keyboard a challenge. I love a good challenge." He kisses my forehead. "I'll be back in a bit. I just need to reply to a few emails."

Sleep drags me back under before I can protest, and when I

wake again, he's wrapped around me and his breathing is a deep, even rhythm that lulls me back to unconsciousness.

The next morning, Lincoln wakes me holding a banana and a glass of water. He places them on the bedside table. "Rise and shine, gorgeous."

"Come back to bed." I reach out and take his hand and try to tug him down beside me. He doesn't budge.

"Can't. I need to stop by Gram's before we head to the course."

"Everything okay?"

"Yeah, she's just being stubborn and threatening to climb a ladder and pull down her boxes of Easter decorations on her own." He uses my hand to pull me upright. "It won't take long. Hopefully."

Truth be told, I don't mind at all. I adore his grandmother.

We've barely walked in the door when Milly pulls me against her soft, pillowy chest. "Keira, it's so good to see you again, dear." She smells of flowers and hairspray, and her embrace is so warm and loving that I instantly feel at ease around her.

She shows Lincoln and me to the garage and points to the boxes that contain Easter and spring decorations and then announces her plan to make us breakfast.

"We already ate, Gram."

She waves him off and disappears inside.

"That woman." Lincoln shakes his head. He grabs a ladder and moves boxes from the shelving along one side of the garage.

"She's amazing."

"I think she's a fan of yours as well."

"I think she'd be a fan of any woman you brought around."

"*Humph.*"

"Still no more blind dates?"

"Not yet." He hands me a box labeled "Spring Wreaths."

I take it inside to the living room and return to the garage to find he's pulled four more boxes with varying season-related labels: Easter Bunnies. Easter Plates. Spring Outdoor Decorations. Easter Baskets.

We take them all inside to the living room and then Gram calls us into the kitchen, filling our plates with eggs, turkey bacon, and toast before setting a bowl of fruit between us.

"Thank you."

She smiles lovingly between us. "Lincoln tells me you're doing the sectional qualifier."

"I am." I swallow a bite of eggs, but the reminder of the qualifier has my food settling like a brick in my stomach.

Lincoln lightly nudges my shoe with his under the table. "She's gonna do great."

His confidence in me helps a little, and I take a few more forkfuls of egg and a nibble of toast before I politely push it away. "That was delicious, but my stomach is too tied up in knots for me to eat another bite. I'm sorry."

Lincoln's grandmother doesn't miss a beat. She takes the plate in one hand and runs her free hand from the top of my head down my hair. "If Lincoln says you're ready, then you are. He isn't much of a bullshitter."

I laugh at her cursing, and she grins, pleased that she lightened my mood a bit.

Before we leave, Gram clutches me to her chest again and then reaches for Lincoln

"Thank you." She cups his face and smiles at me. "Take care of that one and make her eat something later."

One side of his mouth lifts before he drops a kiss to her cheek. "Will do, Gram."

"Good luck." Her arms grip me firmly with a freakish strength despite her age.

"Thank you."

Lincoln and I drive to the course in silence. I'm mulling over something he said earlier in an attempt to avoid thinking about golf.

"Does Gram know we're..." I wave between us.

He smirks. "Does she know we're what?"

"Don't make me say it."

He chuckles and then shrugs. "Maybe. She hasn't said anything, and I'm not in the habit of talking to my grandmother about my sex life."

We pull into the parking lot, and he kills the engine. He jumps out, and I'm slow to follow, while I try to sort through the emotions swirling around me. I can't help being disappointed even if it's unjustified. I haven't told my family about him, so why am I annoyed he hasn't mentioned it to his grandmother?

I'm still working through my feelings as we grab a large bucket of balls from the pro shop and head over to the driving range. Lincoln sets up his camera to capture my swing, and I stretch.

"Do you think she'll set you up on more blind dates eventually? It's been what, two months since the last one?"

"The one you crashed?" He smirks. "Probably. I'm sure there's someone at the country club she hasn't hit up for single daughters or granddaughters yet." He's all set up and faces me. "Ready?"

"Why don't you just tell her we're . . ." I tread carefully. I know he doesn't want anything serious, but whatever we are is more than fuck buddies. "Dating or hanging out or whatever you want to call it."

He doesn't respond at first, and I get my driver and tee up the first ball.

"Trust me, you don't want her knowing. She'd probably start picking out names for her great grandchildren."

When I'm silent for too long, he adds. "I'm not ready for that."

"I know, and I'm not asking for that, but we're *something*. I don't understand why you wouldn't say something to get her off your back."

"Is this about me seeing other people? Because I'm not sleeping with anyone else."

"No, it isn't that."

He lowers his voice and walks closer. "Then what is it?"

I shrug one shoulder. "Things are good between us, or at least they are for me. We're spending lots of time together, and I really like you. I guess I'm wondering what happens when we're done working together?"

He rakes a hand through his hair and doesn't quite meet my gaze. "I'm not sure."

The pit in my stomach grows.

"Come on," he says, "let's get you through the qualifier and then you can start thinking about the day you're gonna be free of me." He says it teasingly, but I'm hurt that he is so easy to dismiss whatever is going on between us.

I nod my agreement, and we get started. It's painful working together the rest of the morning. I go through the motions while Lincoln stands back, seemingly unaffected. Though I know he can tell the difference in me. I'm not exactly subtle about my dark mood.

"Nice. That looks really good," he says after my first drive off the back nine. Smiling, he raises his hand to give me a high-five, and I slap my palm against his softly. He captures my fingers, and I meet his gaze. "How'd that feel?"

Numb is what I think, but I say, "Okay."

He doesn't bring up my sour attitude until I miss the fairway on fifteen. "What's going on in your head? You're getting sloppier with each swing. If this is about anything but golf, push it away for later. Next week is it—everything you've worked for."

"Maybe you can compartmentalize your life like that, but I can't."

"Damn it, Keira, I won't let you sabotage yourself like this. You can do this, but you can't break down now. This is it."

"And then what? I go pro and live a lonely existence where I never let anyone get close like you do?" I brush past him and put my driver into my bag. I know I've gone too far when I turn and see the pain in his eyes. "I'm sorry, I didn't mean that."

He faces off with me, keeping a few feet between us. "I've never lied to you about who I am or what I want."

"I know. I just thought somewhere along the way things changed. I guess they only changed for me." I feel foolish. Not because of my feelings but because I never expected him to not be able to own up to his.

"Keira—"

"No. It's okay. You're right. This is my fault. I'm days away from the biggest event of my life, and I need to focus. Nothing else matters right now."

He nods. "Okay, let's get back to work then."

I unbuckle my golf bag from the cart and sling it over my shoulder. Acceptance, defeat, determination—they each take their turn forcing one foot in front of the other as I realize I'm responsible for what I allow or don't allow to mess with my head.

Lincoln was right about one thing; I have to push everything else aside and focus on golf.

"I think I need to do this on my own."

He looks as if he wants to argue, so I say the only thing I can think of to stop him and protect myself. "You're fired."

CHAPTER THIRTY

Lincoln

"Did you hear what I said?" Kenton asks, and I glance at my laptop.

"No, sorry, what?"

He chuckles. "Jesus. What in the hell is going on with you? I've never known you to be so disinterested in talking business before. You watching porn or something?"

"Sorry. Sorry." I shake my head and force myself to focus on the report we're supposed to be reviewing. "What was the question?"

"Doesn't matter. You don't really need me to review the business shit. Any questions I come up with are ones you probably already asked."

That is usually true, but today I'm not so sure about that, which is why I'd forced him on the phone to talk it out.

"Keira's qualifier is coming up, right?"

"How do you know about that?"

"Gram."

"Ah." I nod. "Yeah, it's on Thursday." I fiddle with the yo-yo on my desk.

"That's awesome. If she qualifies, it'll be great publicity for the company."

"That isn't gonna happen."

"Wow, bro, way to have confidence in your mad coaching skills."

"Not that. Keira's fantastic and has a good chance of qualifying, but we aren't working together anymore."

"Oooooh. Shit. I'm sorry. That's why you look like someone told you golf is for pussies."

"She'll be all right. She's ready."

"Yeah, but what about you?"

"There's no shortage of clients. In fact, I might have to hire another golf coach to handle the overflow."

"Come on, Linc, you and I both know she wasn't just some client. Even you aren't that much of a dumbass to believe that. You like her. She's different. Gram said you've brought her over a few times. The last person you brought to Gram's was Lacey."

"And you know how well that worked out," I say dryly.

"Fix it. Whatever you did."

"There's nothing to fix, so drop it, okay? It's for the best. I'm not looking to get involved beyond a certain point, and I passed that point with her a month ago. She wants things I can't give her." Every word burns like acid.

"Can but don't want to because Lacey was a giant bitch."

"I gave her a lot of reasons to be a bitch. The divorce was my fault. I'm not capable of shutting off work. When I was playing, it was all I thought about. Same with work. Lacey was a distant second. It wasn't fair, and I won't do it to Keira."

"So, don't. I'm not telling you to be a selfish prick. I'm telling you to get your shit together and do better. You're clearly upset about losing her, so do something about it."

"I have to jump on another call."

He shakes his head slowly. "I just wanna see you happy, bro. So does Gram. It's why she's always setting you up on dates. Since you brought Keira around, she moved on to me, and I'm loving it. I don't even have to leave my house anymore to find chicks."

"Oh yeah? She sending you dates in Los Angeles?"

"Sort of. One of her friends has a granddaughter out here, and they've been badgering us to meet up. Anyway, the point is, I'm happy with the setups. Someone else is doing all the work and I just get to date awesome women. Don't screw this up for me."

I laugh. "Good luck with that." My phone beeps with my next call. "Gotta go."

"Later, bro."

I click over to Heath. "Hey."

"Hey, old man, what's up?"

"The usual. What about you? Managing to fill your time since the season's over?"

"Eh." His response is about what I'd expect for bringing up their season ending. They finished with a brutal loss in the conference championship.

"I have a couple of camps looking for coaches again this summer, including Deerwood. You did a great job for them last year."

"When would I have to decide? I'm hoping to get invited to the Coyotes developmental camp in July."

I sit up straighter. "Yeah? Wow, Heath, that's awesome."

"Well, I haven't been invited yet, but Coach Meyers thinks it's likely."

"That's really cool. Best news I've had all week." I make a note to look for some other guys I can recommend to the camp should Heath not be available. "I can probably hold Deerwood off on finalizing staff until the end of the month."

"'Preciate it."

I can usually count on Heath to carry our conversations with his usual antics, but he seems to have as much on his mind as I do, and we wade through the usual business stuff in less than ten minutes.

"What else is new?" I ask before he can push me off the phone. "Still managing to show up to class?"

"They haven't kicked me out yet, so I guess I'm doing okay."

"That's encouraging."

"I'm kidding. Geez. Yes, grades are good. Everything is good. Next year, are you and Nathan gonna get off my case?"

"Not likely."

"Didn't think so. Well, on that note, I gotta go. I'm going to a party where there'll be booze...lots and lots of booze and opportunities for all sorts of shady decisions."

"Stay out of trouble." I can't help but add the one last order. "Where are you heading tonight?"

He hesitates a second, probably because I never ask specifics. "Why? Are you planning to stop by to check in on me, old man?"

"Just making polite conversation." And wondering if he's going somewhere that he might run into Keira, but I'm certainly not telling him that. I don't even want to admit it out loud to myself.

He laughs and disconnects without answering, and I spend the next few hours taking one call after another. When I'm finally able to toss my phone onto the desk and breathe a sigh of relief, I look up at the boxes from the storage unit lining the far wall in my office.

I'm tempted to throw all of it into the dumpster just to be rid of it, but I know there are probably a few mementos from my childhood I'd be sad to lose.

I stand and cross the room. I can't feel any worse, right?

Wrong. I pull back the flaps on the closest box and stare down at an eleven by fourteen framed photo of my wedding day. A young, happy couple stares back at me. Lacey's smile is big and genuine as I bend her backward in a kiss-the-bride pose. God, we look so happy and totally unaware of the shitstorm that lies ahead.

And that's why I need to let Keira stay pissed at me. She has her whole life ahead of her, a golf career and love. I choke on the last word, already bitter picturing her with someone else. She deserves it all.

My phone vibrates on the desk and I ignore it as I let the flaps fall closed and walk out of the office. I don't let my mind wander to what other treasures might be waiting for me in those boxes. I don't answer clients. I don't beat myself up over the work I should be doing instead of crawling into bed. I don't question it when I close my eyes and inhale her faint scent.

And I don't call Keira, though that one is much harder than all the others.

CHAPTER THIRTY-ONE

Keira

After our practice on Tuesday, a local reporter stops by the campus course to talk with Cassidy. Erica stands beside me as we watch Coach beam with pride next to Cass as she's being interviewed about her invitation to the amateur championship.

"You'd think they were recognizing him." I don't have to look at her to know she's rolling her eyes.

"Yep. I'm sure he's figuring out a way to make it all about him."

We grab our bags to head out. "Are you coming over tonight for Cass's party?"

"I can't. I'm heading up to Scottsdale as soon as I pack."

"Oh, right. The sectional qualifier is this week."

"Yep. It's Thursday, but I have an early morning practice round on the course tomorrow."

"I wish I could come watch. You're gonna kill it, you know that, right?"

"I wish I had your confidence. Practice this week has sucked."

"You're just in your head. When you get there and your handsome coach is by your side, you'll get your confidence back."

Thinking of Lincoln makes my heart hurt. I haven't told the girls we aren't working together anymore. If I did, they'd want to talk about it, and I definitely don't want to talk about it—at least not this week. Next week, I'll let them take me out, and I'll word vomit all my feelings. But not yet.

"Keira Brooks?"

I turn to find the reporter walking toward me.

"Um, yeah, that's me."

"I'm Ernie with the Valley Daily Newspaper. Do you have a few minutes? I'd love to talk to you about your season."

"Sure." I look from him to Erica.

"See ya later, superstar." She nudges my side and shoots me a big smile.

Ernie goes straight into his questions. "Congrats on your season. You've had a great showing recently with the win last month and a second place finish two weeks ago in Texas, how are you feeling?"

"I feel . . ." Heartbroken. Annoyed that I'm heartbroken. Determined. "I feel good."

"Rumor has it you're heading to the sectional qualifier in Scottsdale this week. Any truth to that?"

"Yes, I am." I force a big, excited smile.

"How have you been preparing for an event of this magnitude?"

"Wow. I don't know." My heart thumps wildly as I scramble for something coherent to say. "I've been focusing on taking each moment as it comes. Lots of practice and visualization to think through different scenarios."

Coach Potter walks up as I'm finishing my answer.

Ernie looks to him. "Keira was just telling me how she's preparing for this weekend. You must be pretty proud to have so many talented girls on your team this year. One headed to the amateur championship and another making a run for the US Open. Pretty exciting for Valley U golf."

"Yeah, of course. I'm extremely proud of Cassidy and of Keira too. It's brave of her to enter and get the experience. People are going to see a real difference in how far she's come this year."

My face heats at his wording. The pseudo compliment is his way of trying to take credit for Lincoln's work, which is total bullshit. He might as well tell this reporter I don't have a shot in hell of winning.

"You've done great work with them, Coach." He extends a hand, and I bite my tongue as they shake and say goodbye.

After Ernie leaves, Coach walks off without so much as a good luck to me. Screw him. I don't need him or his support.

I'm still seething as I get back to my dorm. Abby left a note wishing me good luck on my desk with a new box of Pop-Tarts. I dig into them as I pack my bag and that lifts my mood some.

I'm on autopilot as I drive up to Scottsdale and nearly make the turn to Lincoln's apartment without thinking. I miss him and I'm so freaking mad at him.

The hotel near the course is busy when I arrive. I spot a few golfers I know and others I just recognize as I make my way through the lobby and up to my room.

Once I'm settled, I call my mom.

"Hey, honey," she answers. "How are you?"

"Fine. Nervous. I'm playing the course tomorrow morning to get a feel for it."

"I know. Well, it slipped my mind but it's on the calendar and your dad sent me a text a little bit ago to make sure I remembered. The man doesn't have an organized bone in his body except when it comes to tracking your golf schedule. We're really proud of you, honey."

"Thanks, Mom."

I expel a breath and a little of the tension.

"Want me to sing to you like I did when you were little and scared to sleep in your own room? Do you remember that? I'd sing Twinkle, Twinkle Little Star."

"And then I'd make you do it over and over again in different funny voices."

We both laugh into the phone.

"Good luck tomorrow, Keira. I love you."

After we hang up, I order room service and turn on the television for noise. I'm too scatterbrained to focus on anything for long. The time passes as I alternate scrolling through my phone and flipping through channels. I ignore the part of me that wants to call Lincoln knowing he'd be able to soothe and comfort me in that way only he can.

I go to bed at eight, but I see every hour, dozing only in short increments before waking in a panic that I'd somehow overslept.

Needless to say, I'm tired during Wednesday's practice round. I take the course at a slow pace, trying to figure out the best way to play each hole. My anxiety grows with each swing, and by the time I make it back to my room, I'm a mess.

My phone rings, and Lincoln's name on the screen makes my weak heart race. I'm too tired to be angry.

I take a deep breath and force myself to wait until the third ring to answer. "Hello?"

"Hey." His deep voice rumbles, and I close my eyes, trying to fight off the emotions it stirs in me. One word, and it all comes crashing back. I want to be mad, but it's really a deep hurt and sadness I feel without him.

"How are you feeling?" he asks sounding upbeat and optimistic. "Ready for tomorrow?"

"I think so."

The awkwardness that hangs between us is unfamiliar and painful.

"You're gonna be great. Just go out there and have fun."

Fun.

I haven't had a lot of that over the last few days. For a guy who's so serious and work-focused, Lincoln became a big part of the joy and excitement I've had playing recently. Loving golf and having fun while playing haven't always gone together for me.

It's silent again while I struggle with what to say. I don't want there to be this weirdness between us. I respect him too much, and he gave me a lot. Too much and not enough.

"Thank you for everything. I wouldn't be here if it weren't for you. I hope I can do your coaching justice."

"You already have. It was my absolute pleasure, Keira." He sighs into the phone, and I can picture him running his fingers through his dark hair. "I just wanted to wish you luck and let you know that I'll be rooting for you. Gram too. She asked me to bookmark the live scoring website so she can follow along."

"She did?"

"Yeah, you made quite an impression on her. Keira, I . . ." He curses lightly away from the phone and then clears his throat. "I should let you get some sleep."

Disappointment and resolution center me, and I finally feel like sleeping. "Yeah, okay. Thanks for calling, Lincoln."

Ending the call, I curl into a ball on top of the scratchy comforter and fall asleep, wishing Lincoln's arms were wrapped around me. When my alarm goes off early the next morning, I rise like the dead, shower, and get ready.

Conditions aren't great today. It's sunny, but dark clouds in the distance threaten rain. It's also hot and muggy, making it hard to breathe. But I can't let that stop me. I've done all the work. Today is about battling my head. There's no room to wish or hope for any aspect of my life to be different.

Me, the ball, and my golf clubs. They're all I focus on. They are all I need.

I'm in a later starting group, so I'm able to watch some of my competition. Among them are girls I've played against, girls I've looked up to, and a few I've never heard of before.

A senior at Arizona State, Martha, is putting up a strong performance. Each swing looks better than the last. She's unbeatable, or that's what everyone whispers as they watch her dominate for the first hour of the day. She has skill and confidence that makes others feel timid and weak.

In hindsight, I probably shouldn't have watched her because, by the time it's my turn to tee off, even I'm shaken by her strong showing.

I step up, place my tee and ball, and let out a deep breath. I stare down the fairway to the flag, visualizing my ball exactly where I need it to be—where I know I'm capable of hitting it.

This is it.

I scan the crowd without realizing I'm looking for him, but when I don't see Lincoln's dark head, frustration and anger sets in. Not at him, but at myself for being disappointed about anything during the biggest moment of my life.

I'm angry for most of the front nine, but it works for me. I hone it into a focused desire to do well despite his absence, to do well for myself.

It's so disgustingly hot out and that pisses me off too, so I add it to the list and let it drive me to work even harder.

I first notice Coach Potter walking along the course at the tenth hole. I shouldn't be surprised he decided to deign me with his presence. He'll want to be here in case I pull off a miracle so he can pretend he's a loving and supportive coach.

I falter at twelve with a bogey, but I'm able to recover on the last five and finish five under and tied for second place.

I sign my card in the clubhouse and make my way toward the player rest area. I have a short break before my second round, and I need to eat and drink a gallon of water. It's only gotten more humid as the day progressed.

I check my phone, trying not to be sad that Lincoln hasn't texted. I know it's possible he isn't tracking the tournament, though some part of me refuses to believe that. That part is still hopeful and closely tied to my need to believe what Lincoln and I had went beyond obligation and a casual fling.

My body aches, and I'm so tired when I spot Potter waiting for me with a big pleased smile on his face that I don't bother to try to avoid him. I'm so hot, but my skin feels dry instead of sweaty when I wipe my hand across my forehead. I suck in a deep breath that doesn't do anything to get oxygen to my lungs.

Coach Potter rests an arm around my shoulders, and I try to move out of his hold, but there's nowhere to go and my legs are shaky underneath me. God, if he'd just stop touching me, maybe I could catch my breath.

My mouth is gritty, and my throat aches as I try to swallow. Dots blur my vision. I really need to eat something.

If I could just get to a quiet area and relax for a few minutes, then I would be okay. My stomach twists violently, stopping me in my tracks. Bile rises, and I heave. My throat is so dry it takes three attempts to bring up my breakfast.

I'm aware that I've puked on Potter's shoes, but the pain is so intense I can't even be happy about it. My legs give out, and I collapse.

I'm out only a few seconds, I think, but when I open my eyes again, two people in tourney polos are carrying me into a private room. Potter elbows his way into the room behind them.

A lady, who introduces herself as Mary, assures me she's a doctor and then asks me a bunch of questions. I answer in a daze. There's a real threat of puking every time I open my mouth.

"Can I have some water?" I croak.

One of the polo dudes hands me a bottle of water, even going as far as to unscrew the cap for me.

"Keira, I think you have heat stroke," Mary says. "I have a car waiting for you."

I lift my head and see the seriousness in her expression as she places a cool washcloth on the back of my neck. "It's just a precaution."

I want to put up a fight, but I can't seem to form the words. The room is spinning, and it feels as if I'm burning from the inside out.

I'm helped to my feet and taken out a back exit to a waiting car. I have enough wherewithal to realize I probably need to text my parents and let them know what's happening, but I can't remember if I actually do it.

Potter slides into the back of the car with me, and I can't help but think his presence isn't helping at all.

CHAPTER THIRTY-TWO

Lincoln

I'm on the phone with a client when I get the call about Keira. The fact that Gram knows before I do would be obnoxious if I weren't so pissed that I wasn't there. I wrestled with going all morning, finally deciding it was best for Keira if I didn't show. She didn't need any distractions.

"Is she okay?"

Gram does her best to sound calm, but I can hear the worry in her voice. "I'm not sure, but they took her to the hospital."

I grab my keys and head out the door at a run. "Which hospital?"

I jump into my SUV and am starting it and slamming the gear into reverse before the door is even closed. Dark clouds hang low and rain spits onto my windshield just hard enough that I have to use the wipers.

I don't remember the drive over, parking, or running through the hospital, but I'm panting when I get to the emergency room. The woman behind the front desk looks at me as if I might be the one in need of help.

"Keira Brooks."

"Are you family?"

"No." I grind my teeth.

Her flat smile tells me I'm not getting back there. "If you have a seat, I'll let the nurse know Miss Brooks has a visitor."

A woman in scrubs stands holding the door to the emergency room open as she calls the next patient. Fuck it. I run past her.

"Sir. Sir. You can't be back there, sir."

Over the intercom, they call for security, which means I have to find her fast.

"Keira," I call out.

Curtains are pulled, giving privacy to patients. There are a handful of nurses and doctors who have stopped what they were doing to stare at me, so I stop in front of them, asking, "Keira Brooks?"

My heart is pounding so hard I might need to lie down in one of these beds. But only after I find her.

A big dude in a security uniform approaches before anyone answers. "Sir. I'm gonna have to ask you to leave."

"Keira," I shout a little louder, desperation and panic clear in my tone.

This time, she responds. "Lincoln?"

I run toward her voice and find a doctor giving me a disapproving look as he holds the curtain open. Keira's in the bed behind him, and Coach Potter in the chair beside her. I bypass the doctor and his dirty looks, ignore fucking Potter's existence altogether, and go to her side.

"Oh my God." I lean down and lightly run my hand across the top of her head, breathing her in.

"Sir." The security guard stands outside the curtain.

"I'm not leaving."

"Sir, we—"

"It's okay. He's okay," Keira speaks up. Her voice sounds small and weak, but the security guard reluctantly retreats.

"What happened? Are you okay?" She's hooked up to an IV, and her face is flushed red, but otherwise, she looks okay.

"I got overheated and dehydrated. I'm fine."

The doctor clears his throat. "Fine might be a stretch. Your potassium was dangerously low. Fortunately, everything else looks okay. We're going to move you up to a room so we can monitor you a little longer. If everything looks stable later tonight, we can get you discharged."

"No." She moves to sit up, but I can tell it pains her. "I have to get back to the course before I'm disqualified."

"Uh, actually, I just got word that there's a weather delay. So, everyone who was slotted for this afternoon will tee off first thing in the morning." Potter reads from his phone.

The doctor looks to Keira and speaks sternly. "You need time to recoup. We're giving you fluids, but you were severely dehydrated." He shakes his head. "Even for someone young and active, you aren't going to feel one hundred percent for a few days. Don't push too hard or you'll end up right back here."

"But she *could* play tomorrow?" Potter asks. "We have a chance to win."

"We?" I ask, not hiding my disdain.

He glares at me but doesn't answer, so I focus my attention back to Keira.

She lets me hold her hand for the next few hours while they pump her with fluids. She dozes on and off, but it feels like every time she gets comfortable someone wakes her up to check this or that.

It's after seven before the doctor releases her. A nurse makes her sit in a wheelchair so she can wheel Keira out to the parking lot, and Potter and I flank her on either side.

"I'll bring the SUV around."

She stands, and I lead her to a bench to wait while I get the car. Rain comes down in a steady pour and it doesn't look like it's going to break anytime soon.

"I already called a cab to take us back to the hotel," Potter says.

Keira looks between us. Even on my worst day, I'm a hell of a better option than Potter.

"You can't stay at the hotel. Come with me. You'll be more comfortable at my place, and I can keep an eye on you."

She stares at me blankly.

"Nonsense. I'm staying at the hotel too and I can keep an eye on her."

"Like you did today?" I step to him. I've easily got three inches on him and I use every single one to make him feel small and worthless. "Where the fuck were you? Why weren't you looking out for her?" I hate him for letting it happen, but only a fraction as much as I hate myself.

I can see the anger on her weak frame as she says, "I'll be fine at the hotel. I don't need either of you."

The weight of that statement slams into me. I kneel in front of her and take her hand. "Come with me. Please. I'll take you to Gram's if you prefer. I just need to know you're okay and that someone is there if you need anything."

Potter scoffs. "She just needs a little rest. She can do that at the hotel and I'll be there if she needs anything else."

I wouldn't trust this guy with a pet goldfish, let alone my favorite person in the world.

She bites her bottom lip but doesn't outright turn me down, so I take that bit of leverage and run with it. I dial Gram and put the phone to my ear. She answers on the first ring as if she were waiting for news. It seems right somehow that she's concerned too.

"Gram, I'm gonna bring Keira to your house for the night. That okay?"

"Yes. I'll get the spare room set up and make soup. Do you think she could eat some homemade bread? I'll make some anyway, just in case."

Keira watches my face as I smile and nod. "That'd be great, Gram. Be there soon."

"Ready?" I stand and hold out my hand. She puts hers in it slowly, and I lean down and sweep her legs out from under her so I can carry her to my SUV. I don't say another word to Potter before we leave him standing there to wait for his cab.

I hold her hand as I drive, but neither of us speaks. I want to tell her everything is okay, but nothing is okay, and I won't make things worse by lying to her.

When we get to Gram's house, she's standing at her door, waiting for us. Gram pulls her into a hug, and Keira surprises me by wrapping both arms around my grandmother and leaning into her. Her shoulders shake and sobs wrack her tired body.

Gram meets my eye and pats Keira lovingly. They stand that

way for several long minutes before Gram leads her into the house. I follow, chest aching at not being the person she wants to lean on.

I don't want her to cry, but when she does, I want to be the one to wipe her tears.

"Lincoln, can you check the soup and the bread, I'm going to get Keira settled."

I stand alone in the hallway as Gram and Keira go into the spare room and shut the door. After checking the food, I grab a beer from the fridge, open it, and take a long swig before abandoning it on the counter.

Pacing the hallway, I wait for either of them to emerge or to call out for me. Anything would be better than standing here helpless.

When Gram finally comes out, she turns the light out and closes the door quietly. As I step forward, she stops me with a shake of her head. "She's resting."

"But—"

She shakes her head again, and I know my grandmother well enough to know she's as likely to let me through as she is to stop trying to find my next wife. I drain the rest of my beer, grab another, and follow Gram into the dining room. She instructs me to sit and then puts soup and bread in front of me.

"I'm not hungry."

She raises a brow and waits.

Grumbling, I pick up the spoon and take a few bites. I taste nothing, which is a real tragedy because I'm sure it probably tastes amazing.

"How is she?"

"She'll be okay. You did the right thing bringing her here."

"She wants to play tomorrow." I wave a hand outside. The rain has slowed, but still pelts the ground. "Assuming it isn't further delayed."

Gram nods. "She told me. I don't think anyone is going to be able to talk her out of that."

"I should have been there. If something happened to her…" It's hard to breathe as I contemplate that.

"Lincoln, honey, I don't know what happened between you and Keira or why you weren't there today when I know there's nowhere else you'd have rather been, but I have a sneaking suspicion it all leads back to one thing." She pauses to look me square in the eye. "Lacey."

I groan. Here we go again.

"You have to stop beating yourself up for things that happened in the past and start living your life. It wasn't your fault. I know it, Lacey knows it, heck, you're probably the only one who doesn't know it. But that isn't the point. You either need to believe that or decide to forgive yourself anyway so you can move on."

"I'm a workaholic with a schedule that makes it damn near impossible to date, let alone be in a serious relationship."

"Then why are you upset?"

I grind down on my molars.

"Keira isn't Lacey. Don't make the mistake of pushing her away because you're scared. You've never been a coward. Don't start now."

"What if I hurt Keira the same way?" I shake my head, the thought physically painful.

"You won't."

"How can you know that?"

"Because you're too smart and too stubborn to make the same

mistake twice."

I wish I could believe that.

After dinner, Gram makes a plate for Keira and takes it into the spare room in case she wakes up hungry.

"Are you staying?" she asks as she turns out the kitchen lights.

"Yeah." I grab the throw blanket off the back of the couch, and Gram brings me a pillow. "Thanks."

She kisses my cheek, gives me a sad smile, and heads to bed.

Once I'm settled on the couch, I stare up at the ceiling as silence falls over the house. I think about what Gram said, trying to make it fact in my head and heart, but I know to my core I didn't do right by Lacey.

I didn't fight for her or for us. I was relieved when it was over because it was one less responsibility and distraction. That's a shitty realization—to know your marriage has gone up in flames and you're happy about it.

Nowhere near sleep, I throw off the blanket and quietly head down the hallway. I rest my hand on the wooden door and try to talk myself out of going inside. I rap my knuckles lightly and then push the door open just enough to see through a crack. The room is dark, save for the dim light coming from the lamp on the bedside table that casts her small frame in shadows.

She's turned away from it, and the comforter is askew and bunched up at her feet. Moving to the bed in two long strides, I settle in behind her and pull the blanket over us. Wrapping my arm around her, I breathe easy for the first time in days.

CHAPTER THIRTY-THREE

Keira

I already know he's gone before I open my eyes. His scent lingers, but the bed is entirely too cold and quiet without him. I don't know when he joined me, but I woke in the middle of the night with Lincoln wrapped around me like a cocoon.

I should have told him to go so I wouldn't have to feel the sadness of losing him all over again, but instead I let myself enjoy one more night in his arms.

A plate of food and two water bottles sit on the nightstand, and I down one of the waters before getting out of bed. I tear off a hunk of bread and chew it while I put on my shoes. My body is achy, and I definitely don't feel one hundred percent, but I'll survive. I have to. I need to block out the pain, swing by the hotel, shower, and get to the course.

"Good morning. I made breakfast," Milly says as I tiptoe through the living room, trying to make an escape.

I turn, plastering a thankful and convincing smile on my lips. "I have to get going. Thank you so much for letting me stay last night. I feel much better after a good night's sleep."

My eyes dart around the living room, kitchen, dining room, and then finally the patio, but I don't see Lincoln anywhere.

"He isn't here." She sets a plate on the dining room table. "Come on. You'll be dropping at the third hole without a good breakfast."

"Where is he?" I follow the scent of hash browns and eggs.

"Some sort of work emergency. He said to tell you that he'd see you at the course."

Work. Of course.

"You didn't need to do this but thank you. It smells delicious."

Milly doesn't linger in the dining room while I eat, which makes me insanely grateful. I don't really feel like talking or thinking about anything except golf. I cried ugly tears last night in front of this woman, letting all my fears about golf, Lincoln, life pour out of my eyeballs.

I eat slowly and manage to finish everything Milly puts in front of me. Now I'm ready, I tell myself ignoring the way my hands tremble as I carry my dirty dishes into the kitchen.

"The rain stopped early this morning, and it promises to be a beautiful day." She takes the plate and glass from me and hands me a brown paper bag. "Take this with you for later."

I look inside to see a banana, a sandwich that looks like it might be peanut butter and jelly, and a Gatorade. I reach out with one arm and wrap it around her neck, surprising us both with how tightly I hug her. When I pull back, there are tears in my eyes. "Thank you."

"I know that there's no talking you out of playing today, but listen to your body. There's no shame in taking care of yourself.

There will be more tournaments. Your time is coming. I can feel it."

"I will," I promise.

"Let me grab my keys, and I'll drive you."

"No need, Uber's on the way."

She nods. "Good luck."

Once I'm in the back of the Uber and headed to the hotel, I call my mom.

"Honey, I'm so glad you called. I wasn't sure how long to wait before I worried. You sounded so tired last night. Are you okay?"

"Yeah, I am." I close my eyes and lean my head against the headrest. "I had a good night's sleep and a good breakfast. I'm going to try to play today."

I wait for her to chastise me or tell me that isn't a good idea, but she laughs lightly and says, "Of course you are. I wish I were there to see you. Bart and I'll be there at the Open though. He's already memorizing the course and checking out the local restaurants."

"You're coming?"

"Yeah, your coach sent us all the details, booked us flights and hotels. Your dad, too. Honestly, honey, I didn't know how much you wanted us there, but he said it would make you happy if we were there to cheer you on."

"He did?" I'm confused as to why Coach Potter would call her and make these plans, but then I realize she's talking about Lincoln. "When?"

"Last week."

My heart clenches at the thought of him going to all that trouble for me because he was so certain I was going to make it.

What if I don't? I keep the question inside for fear that voicing them will somehow make it more likely.

"I can't believe you're really coming."

"Of course. Don't sound so surprised."

I nod and wipe a tear away. I'm a freaking faucet lately. "I know it's hard to get away. You have work and lives."

"I have some vacation time saved up, and I can't think of a better way to spend it than watching my baby go after her dreams. Also, I googled the event and I saw that sometimes celebrities attend. Maybe I can trade in Bart for a Ben Affleck look-alike."

We both laugh, and the weight I'm carrying lifts a little.

"I'm so proud of you, Keira. And I miss you. I don't know when you got so big on me."

I hear a page for a doctor in the background and can picture her walking the halls of the hospital in her scrubs. I used to love to curl up beside her on the couch when she'd get home from working late shifts. "Listen, honey, I have to go, but good luck today and call me when you can, okay?"

"I will. Thanks, Mom."

At the hotel, I shower and dress for the day and then head to the course. It's still early, but many of the players in the first tee time groups are already warming up. I stretch first, not even touching my clubs for the first fifteen minutes.

I avoid the questions about how I'm feeling and the sad looks from people who are already discounting my ability to play today. Their doubt wears at me, nicking away my confidence one sad glance and soft, condescending word of encouragement at a time.

I head to the putting green. The club feels cold and heavy in my shaking hands. Zipping up my jacket and flipping the collar up to block the breeze, I take a few deep breaths to get my focus.

I fall into my usual routine, but nothing goes right. I don't know if it's my body or my head, but I'm off, and it shows. My line isn't right on my short or long putts. I head to the bunker with similar results.

By the time I walk to the driving range, I feel as if I'm going to throw up. Coach Potter joins me as I take the first swing with my driver. His eyes light up with excitement as he nods to the lady with a microphone and the accompanying camera guy. "Keira, they want to ask you a few questions."

I step back, and the reporter introduces herself. "Hi, Keira. I'm Belinda with KTLR, how are you feeling today?"

"I feel good." My voice quivers, so I smile as big as I can to overcompensate and twist and turn the pink, unicorn scrunchie on my wrist.

"You've had an exciting month, winning the Valley Invitational tournament and placing second at the University of Texas tournament. What's contributed to your recent successes?"

Lincoln's face flashes before me, smiling back at me through the computer screen all those nights. I open my mouth to speak, but Coach interjects, "She's a hard worker. We had a rough start to the year, but she's really listened to the feedback, and I think it shows just how far a person can go with the right guidance."

My face heats at him trying to take credit for Lincoln's work. Belinda looks to me to verify his statement.

"I have a great coach," I say simply. "I wouldn't be here today without him."

That much is true. Potter smiles smugly, but it doesn't matter. If I win, I'll set the record straight, and if I don't, people can believe my failures are at the hands of Potter. Lincoln has never once tried to take credit, which is just one more reason in a long list of why he's a better coach and man.

"Do you think you'll be able to play at the level you need to today to win?"

I suck in a breath because, isn't that the question of the day? "I'm going to give it my best shot."

"Thank you, Keira. It was a pleasure to meet you. Good luck today."

I walk back to my spot on the range, Coach Potter standing behind me just like he did all those times for other girls on the team. I always imagined what it would be like to have his undivided attention before a tournament, but I have to say that it doesn't feel any better with him by my side.

His presence doesn't encourage or soothe me like Lincoln's does. In a moment of weakness, I look around for him. But even before I finish scanning the small crowd, I can feel he isn't here.

Focus. Only golf.

I tee up another ball, blow out a breath, and swing. I know I'm holding back, but I can't seem to access that gut-deep power and determination I usually can.

"That was short." Coach Potter's brows draw together, hands on hips. "Try it again."

I hit five more balls and then take a break since I'm already out of breath and sweaty.

Coach looks me over and shakes his head. "You can't do it. You don't have it today."

Then he just walks away. Now that I'm not performing at peak level, he isn't interested in standing beside me. It doesn't shock me, but it does hurt.

Of all the times he's doubted my ability, this is the only time I've ever believed him.

CHAPTER THIRTY-FOUR

Lincoln

"Any update?" I pace the office with a club in my hand in case I decide to completely lose my shit and break everything in sight.

"Not since you asked thirty seconds ago." Will chuckles and then his voice is serious again. "I'm working as fast as I can to figure it out. We'll get it back up."

Four hours ago, our server crashed. The whole website down. *Kaboom.* I kept picturing it like a car explosion in an action movie, but instead of walking away like a badass, I'm in the car going up in flames.

I'd woken with Keira nuzzled into my side and so many voice mails it used up all my phone storage. Begrudgingly, I left because that's what you do when you own a business. You get out of bed or stop whatever it is you're doing and you deal with it.

I've already typed out an email to every member of Reeves

Sports, letting them know we're aware of the problem and working quickly to get the site back online. I emailed my clients personally, as well as my staff, and now I'm helping Will any way I can, which is basically just staying out of his way. It's harder than it should be since all I want to do is to barrage him with questions as I pace.

We redirected traffic from the website to our dark site, which explains the outage, but with thousands of members waiting to hear back from coaches and hundreds of potential new clients not being able to sign up—this is a nightmare.

I click refresh on the browser again just for fun. The golf ball stick figure with a sad face frowns back at me. Once upon a time, I sat on a call and smiled at that graphic. How clever, I thought. That'll make people feel better when they can't access the site. Now I wanted to smash the cute cartoon figure in his adorable face.

Stand, pace, check the time, sit, click refresh, ask Will for update.

I shower, leaving my phone sitting on the counter and the ringer turned up so loud it'll likely let the whole neighborhood know if I get a call.

Keira's probably already at the course warming up. I know she's going to play—it just isn't in her to give up. I hate the way my skin prickles with guilt not being there with her. I'm not even sure she wants me there, but it doesn't change how awful I feel for missing it anyway.

Dressed so I can leave for the course as soon as I'm done working, I head back into the office. Will sends me an update that they think they've figured out the issue and I need to jump on a call with him and the rest of the team to lay out a plan.

I'm back to pacing with my club in hand, but with a slightly less ragey grip, while Will outlines the problem and possible solutions.

Finding the issue was only step one.

We brainstorm, me mostly just listening. I hire the best, so I don't have to be an expert on everything, but right now I'd trade my left arm to be a computer engineer.

"Worst case scenario, how long until we're back up?"

Will takes his time answering. "I'm not sure. An hour, maybe longer."

I kick the closest thing to me, which happens to be one of the many boxes stacked up in my office. The box on top of it falls to the floor with a metallic clank, contents spilling out in my pacing path.

"Shit," I mutter and squat to clean it up.

Trophies and medals from tournaments dating back all the way to my first junior tournament are spread out in front of me. I pick up the closest one, a medal from a high school tourney, running my thumb along the raised lettering.

I right the box so I can put everything back and dig through the papers at the bottom. Receipts and warranties—stuff from our filing cabinets that Lacey must have found and put together for me. Most of it's trash, but Pop's familiar handwriting makes me pause.

A few days after my first pro tournament, when I was still wallowing in self-hate for all the stupid mistakes I'd made, he'd stopped by, told me he was proud of me and handed me this folded piece of paper.

"Focus on remedies, not faults."

Pop wasn't much for speaking his heart, but that single line said it all. It was everything he believed about golf and about life. When you screw up, take a moment to be sad or pissed, and then figure out how to fix it.

And I had. It was exactly what I'd needed to stop obsessing and get back to work.

"Lincoln? Boss man?" Will's voice brings my attention back to the call.

"Yeah, sorry, I'm here."

I carry the paper with me to my desk and sit behind my laptop to get back to work. I'm asking questions and taking notes, but my eyes continually drift back to Pop's words.

Focus on remedies. Simple advice that I'd put into practice in every aspect of my life.

Except one.

Fuck.

I'd let all my faults get in the way of the thing I wanted most. Keira.

And of course I want to be with her. Despite everything. Because of everything.

I want her more than I've ever wanted anything. Ever. Period.

I fold the paper and slide it into my pocket as I stand. "Will, I gotta go. You guys got this."

There's silence on the other end of the phone for two long seconds. "You're dropping off?"

"Yep. I have somewhere important I need to be." I smile as I picture their surprised faces. But no one is more surprised than I am. "I trust you to find the best solution. Do what you can and I'll check in later."

I just hope I can get there in time.

At the course, I park and run out to the area between the warm-up area and hole one. Fuck, I hope she hasn't already teed off.

I weave between players and spectators, tournament officials in their matching polo shirts. I finally spot her hanging back, all by herself.

"Keira," I call out. "Keira." I reach her, out of breath and shaky from adrenaline. "Thank God. I made it."

She shakes her head slowly. "It doesn't matter. I'm not playing."

"What?"

"I can't do it." She shrugs looking defeated. "Not like this. I'm not even close to one hundred percent, more like fifty. Weak, anxious, in my head—"

"I love you."

Her eyes widen, and her lips part in surprise, so I repeat it. "I love you so much. I'm sorry I didn't tell you before. I was scared that I'd fail you somehow and you'd hate me. Still am scared, if I'm being honest."

"But…" Her mouth opens and closes like an adorable baby fish.

"I was a bad husband. My priorities were fucked up, and I stopped trying. I gave up. It was easier than admitting it wasn't what I wanted anymore. I swore I'd never do that to anyone else. I tried to keep you at arm's length because I knew that, if I let you in here"—I place a hand over my heart—"I'd never be able to walk away. So, I pushed you until you walked away from me, and I've hated myself every moment since."

She smiles the tiniest bit. This stunning woman that's somehow become more important than anything else.

"You needed me to push you, to show you that you were capable of doing anything you set your mind to, but I wasn't expecting you to push me the same way. I'm in. All in. Without you, nothing else matters."

A guy in a white polo shirt with the country club logo walks up behind Keira and says her name. She looks from me to him and then back to me. I can see the panic on her face and feel the anxiety bouncing off her.

"If you don't feel up to this today, I'll spend every day for as long as it takes helping you get back here. Say the word and we're out of here. But, baby, you can do this. This is your destiny."

I take out the note from Pop, unfold it so she can read what it says, and hand it to her. "I want you to have this. My grandpa gave it to me after my disastrous pro debut. It's a Jack Nicklaus quote that he said fairly often. I carried it every time I played after that, but I never really felt the weight of his message until today. I have a hundred faults, but I promise I'll keep working to be better for you. So I can push you when you need it and help you get everything you want and deserve."

"It's almost time." Polo guy smiles and nods for her to approach the tee box.

"Just one more second," I tell him and take her gloved hand, running my thumb over the leather. "I love you. You can do this. You don't need me, you never did, but I'm glad as hell you found me anyway."

I can't read anything on her face but shock that I just dropped my heart at her feet and nerves that she isn't in any shape to play golf today.

"Keira," the tourney dude says again in a quiet, serious tone as he moves to stand at her side.

She nods to polo asshat. "I'm coming."

Lifting Pop's note, she glances back at me. "Thank you for this." She moves toward the tee box, turning before she steps onto the grass. "You're staying, right?"

"Nowhere else I'd rather be."

She smiles and marches up to the tee box as I move over to watch with the other spectators.

And it's exactly where I plan to stay, right here on the sidelines making sure she gets anything and everything she wants for as long as she'll let me.

CHAPTER THIRTY-FIVE

Keira

I find Lincoln standing to the side, exactly where he said he'd be, and he nods encouragingly. I wave to the crowd and then tee my ball. I stare down the fairway to the flag and visualize the flight of my ball and the exact spot for it to land that would put me in the best position for this par four.

I take a few practice swings back from my ball and exhale a long breath. With it, I push out all the negative thoughts that have plagued me. I'm not in top shape today. Everyone here knows it, but they don't know how much I want this.

Lincoln does.

I glance once more at him before I take my place. With him cheering me on, I feel unbeatable. He fuels my desire to push through, and I know that, win or lose, I'm going to give it everything I have.

The crowd quiets until the only sound is the whisper of a breeze and my own breathing. Lincoln's voice is in my head, encouraging and pushing me.

I check my line one last time and swing.

The crowd claps as I watch the ball flight. It's shorter than yesterday's drive and slightly off target, but it isn't awful.

My second shot brings me onto the green, but I have a slippery downhill twelve-foot putt. I miss it but manage to leave myself in decent position and save par.

The next three holes are about the same. I'm playing safe, but it still feels as if I've run a marathon, and my throat burns from sucking in air. I'm still tied for second place, but there is only one stroke that separates us.

Lincoln stands, hands crossed over his chest, white hat pulled low so I can't see his eyes with the shadow, but I still know he's looking at me.

Hole five is a par three at one hundred fifty-three yards. Yesterday, I hit my nine-iron low and controlled and then was able to make putt for birdie, but it was risky. The greens are playing fast today, and a bad bounce could put me in an awful spot. I can't miss long.

I waver between clubs, ultimately sticking with the nine-iron. My caddy nods. He's one the tourney provided for me, so we haven't chatted much, but he seems to approve.

I tee my ball and stare the flag down. I strike the ball flush, and it flies high and straight. The crowd claps heartily and then groans as it rolls off the green. I end up with bogey.

Going into the back nine, I'm tied for third place. The crowd builds at each hole. The earlier tee times are finishing, and there are only three groups left ahead of us.

Lincoln walks alongside me from the rough, looking just like the boyfriend on the sidelines I always wanted.

Coach Potter is in the crowd too, hanging back as he plays the role of supportive coach. One thing is certain, no matter how today ends, I've decided I'm taking a page from Abby's book and quitting the team. Four months working with Lincoln was more helpful than all the coaching Potter's done his entire career. Times ten.

After drinking some water and taking a few deep breaths in the shade, I pull out my scorecard and course map so I can study the tenth hole. I don't need to since I have it memorized, but it gives me something to focus on.

It's a par five with an elevated green. There are two bunkers running along the right side of the fairway, and trees line the left just beyond the rough. It's a beautiful sight, but there are so many ways to screw it up.

When I shove the scorecard back into my pocket, my fingers graze the piece of paper Lincoln gave me. I don't take it out, just hold it in my hand. I know how much his grandfather meant to him, and the fact he gave this to me touches me deeply.

I think about the words scribbled on it and how hard I've worked to get here, how hard Lincoln worked to get me here. He may be unwilling to take credit, but I wouldn't be here without him. I think he wants this for me nearly as much as I want it for myself.

My driver is heavy in my hand as I stare between two points on the fairway. One safe option and another fifteen yards beyond that, if I strike the ball pure, it should give me a chance to get home in two.

Oh god. I'm gonna go for it. I think this and try to talk myself out of it, but know it's as good as done. All out. Not just for me but also for the man who apparently loves me.

I haven't let the words sink in yet. They're too big coming from him.

The crowd's interest has waned, but Lincoln's still watching. He adjusts his hat, giving me a better view of the smile on his lips. It's encouragement in the exact moment I need it. If I don't make a move up the leaderboard now, it's going to be too late to make a run.

There are two spots, but I don't just want to qualify, I want to win today.

CHAPTER THIRTY-SIX

Lincoln

Something changed in Keira on the tenth hole. She stopped holding back. There's no indecision in her club choice or her swing, and she moves down the course like a machine.

It's the most beautiful thing I've ever seen. I can't take my eyes off her, not even as the ball flies through the air. I judge the lay by the cheers and the hint of a smile on Keira's lips. Then she's all business again and practically sprinting up the course.

The energy of the crowd buzzes as she and the girl she's paired with arrive at the eighteenth hole. Keira only needs par to tie for first and secure a spot at the Open.

She glances around as if she's seeing her surroundings for the first time in a while, and the crowd roars as she scans it slowly, hopefully letting the moment sink in. I can see her exhaustion as her chest rises and falls with a deep breath.

She's tired. She has to be. The fact that she's pushed through after her body was so depleted yesterday is catching up to her. The adrenaline is probably wearing off too. You can only ride the high for so long.

"You got this, baby," I quietly mumble, lift my hat, and run my fingers through my hair before putting the hat back on. I'm more nervous watching her than I ever was for my own events.

I stay in her line of vision, always where she can find me if she needs a familiar face. I'm honestly not sure if my presence is helpful or a hindrance after I ran in and professed my love seconds before the biggest day of her life. Not my finest moment, but I couldn't hold it in a second longer.

The eighteenth hole is a straightforward par four. She needs to birdie in order to win outright.

The other girl, whose name I should remember but don't, drives the ball well. Not as long or consistent as Keira, but her short game is as good as anyone I've seen. She's made more saves with chips and putts today than should be humanly possible.

Weston? Waston? Watson? Yeah, that sounds right.

Keira goes first. Her drive is a little shorter than she's capable, but it lands just off the center of the fairway. Watson pulls out a monster, and for the first time today, her drive is the longer of the two.

Keira looks angry as hell as they walk down the course. The crowd keeps cheering them on because, no matter what happens in the next few minutes, it's been a great tournament and they're going to see more of these ladies.

Their approaches vary only on direction. Both of them get up just off the green, but in the fringe. Watson has a slightly better lie in that she'll be putting on a mostly flat area. Keira's closer but will be working downhill where the slightest miss can end up rolling to no-man's-land.

Watson takes her time lining up her shot, and we all hold our breath as her ball inches toward the hole. There's a collective "oooh" as the ball hits the rim but fails to fall in. She knocks it in for par, securing a tie unless Keira can make the next shot.

The pressure of the moment hangs in the air. Watson stands off to the side, and even those who have counted Keira out are watching. All eyes are on my girl.

Putter in hand, she walks to her ball and crouches behind it to get a good look at the angle. When she stands, she wobbles off balance, and the lady next to me gasps and clutches my arm.

"Sorry," she says and removes her hand as soon as she realizes what she's done. I nod my acceptance of her apology, but I kind of wish she'd keep squeezing my arm to distract me from how weak Keira looks.

I'm fighting every urge to charge onto the course to make sure she's okay. My pulse thrums and anxiety vibrates inside my chest.

Keira takes a moment to regain her composure, but her body's failing her and that's gotta be messing with her mind.

"Take your time, baby."

The forearm-clutching lady beside me doesn't look at me as she says, "You know Keira Brooks?"

"She's my…" Girlfriend? It doesn't seem like enough. "She's my everything."

I feel her eyes on me briefly, but when Keira gets into position to take her putt, everything else ceases to exist.

Keira stares at the line and adjusts her grip, but instead of taking the shot, she steps back. The indecision has us all worried. Everyone's rooting for her at this point, the underdog who didn't let anything stop her.

When her eyes lift and find mine, they are brimming with worry and nerves. I do my best to reassure her, nodding and smiling. If she had any idea how confident I was in her ability to make this shot, she wouldn't have any room for doubt inside her.

Win or lose, it doesn't matter, but I want her to win for herself. I want her to feel that ultimate satisfaction of having her hard work pay off in a big, big way. No client has ever made me this proud, no woman has ever made me want this much.

She holds my gaze for a few seconds more and then her eyes close and her chest rises as she takes a deep breath. When she opens them, she moves with purpose into position, allows a second to adjust, and then takes her shot.

I'm pretty sure the world stops. I know my heart does. The ball rolls along the green to the hole in no hurry. It teases us, drawing out the seconds and the suspense, until I feel like I might faint.

I switch my gaze to Keira just before the ball makes its final decision.

The crowd roars, my heart restarts, and Keira raises her hands in victory. Tears stream down her face as she tilts her head back and looks to the sky.

The woman next to me nudges me with an elbow. "Congratulations."

"Thank you."

Keira hugs her caddy, shakes hands with Watson, and then heads off the course. I walk along the rope just ahead of her. Though she doesn't see me right away, her eyes scan until she finds me. Her smile hits me in the gut, and we move toward each other at a jog. My hands wrap around her waist and hers find my neck.

"You did it."

She's still crying, happy tears that mark her face and slide down to her upturned lips. "Was there any doubt? What happened to all that *it's your destiny?*"

"That was before I realized some idiot rushed in here minutes before you were supposed to tee off and unloaded on you, not to mention the whole recent hospitalization thing."

"I had to win. It had to be today."

"Why?"

"Because I needed to make sure that when I told you that I love you too, you knew it wasn't because I needed you to coach me." Her hands cradle my face. "I love you so much."

My head falls back, and a laugh rumbles from my chest. "Nice try, we have a lot of work to do before June."

"Can you kiss me first?"

I crash my mouth down onto hers, holding nothing back. I don't know how I lived without her, but I don't plan on ever letting her go.

EPILOGUE
Two Months Later...

Keira

I stand on the golf course at the ninth hole right outside of Lincoln's grandmother's house. What feels like a million people are gathered around me. Some talk to me and others only about me.

"Just act natural."

"But try to smile."

"I think she needs a little more blush."

"How's the black shirt? Should we have her in white instead?"

"Can I have a minute with Keira?" Lincoln's voice cuts through the others, and I want to fall into him the second everyone else walks off and it's just us.

"Nervous?" he asks.

"Yeah, when you said we were gonna shoot a video for the site, I thought it'd just be you and me." I gesture toward the people and equipment. It looks like we're shooting a music video. "Is all this necessary?"

"Nothing but the best for my star client. Ignore them and just show off for me, sweetheart." He hands me my wedge and a ball, drops a kiss to my cheek, and calls everyone back.

When I'm given the go ahead, I take a breath and start.

Tap. Tap. Tap.

The noise soothes and excites me. Body poised, right forearm extended slightly in front of me, the tip of my tongue between my teeth, and my man standing on the sidelines watching me. I move through the trick, forgetting about the cameras.

After five takes, the guy holding the camera calls, "We got it."

As the crew packs up, I stand off to the side and watch Lincoln thank everyone. He's so good at being in charge, at making people feel his thanks and respect, and ultimately getting them to do what he wants in the exact way he wants them to do it.

"Seems like a lot of manpower for fifteen minutes of shooting," I say when he walks over to me.

He takes my hand and leads me to the golf cart path. "Take a walk with me?"

"What about all our stuff? Shouldn't we help pack up?"

"Trust me, they don't want us touching their equipment. Leave your clubs here; we won't be long."

The sun sets in front of us, and we walk with our hands linked. It's the perfect ending to a chaotic week. The Valley semester ended, and school is out—forever for me. I'm going to finish my degree eventually, but since meeting Lincoln and realizing what's possible, it no longer feels like the right path for me. I have new goals and dreams, starting with playing in the US freaking Open next week.

Also, I moved in with Lincoln. A big step for us, but another one that just felt right. I'm attempting to hide the extent of my messiness for at least another month or two so he doesn't change his mind.

But so far, it's been bliss. He works a lot, but I've instituted a shirtless workplace, and that's helped morale a lot, if I do say so myself. And when he forgets to take a moment to breathe, I just crawl into his lap, wrap my arms around him, and remind him.

"I really love it out here. Think Gram will mind if I start sleeping on her patio every night?"

"No." He chuckles. "She'd probably be thrilled."

I close my eyes and breathe in the scent of jasmine and grass. "Someday I'm going to live on the golf course where I can just walk out and play golf any time I want. We can sit on the patio and you can critique swings of everyone who passes by."

"I bet they'd love that."

"Not to them, just to me. For fun."

"I can think of a lot of things to do in this hypothetical house that would be a lot more fun than that."

"Oh yeah? Like what?"

"Like surprising the hell out of you by telling you it isn't so hypothetical." He stops walking and turns to face the back of a house across the fairway from Gram's. It's down from the tee box a hundred yards or so and has a big For Sale sign hanging just off the course.

"Gonna buy me a house someday, sugar daddy?" I joke and lean against him. "That one is nice. Good patio. That pool is great too. Yep, one just like this will do. Got a cool million I could borrow?"

"It won't cost you quite that much."

I pull back and look up at his face because he's gone along with this charade far too long and sounds far too serious.

"What'll it cost me?" I ask tentatively, my pulse speeding.

He takes out his yo-yo, which makes me laugh.

"I have to learn a trick? You know I'm hopeless with that thing." He's tried to teach me a few basic tricks, but it seems that I can add yo-yoing to the list of things I'm not very good at.

He takes my left hand and guides my ring finger through the slipknot, still holding the yo-yo in his palm. "Ready?"

I nod. I have no idea what he's up to, but I'm ready for it all—anything he wants to throw at me.

"It'll cost you forever." He opens his palm, and a beautiful platinum ring slides down the string and onto my finger.

I gasp as Lincoln gets down on one knee. His lips are wrenched into a tight, nervous smile, and he looks at me with such hope and want that I'm utterly floored.

"You're sure?" I have zero doubts that the man loves me, but this? I'm stunned.

"I've never been more sure of anything." He pushes the ring down my finger. "I want us together in this house." He nods toward the home behind us. "I want your stuff strewn all around it, and I want to wake up every morning and try to figure out how to be the best husband and coach that I can be. I'll never stop wanting you. Never stop wanting to be better for you. Not in a million lifetimes together. Marry me?"

"Yes! Yes, of course, I'll marry you."

He stands and brushes a quick kiss against my lips before tipping his head back and screaming, "She said yes! She said yes!"

I'm laughing as he sweeps my legs out from under me and carries me back toward Gram's house, kissing me and telling me how much he loves me the whole way. When he sets me down, he does so in front of a bunch of people who are all smiling and holding champagne glasses.

"What if I'd said no?"

He smiles. "It was going to be a really lame party."

"Dad?" I spot him off to the side dressed fancier than I've maybe ever seen. I rush to him. "What are you doing here?"

"Heard my baby girl might be getting engaged."

Lincoln's at my side and extends a hand to him. "Good to see you again, Mr. Brooks."

"Now that you're getting married, I think Dan will do just fine."

I squeeze my dad and then pull back and check him out. Face clean-shaven, and I think I smell cologne. I pat the pocket on his button-down shirt. "You clean up well."

Leaving him was the hardest part of moving away from Valley.

"Dan," Milly calls as she walks toward us. A woman follows closely behind her. "Dan, have you met Addison yet?"

Addison blushes a bright red that almost matches the shade of her hair and holds her hand out to my dad. "Milly has told me a lot about you."

Lincoln leans down and whispers in my ear. "Looks like Gram found someone new to play matchmaker with."

I glance to her, and she gives me a mischievous wink, which has me grinning like a fool.

"Come on, my parents are around here somewhere."

He sweeps me away and we make our way through the small crowd until my eyes land on a man who looks like an older version of Lincoln.

"Keira, these are my parents, May and Jim."

"It's so nice to finally meet you," I tell them.

"You too. Welcome to the family." Lincoln's mom pulls me into a warm hug, and then his father does the same.

"What'd I miss? Did she say yes?" A man comes to a stop next to Lincoln's parents, adjusts his tie, and then finally looks between Lincoln and me. A cocky smirk pulls his mouth into a wide smile.

"Keira, this is my obnoxious little brother, Kenton," Lincoln says before grabbing him playfully and hugging him.

"Nice to meet you, Keira," Kenton says. "If you want embarrassing stories on this one"—he punches Lincoln in the arm—"I have you covered."

"Don't even think about it," Lincoln warns him.

"What? She can't agree to marry you without hearing about the time you peed the bed and blamed it on the dog."

Lincoln hangs his head and mutters under his breath. He wraps an arm around my waist and pulls me away, shouting over his shoulder, "Thanks a lot, man. Enjoy the party."

Abby, Erica, and Cassidy sit off to one side with Smith and Keith. After I've met all of Lincoln's family, I sneak away to join them.

"Congratulations." Abby stands and squeezes me hard.

The other girls do the same, and I take a seat next to Keith.

"Congrats," he says. "Senior year won't be the same without you."

"I *am* an awesome lab partner." I bump his shoulder with mine. "I got you a present to make up for all the stress I've caused you over the last three years."

He raises a brow in question.

"Reeves Sports all access, unlimited membership for life."

"No way?"

"Yes way. Thanks for always having my back."

"I, uh, have something for you, too." Keith stands and produces a folded newspaper clipping from his front pocket. He holds it out to me. "I thought you might want to frame it."

As I unfold the paper, Erica moves so she can see and busts out laughing.

"What is it?" Abby asks.

I hand it to her. "It's the correction the paper issued from that interview I did at the qualifier citing Lincoln Reeves as my coach instead of Potter." I smile at Keith. "Thank you. I knew you had a little rebellious streak in you."

It's hours before Lincoln and I get back to the apartment, and when we do, I drop onto the couch exhausted and happy. So freaking happy. I hold my left hand up, admiring the big rock on my finger. It's beautiful and a little heavy.

"Do you like it?" he asks, taking a seat next to me. "I've never seen you wear jewelry, so I had no idea what to pick."

"I love it."

"I'm glad. That ring belonged to Gram."

"It was your grandmother's?" I ask. "It looks brand new."

"Pop gave it to her for their fortieth anniversary. She wore it for a month or two and then went back to her original set. Sentimentality won out over the size of the rock, I guess. Anyway, when I asked her for help finding a ring, she offered me that. I thought you'd like having something that was hers."

"I do." I hold it against my chest. "It's perfect." Moving so I can face him, I ask, "You're sure about this? Really? I'm not sure you know what you got yourself into. I'm messy, and I get hangry. I like to eat in bed, and I—"

He presses his lips to mine mid-sentence, kissing me hard and making me forget what I was going on about. When he pulls back, it's to say, "Stop trying to scare me off. I know exactly who you are."

"You do?"

"*Mm-hmm*. You're the girl who's stuck with me. I'm not going anywhere." He stands and tugs me to my feet before leading me to the bedroom. "Well, except to bed so I can sex up my new fiancée."

Calloused fingers gently lift my shirt over my head and push my skirt and panties down to the floor. I step out of them and unhook my bra before he can get to it, tossing it to the ground.

Instead of throwing me onto the bed like it looks like he wants to do, he draws my naked body against him. "I love you so damn much."

"I love you too." We stand together, leaning on one another and soaking up all the feelings and things words can't say. "What's next, Coach?"

I feel the laughter from his chest, and his mouth descends close to mine. "Sex. Lots and lots of reps. I'll let you know when to stop."

Acknowledgments

Another book that absolutely could not have been written without so many other people's help.

To my husband, I never would or could have written a golf book without you. This one is definitely for you <3

Ann, writing would be lonely without you. Thanks for pushing me along the way.

Becca, I'm never letting you leave me. *Darcy hand flex*

All my family and friends who support and love me even when I'm holed away in my office for weeks at a time—I love you so much. Who has the tequila?

And special thanks to Michelle B. and Kathy P. for their help in researching this book.

Made in United States
North Haven, CT
12 September 2023

41472271R00167